EGYPT'S FIRE

THE CURIOUS LEAGUE
OF DETECTIVES AND THIEVES

EGYPT'S FIRE

TOM PHILLIPS

PIXEL✚INK

PIXEL✚INK

Text copyright © 2022 by Thomas Theodore Phillips III
All illustrations copyright © 2022 by TGM Development Corp.
Bowler hat and umbrella illustration by Thomas Theodore Phillips III
All other illustrations by Stephen Gilpin
All rights reserved

Pixel+Ink is a division of TGM Development Corp.
www.pixelandinkbooks.com
Printed and bound in April 2022 at Maple Press, York, PA, U.S.A.
Book design by Jay Colvin

Cataloging-in-Publication information is available from the Library of Congress.

Hardcover ISBN: 978-1-64595-105-6
E-book ISBN: 978-1-64595-107-0

First Edition

1 3 5 7 9 10 8 6 4 2

For Big Tom, the greatest father who ever lived

PROLOGUE

The time you discovered the greatest detective who ever lived.

M OST DETECTIVE STORIES start with a phrase such as "It was a dark and stormy night" or "The moment she walked through the door, I knew she was trouble." But this story, I dare say, is not like *most* detective stories.

This is the story of the greatest detective who ever lived, and whom you've never heard of.

Now, before I continue, I'll answer a couple of questions: First, the set of keys your mother is frantically looking for can be found under the left cushion of your couch, and second, the reason why you have never heard of the detective in question is that you haven't read this book. But I am sure after you do, you'll agree with me.

And who am I? Just a humble observer who feels compelled to set the record straight.

Throughout my lifetime, I have witnessed, collected, and recorded mysterious events all over the world, but the strange happenings I am about to recount are by far the most interesting I have ever laid witness to. I've changed some of the names to protect the not-so-innocent, but every other detail is exactly as it occurred.

It all began with a lonely boy, a priceless ruby, and an inspector named Toadius McGee.

CHAPTER ONE

The time when an orphan almost caught a master criminal.

IN A CRAWL SPACE above the bathroom on the fourth floor of the New York Museum of Natural History lived an orphan named John Randel Boarhog. He had been living in the museum for about six months. At eleven-and-a-half, John had decided that he would be better off on his own. He was done with orphanages, foster homes, and grown-ups. He was tired of other people deciding what was best for him. John knew what was best for himself—living with his mother. Unfortunately, that was now impossible.

If you've ever tried to live in the ceiling of a museum,

you know how difficult it can be. Living in the ceiling of any building is tricky, but museums are perhaps the most challenging, even for expert ceiling dwellers. John had discovered that if he followed the same routine every day, he could reduce the chance he'd be caught, so he'd learned the schedules of every janitor, scientist, and security guard involved in the running of the institution.

On the day in question, John rushed up the museum steps. He was late. The sun was already setting, and its golden rays bounced off the skyscrapers, casting a maze of shadows around him.

He arrived at the top of the stairs and stopped to catch his breath, pausing to rest beneath the giant stone words TRUTH, KNOWLEDGE, VISION, which were engraved high above the entrance of the building.

"Watch your head!" a voice called from above him. John looked up to see a man on a scaffolding. John had been so busy being late, he hadn't realized they were changing the banners on the outside of the museum. "Look out below!" the man yelled as he let the banner fall.

John's breath left his body as it unfurled. The crimson seemed to glow in the golden light. EGYPT'S FIRE AND THE SECRETS OF AN EGYPTIAN TOMB! it proclaimed in bold white letters.

"Wow," John said.

"Are you coming in or what?" a security guard called to the boy.

"Sup, Al." John smiled at the stocky guard.

"Good evening, John," Al replied, winking and tipping his hat. "I'm afraid the museum is about to close, though."

"I know, but I have to give Ms. Wingfield her book back."

"How was school today?"

"Good," John lied.

"What did you learn?" Al had asked an innocent question, but John didn't have an answer. The truth was, John hadn't been at school that day. He hadn't been to school in a very long time.

"Looks like they're finally about to open the new exhibit," John said, quickly changing the subject.

"Yeah, and in the nick of time if you ask me." The security guard laughed. "Rumor is they mixed up the exhibit pieces with props for that new show on Broadway."

"Oh no. That's terrible."

"Not as terrible as the play. It's called *Asp Me Why I Love Her*, and it's about a museum curator falling in love with a mummy." Al shook his head. "I guess the big dance sequence was pretty interesting, and Ms. Wingfield enjoyed the production's dedication to historical accuracy."

"It sounds awesome." John liked musicals. He'd thought about living in a theater, but as everyone knows the only worthwhile place to live in a theater is in the basement, and they're usually occupied by phantoms.

The old guard blushed. "You were right about the flowers. She loved the purple roses."

John smiled. "I thought she would."

"How did you know?"

"She has purple roses on her phone case," John said with a shrug. "See ya later, Al-ligator."

"After a while, John-a-dile." Al saluted as the boy slipped through the doorway.

They say you never know how much you'll miss something until it's gone. John had found this to be true. Once he'd moved into the museum, he couldn't return to school for fear of being caught and sent back to the orphanage, another foster home—or, even worse, to juvenile detention. He missed his classes more than he'd ever expected to, so he'd had to find ways to learn on his own. And that's where Ms. Wingfield came in.

John entered the gift shop, where a silver-haired woman was locking up for the night. He reached into his bag and pulled out a book entitled *Egypt: Not Just Another Pyramid Scheme*. Ms. Wingfield, the manager of the gift shop, had developed a habit of lending him books about the exhibits in the museum. She loved to learn, too.

"Hello, Mr. Boarhog." From her voice, you could tell

that Ms. Wingfield used to be either a librarian or a drill sergeant.

"Hi, Ms. Wingfield. Thanks for letting me borrow this."

"Did you like it?" she asked taking the book.

John grinned. "I did."

"Which parts?"

"Um . . . I liked reading about how the Egyptians mummified their dead, how they built the pyramids, and most of all, how they created one of the first written languages."

"Speaking of languages"—she pulled out another large book—"try this one on for size."

A Picture Is Worth a Thousand Words: Hieroglyphics for Beginners was printed on the cover in gold along with some very strange drawings.

"Hieroglyphics. That's the written language I was talking about."

"Please make sure you bring it back in one piece." Ms. Wingfield touched his hand. "Oh, and John, thank you."

"For what?"

She blushed. "For telling Al I like purple roses."

"I have no idea what you are talking about," he replied with a knowing smile.

"Aren't you a rotten liar." She winked.

Just then, a bell rang throughout the museum.

"Closing time!" a shop worker called out.

"Well, you'd better head home. They'll be locking the door soon," warned Ms. Wingfield.

"Yeah, you're right. Have a good night."

John waited until Ms. Wingfield was out of sight before bolting for the stairs. He knew the museum began shutting down at 5:45 p.m., and the doors would be locked to anyone who didn't work at the museum by 6:00 p.m. sharp, which gave John exactly fifteen minutes to sneak through the museum and get to his hiding place on the fourth floor.

His routine was simple. He'd enter the fourth-floor bathroom, head to the third stall, and climb carefully up on top of the back of the toilet. Above it, there was a loose ceiling tile. John would move it, hoist himself up into the ceiling, and slide the tile back into place. Above the restroom was a giant crawl space. John could easily stand up and walk around as long as he kept to the beams. He'd spent months gathering objects to make the space into a cozy bedroom. It was, of course, impossible to get real furniture up there, so John had been forced to get creative. He'd used clothes from the lost and found to weave together a makeshift hammock. He'd spotted an old lamp in the trash, and with the help of a book on electricity he'd borrowed from Ms. Wingfield, he'd figured out how to get it to work so he wouldn't be stuck living in the dark. It was amazing what you could learn from the right book.

John had just pulled himself into the crawl space when he

heard the door open. He watched though the crack created by a slightly ajar ceiling tile as the two night janitors entered the bathroom.

"Wow, Mr. Van Eyck is in a mood tonight," one of the custodians, a tall man with white hair, complained.

The other janitor, who was far shorter, tried not to trip over his too-big uniform as he crossed the room to empty a garbage can. "Bill, you can't blame the old man for wanting everything to be perfect. They've been trying to get that Egypt's Fire exhibit ready for months. I, for one, am excited to see the ruby."

"Be careful looking at that Egypt's Fire, Bart. . . . The boys downstairs say it's cursed."

That was hogwash, of course. John thought about the book he had just finished. Unlike the real Egypt, with its desert raiders and booby-trapped tombs, this ruby was harmless. *There's no danger in the museum,* John thought.

"Speaking of cursed," Bart said, emptying the last garbage bin, "Van Eyck wants us to clean out the employee refrigerator."

"You can't pay me enough to have anything to do with that science project," Bill replied, grimacing.

"Anything's better than this floor." Bart laughed nervously. "This whole wing gives me the willies. I always feel like someone's watching me up here."

"You and your ghost stories. . . ." Bill held the door for Bart. "I keep telling you this place ain't haunted."

"Then you explain what happened to my uniform."

"For the last time, what would a ghost want with your old uniform?"

John's gut twisted as he eyed a set of coveralls hanging from a nearby beam. As on the pint-size janitor, the uniform was too large, which meant John could use it as a disguise when he wanted to explore the museum undetected. He listened to the men continuing to bicker until their voices finally faded away, leaving only the sound of his empty stomach to keep him company.

At that instant, John's stomach let out a particularly loud growl. He realized he hadn't eaten anything all day, and the refrigerator in the break room, his only chance for food that night, was about to be cleaned out. "Break room it is."

He lowered himself back into the bathroom and slipped on his disguise inside a stall. The uniform pooled over his wiry frame. John pulled Bart's hat down over his drab, brown eyes, then studied himself in the mirror. Until recently, he'd never liked how average he looked. His dark hair seemed to grow in odd directions. His skin was the exact same brown as the dull uniform. But since he'd started living in the ceiling, being average looking made it easier for him to blend in. John yanked Bart's cap down a little farther over his face for good measure, then made his way quickly to the staff break room in the hopes of snagging dinner.

A break room is like a playground for adults, except instead of slides and tire swings, they have coffee machines, employee safety signs, and posters of kittens telling you to *Hang in there*. Cafeteria-style chairs and tables sat in the center of the room. John hurried to make himself a cup of joe. The end of the day meant that the coffee was usually gone by the time he got there. He looked in the machine and found the day-old grounds, then poured hot water through the soggy mess until a light-brown liquid filled his Styrofoam cup.

Then he moved on to the refrigerator, cheering when he found an egg salad sandwich inside. He couldn't believe his luck—he loved egg salad. John looked around the room for something to store his sandwich in, humming happily as he spotted a napkin, and wrapped it around his dinner.

As he gently closed the refrigerator door so no one would hear, he noticed a new sign posted on the wall. It was green with a large blue robot on it, and read, THE WORLD'S GREATEST ROBOTICS ENGINEERING COMPANY, NOFFO. The museum had just spent a huge sum of money to have a high-tech computerized security system installed.

NOFFO's Gotcha 3000 consisted of motion-sensor cameras, four-inch steel self-containing doors, laser grid alarms, and a knock-out gas system. It would report, record, contain, and pacify any thief trying to steal from the museum. It was such a powerful security system that John had to get back into his hiding spot before it was armed each night, which was one of the reasons John read so much—he was stuck in his hidden room from nine at night until seven the next morning.

Reading not only passed the time but gave him an escape from the situation he currently found himself in. In the real world, there were no super villains, death traps, or life-changing mysteries to be solved.

"I see you've noticed our new sign," a deep and sinister voice called.

John turned slowly to find a shadow looming in the doorway. It reminded him of a book he'd read about a count from Transylvania who would float in the shadows, waiting to prey on his victims.

John would have preferred facing a blood-sucking fiend from beyond the grave, rather than the man who stepped into the room: Mr. Viktor Van Eyck, curator and head of the New York Museum of Natural History.

Viktor Van Eyck was a tall, skinny man. What was left of his gray hair was neatly combed over the top of his balding head. With his black pinstriped suit and heavily creased face, he could have walked straight out of a 1930s horror film.

The blood drained from John's face, and his heart began to pound. He was caught.

"Good evening." Van Eyck's voice seemed to echo in John's head. "I thought I would find you here."

"You did?"

"Yes, I've been looking for you all over the museum."

John gulped. "You have?"

"Indeed." Van Eyck crossed over to the coffee machine and opened a cabinet above it, only to find an empty coffee can. "Animals," he muttered.

John cleared his throat. "I can explain—"

"I've run this museum for almost fifty years. When I started here, all I had to worry about was whether the flower in my lapel was fresh and where I'd left my glasses. My face may be a little more wrinkled and my hair, grayer, but I still love this museum, and I will continue to put this museum first."

"I love this museum, too," John replied, beginning to sweat.

"Then please help an old man out and read this label," Van Eyck said, handing over a jar. "I seem to have misplaced my spectacles again."

"Cinnamon," John read mechanically.

The old man frowned. "Just once, I would like to end my day with an abundance of coffee."

"I just use the old grounds," John said, offering his cup.

"That is *not* coffee. *That* is brown water."

"I like to pretend it's an exotic blend, imported from a country where they like their brew much weaker."

"Yes, that sounds horrible." Van Eyck shuddered. "I don't have to tell you that we can't have people running willy-nilly around my museum. That's why I had the Gotcha 3000 installed."

"I understand."

"Good." The curator reached into his pocket and pulled out a slip of paper. "Here is your code. Do *not* share it with anyone."

"Me?" John's hands began to shake as he took the piece of paper.

"Of course, you," Van Eyck replied gruffly. "I need it because it's my museum. Peter in security needs it to program the system. And, of course you need it, because you are the night janitor."

"I do?" John realized Van Eyck's mistake, then tried to lower his tone so as to sound like a grown man. "I mean . . . I *do*!"

Van Eyck squinted to see John more clearly. "Are you feeling unwell? You look a little pale."

"Just getting over a cold, sir," said John, covering his face with his arm, fake coughing, and backing away.

"And because you are the night janitor, it is your job to make sure our exhibits are beautiful. Our newest one is about Egypt. How are we supposed to represent the great country of Egypt with dirt and sand all over the floor?"

John raised an eyebrow. "Have you ever been to Egypt?"

"Of course not. Why would I want to travel to Egypt?"

"You don't want to travel the world? See new countries, meet new people?"

"My silly little man, I run a museum. If I want to see a distant land, I can have it brought to me." Van Eyck clapped John on the shoulder. "Good night. Oh, and I want to see my reflection in the floor of the new exhibit tomorrow morning."

"Yes, sir."

"And, Bartholomew?" Van Eyck smiled. "I can give only one of you access to the exhibit tonight. Whatever the room looks like in the morning will rest entirely on your shoulders. Good night."

JOHN WAS RELIEVED Mr. Van Eyck hadn't recognized him, but he also felt a bit sad. This was the hardest part of the day for him—when everyone else in the museum had gone home and he was truly alone. He reached into his uniform and pulled out a locket from around his neck. The beat-up tin heart was much like his own. He'd unlatched it so many times, the hinge was starting to break off. With the utmost care, he eased the locket open to reveal a picture of a beautiful woman.

His mom had the prettiest red hair and brightest green eyes. She'd been a bartender and poet. He remembered how she would let him sit at the bar and listen to her recite great works from Lewis Carroll and Shakespeare while he did his homework. He missed her so much.

On the other side of the locket was a scrap of another photo. John had always assumed it had been a picture of his father, though he'd never met the man. When John had once asked about him, his mom had smiled and said, "You can't lasso a cloud, Johnny, nor can you tame thunder."

His mom had a way of making things seem better than they were. You didn't get evicted from your apartment; you were just on an adventure. A rainstorm didn't ruin a picnic; it was just an enormous sprinkler to dance in. If she were with John now, she would've told him, "When chins go up, fears go down."

The funny thing about fear is that it can happen only if you *know* you should be afraid. For instance, you're not afraid of the green wombat, a furry animal that lives in stinky gym shoes, because until now, I'm sure you'd never heard of one. Even if you saw one, you probably wouldn't be afraid of it until you noticed its sharp needle-shaped teeth or smelled its funky, gym-shoe breath. But the next time you get out those shoes for second period, I bet you'll look twice, because nothing hurts more than sticking your foot into the newly renovated sneaker-home of a putrid, razor-toothed wombat.

John had experienced all kinds of different fears lately, from wondering where he'd find his next meal to being startled by the rodents that also made the museum their home. He feared he'd be alone for the rest of his life. He feared he'd never amount to anything. He feared that his best days were far behind him. He'd been living with all these fears for two years, because that's when his mother had been stolen from him.

However, unlike other things that can be stolen, there was no way to recover her. John couldn't offer a reward for her safe return. He couldn't replace her with a duplicate, and he certainly was *not* going to be able to buy another mom hastily from the local bodega. John's mother was gone, and he feared that any hope of happiness had vanished along with her.

John was thinking about all this as he walked along the deserted corridor. The echoing sound of his footsteps seemed even louder, as if the museum was confirming he'd be forever on his own. The sporadic dim overhead light, mixed with the eerie glow of the moon, caused odd shadows to form along the walls, and the frozen faces of the statues and paintings seemed to watch him as he slowly passed by.

Even though John had walked these halls every night for the past six months, he still felt a cold tingle of fear creep up his spine as he approached the large stone-framed opening of the Egyptian tomb; two tall pillars on each side held up a giant slab of what appeared to be limestone.

Limestone, if you ever have the chance to encounter it, is not very limelike at all. It isn't green, and it doesn't taste very citrusy. It is, however, what is used to build pyramids, landmarks, and entrances to Egyptian exhibits.

John popped open a panel in one of the pillars, revealing a keypad behind it, then carefully typed in the code Mr. Van Eyck had just given him. The door buzzed and opened slightly. Creaking echoed off the limestone pillars as John slowly pushed into the room. He froze, looking around to make sure no one else had heard the noise, then gently closed the door, leaning against it as he waited for his racing heart to calm.

He shuddered as he unwrapped his sandwich, then, spotting a switch across the room, he crossed the chamber to turn on the lights, all the while imagining what it must've been like for the first explorers to discover this tomb.

The windows had been blocked off by exhibit pieces, and pale-blue moonlight filtered down through a series of small skylights, casting an eerie spell on the oddities and artifacts filling the space, each more mysterious than the last. John moved slowly from one object to the next, each new sight more fascinating. There was a small-scale model of the tomb, a golden funeral mask of the pharaoh Hatshepsut, and even a sarcophagus.

After a few bites, John carefully wrapped the rest of his sandwich in the napkin, returning the bundle to his pocket before moving to get a closer look at the sarcophagus. Unlike the other artifacts, it wasn't held behind glass. Its paint had been restored and the surface shined. The casket had been carved to look like a beautiful woman. John's heart skipped. The face looked so familiar—like his mother's. This wasn't a new experience. John would see his mom in a crowd gathered on the sidewalk or in the crush of the subway. And every time, he'd feel that same sharp stab when the flame of hope that the last months had been nothing but a bad dream was snuffed out.

And so it was with the sarcophagus: as John drew closer, the figure looked less like his mother and more like an Egyptian queen.

John wondered who the woman was—if she had had a family. Though her eyes were painted on, he couldn't help but notice they had a sort of sparkle to them.

"I bet it was cool to be so rich," John said.

The sarcophagus didn't reply, not because it was rude, but because it was an inanimate object. John felt a little silly for thinking it might answer him, even for a moment. Still, he had to admit talking to someone felt nice. But even as he knew the stone woman wasn't real, she had an expression that made it seem as though she were looking over his shoulder. He turned around to see what she appeared to be so captivated by.

A beam from one of the skylights fell perfectly on a glass case sitting in the middle of the room. Inside the glass prison was the most beautiful jewel John had ever seen. The mesmerizing stone was the dark color of blood, and was cut perfectly to catch the light, sending a kaleidoscope of sparkles across the room. John was entranced.

For a split second his eyes swam, and then he felt woozy, like a cartoon character staring into the eyes of a king cobra. He shook his head. Maybe the ruby *was* cursed. Beads of sweat gathered on his forehead. Had the museum suddenly gotten warmer? Now he understood why the ruby was named Egypt's Fire—the stone had left him with a burning desire in his heart. *If only I could touch it. . . .*

Before John could shake off the spell, he was right in front of the jewel's glass prison. He gazed deeply into the heart of Egypt's Fire, swaying helplessly, his image reflected back at him in the stone's many facets, as if he were staring into a thousand vermilion mirrors.

Suddenly, enchantment turned to terror. His heart

plunged and his hands began to shake, for the reflections showed him something he had not been prepared to see.

Someone was behind him.

Before John could scream, his vision blurred and he lost consciousness.

John had been wrong about three things that night: Danger *did* lurk in the museum; he was *not* alone; and he was about to uncover a life-changing mystery.

CHAPTER TWO

The time John met the greatest detective who ever lived.

THE ROOM WAS BATHED in a soft light, and John instantly knew he was dreaming. That's what happens in a good dream. Everyone seems to be in a bright place, and whatever's in the background is often slightly blurry, as if the dreamer remembers what should be there, but not entirely. John found himself lying in his old bed. He looked around the room, transfixed by the gentle glow and smell of fresh flowers.

"How are we feeling?" a voice as warm as a summer's day asked.

Curly red hair glowed in a halo above him, and the cool

pressure of his mother's hand on his forehead felt soothing, as though her touch could magically make everything
better.

She smiled. "I think your fever has broken."

"Mom?"

"Yes, my love?"

"Where did you go?"

"Go? I haven't gone anywhere. I've been here the whole
time." She sat back.

Around her neck, something sparkled. John tried to focus
on it—the locket he'd been carefully protecting.

"Why don't you rest while I read to you?" She reached
over and picked up a book. "Where were we?" She flipped
through a couple of pages. "Ah, here we are:

" 'But how about my courage?' asked the Lion, anxiously.

" 'You have plenty of courage, I am sure,' answered Oz. 'All you
need is confidence in yourself. There is no living thing that is not
afraid when it faces danger. True courage is in facing danger when
you are afraid, and that kind of courage you have in plenty.' "

She reached out and touched John's face. His focus began
to blur again. He wanted desperately to stay awake, but he
was too tired.

"Son, can you hear me?" A familiar voice echoed in
John's head.

"Mom?" John smiled. But as his vision cleared, the groggy

twelve-year-old realized he wasn't staring at his mom but into the grim face of an old man.

"Mr. Van Eyck?" John sat up abruptly.

He was back in the museum. It had just been a dream. Then reality set in. "The *ruby!*"

The director frowned. "It's gone."

The blood rushed from John's head, and his hands began to shake as he looked up at the case. The display that had held the ruby was smashed. Shards were scattered all over the floor, as if someone had thrown handfuls of glass confetti around the exhibit. Instead of the dazzling stone, there was only an empty pedestal. The person John had seen reflected in the ruby must have taken it.

John frantically surveyed the room. Half a dozen police officers were spread out among the artifacts. One was dusting the light switch for fingerprints, another collected glass samples from the floor, and two more were taking selfies with the sarcophagus.

"Hey, someone get me the security tapes from last night!" a stout, brown-suited man bellowed. The round man barked orders at his fellow officers, while a woman with a notepad wrote down everything he said.

John tried to stand, but he slumped back to the floor as another wave of dizziness washed over him.

"Be careful. The Gotcha 3000's gas is potent. You may feel a little woozy for a day or two," Van Eyck said as he helped John to his feet. "Here, drink this." He handed John a cup of strong coffee. "Caffeine will help with the headache. I'll try to find a paramedic."

"As soon as Sleeping Beauty over there wakes up, we'll get some answers," the detective said, turning back to the woman with the notepad. "Should have this case wrapped up by lunch."

"Do you think that the new security system failed?" she asked. Long brown hair cascaded over the lapels of her tailored, white pantsuit, and John noticed her bright-purple pumps matched her hoop earrings.

"Of course it didn't," Van Eyck interjected, steering John toward the detective. "It's the best investment this museum has made since the day we got rid of the student rate." If there was one thing that Viktor Van Eyck hated more than thieves, it was giving a discount to rabble-rousing teenagers. "Bartholomew, this is Detective Doug Brownie."

Detective Brownie was a giant of a man. He was what some would call rotund. His wide face was anchored by a double chin, and his brown suit was wrinkled, as if he had slept in it for several days.

"Who is this?" the detective asked.

"This is Bartholomew, the night janitor."

Brownie scratched his head. "You have a kid as a night janitor?"

"Kid?"

Brownie laughed. "You do realize that this person is a child."

"I'm not a child," John protested.

"Yeah, well you look like one to me," Brownie spat back.

"What are you talking about?" Van Eyck squinted, then reached into his pocket, pulled out his spectacles, and settled them on his nose. The sound that then came out of the museum director's mouth would be talked about for years to come. I can't reproduce the utterance, but if I had to describe it, I would say it was something like two camels singing opera while a cat playing a broken violin yowled after stubbing its toe on the end of a coffee table. "You . . . you . . . are a *teenager?*"

"Not technically, sir," John replied. "I'm twelve."

"Twelve?" Van Eyck sat down crisscross applesauce on the floor and began rocking back and forth. He was hyperventilating.

"Does the museum have a habit of hiring underage employees?" the woman asked, scribbling away in her notebook.

John knew that his secret had been exposed, but he still

didn't want Van Eyck to get in trouble. "I . . . umm . . . don't work here, ma'am."

"Then why are you wearing a janitor's outfit?" she pressed.

"I borrowed it."

"You mean you stole it," Brownie rumbled, "just like you stole the ruby."

"He did?" Van Eyck eyed John as if he were a donkey painted to look like a zebra.

"What? No," John said, holding up his hands. "I didn't steal anything. I swear."

"Then why did we catch you red-handed?" Brownie demanded.

"I—I just wanted to see the ruby."

Brownie pointed his finger in John's face. "So you broke in the night before the exhibit opened to the public?"

"I didn't break in," John said, taking a step back. "I was already here."

"Are you admitting you stayed after-hours so you could sneak in to see the ruby?" The woman made another note.

"Perhaps we should take this conversation to my office," Van Eyck politely offered.

"No need. As I was telling Ms. Star . . ."

John had heard that name before. Jaclyn Star was a famous reporter for *Confidential Informer*, the world's primo magazine covering detectives, crime, and fashion. She was said to have a nose for news. *A nose for news* means she had a knack for finding interesting stories. Coincidentally, she was also said to have an unusually large sniffer, which John found puzzling. He didn't think Ms. Star's nose was particularly oversize. In fact, he thought it looked very nice.

Brownie peered down at the boy. "You better tell us the whole story if you know what's good for you."

"Okay," John began, his voice shaking. "I live here. I've been living here for about six months."

"You *live* in the museum?" The reporter was now writing furiously.

"Yes," John said, avoiding the detective's eye.

"So, you're a squatter as well as a thief?" Brownie pulled out his handcuffs. "I think it's time to take this downtown."

"*No!* I didn't steal anything. You have to believe me, officer. I didn't do it. Yes, I use this uniform so I can walk around the museum at night. I messed up, but I swear I just wanted to see the ruby. When I came in last night, the jewel was right there." John waved at the broken display case. "But I wasn't alone. Someone came up behind me. That's the last thing I remember before I woke up here."

"You saw someone behind you?" Van Eyck glanced over his shoulder to make sure someone wasn't behind him.

"Describe this so-called person," Detective Brownie commanded.

"I don't remember. I didn't get a very good look at them."

"Nonsense," Brownie spat. His breath smelled of rotten eggs. "Your story doesn't hold water. You just 'passed out'? What you really mean is you were *knocked out*. The perp—that's you—set off the alarm. The steel containment doors shut and the security system's knockout gas released. You were the only person found inside the trap. Now, before I lose my patience, what really happened here?"

"I'm telling you the truth. I didn't steal anything. If you would just let me explain—"

"*You* explain something to *me*? *I'm* a *detective*—a third-grade detective. *You* are a *runaway*." Brownie's pudgy face turned red like a tomato. "You're gonna tell me what I want to know, or I'm taking you downtown."

Van Eyck, still sitting on the floor, pointed to a security camera on the wall. "Once we see the security footage, we'll know exactly what happened."

"Or," Brownie growled, "you could save yourself some time and confess."

"*Confess?*" John swallowed. He didn't like the sound of that.

"You must take me for a real igneous," the detective spat.

"You mean *ignoramus*," John corrected.

"What?"

"*Igneous* is a type of rock. *Ignoramus* means a man of lesser intelligence," John explained, then wished he hadn't.

Brownie smiled, but it wasn't friendly. "Fine. If you didn't steal the ruby, then who did?"

"I don't know." John was starting to feel nauseated. "But it wasn't me. I swear. I used the code Mr. Van Eyck gave me to turn off the alarm. Then I walked up to the ruby. I was looking into the case when I saw someone behind me. Before I could do anything, I passed out. I'm actually not feeling all that great right now."

"So, the pink gas didn't knock you out?" Brownie's teeth flashed menacingly.

"I never saw any pink gas—"

"But if the alarm was turned off, then why did the gas eject?" Brownie pressed.

John shrugged. "I don't know."

"The code only turns off the motion sensors," Van Eyck explained. "If someone tampered with the display case, the alarm would still sound. The only way to turn off that feature is by using this remote." Van Eyck pulled a little box from his jacket pocket. "This is my new remote for the Gotcha 3000. NOFFO products are affordable, reliable, top-of-the-line, and come in any color. All their systems include remotes, which is great when you're running around making sure rabble-rousing teenagers aren't drawing mustaches on your paintings."

"Does that happen often?" Jaclyn asked.

"Not yet, but you can never be too careful when it comes to today's youth." Van Eyck seemed pleased with himself.

The room went silent as all the adults turned to John.

"That's not fair. I was living on the street." John clenched his fists. "I just needed a place to crash."

But that explanation only seemed to add fuel to the fire. "I can find you a place to crash at Rikers." Brownie snorted.

"What about my ruby?" Van Eyck pleaded.

Brownie pointed at John again. "Obviously, this punk has it."

"Not necessarily," a voice said from behind them.

Jaclyn's eyes sparkled, as if she'd seen a large diamond. Brownie's face squished up, like he'd just eaten a large lemon. Van Eyck looked confused, as though he'd stumbled upon a large diamond-shaped lemon.

Defeated, John turned to identify the oddity lurking behind him. Only the figure he saw wasn't odd at all. The man's face looked nothing like a diamond, a lemon, *or* a diamond-shaped lemon.

The angular man appeared to be in his mid-thirties. He had brown skin and was dressed from head to toe in navy blue. A bowler hat rested on top of his head, and a red necktie was neatly tucked into his double-breasted suit. On his lapel, he wore a red pin inscribed with three letters, *S.O.S.*

Turning back to Brownie, John caught the detective looking hungrily at the pin, like he was about to dig into a birthday cake.

Brownie shook his head. "What are you doing here?" John noted that the detective's voice sounded a bit less confident.

"What am I always doing at a crime scene? Why, I'm here to solve a crime of course." John noticed the man's voice had a very eloquent English accent to it, like James Bond's or Danger Mouse's. The man surveyed the room and its inhabitants, smiling when he spotted Ms. Star. "Jackie, I like the new nose."

"I'm sure I have no idea what you're talking about," Jaclyn said primly, checking her reflection in the glass of a nearby display case.

The blue-suited man ignored the comment, instead moving toward the old man still seated on the museum floor. He reached out his hand. "Shall we, Viktor?"

"If we must." The museum director collected himself, then clasped the strange man's offered hand. With lightning-like reflexes, the man pulled Van Eyck up and into his arms, striking a pose.

Brownie was clearly not a fan of these theatrics. "That's enough. We don't have time for your—"

Before Brownie could finish his sentence, the two men began to waltz around the room. For an old man, Van Eyck was surprisingly light on his feet.

To an untrained eye, the men's steps would have appeared chaotic and absurd, but John couldn't help but notice they were following the same path he'd taken the night before.

The bowler-hatted man spun Van Eyck, leaving him at the model of the tomb. Viktor grabbed the edge of the display, trying to catch his breath.

The strange man struck another pose, then swept Jaclyn Star into his arms, pulling her close before the two began to tango.

"Inspector?" Jaclyn laughed as he danced her up to the sarcophagus.

Brownie once again tried to take control of the situation, but instead found himself the next unwitting dance partner of the mysterious new detective.

"What the—" Brownie clung to the odd man, trying to keep up with his footwork.

The two kicked and spun, spun and kicked, until finally they ended up in front of the Egypt's Fire display case, where the inspector dipped Brownie low. The other officers applauded as the pair held the pose for a moment, before Brownie was abruptly dropped to the ground.

"Hmm," the inspector said, bending down to pick up

a small hammer resting near the shattered display case. He stared at the tool for a second, then looked past it, his focus settling on John. "I don't believe we've met. My name is Inspector Toadius McGee."

CHAPTER THREE

The time John stole a billion-dollar ruby.

"CAREFUL, DOCTOR," Toadius said, as he shook John's hand and guided him out of the way of two officers taping off the crime scene. "May I start by apologizing for my colleague. He is, as they say in France, an idiot."

"I'm not a doctor." John didn't know what else *to* say.

"And *idiot*"—Toadius winked—"isn't a French word."

"But it is a French word."

"McGee, you're too late. I already solved this case." Brownie had risen from the floor by then, and he was furious.

"You did?" Toadius leaned in, his eyes gleaming. "Who did it?"

"Him!" Brownie stated forcefully, jabbing a finger at John.

Toadius burst out laughing. The other officers joined in. After all, laughter is infectious. The inspector gestured toward John, then doubled over, holding his stomach. *"Him?"* Suddenly, he stopped laughing as though he had never started. "Oh, you're serious."

Removing his hat, the inspector studied the detective as he would a piece of modern art. "It must be so lonely to be one of your thoughts." He reached out and gave Brownie's chin a soft tap. "Just keep swinging, slugger. You'll get your home run one day."

Brownie's mouth opened, but all that came out was a low groan.

Toadius placed his hand on John's shoulder. "There is no way that this young man tried to steal the ruby."

Jaclyn Star raised a skeptical eyebrow. "He had the means, as he knows the museum layout," she said, consulting her notebook. "He had opportunity. He was alone with the ruby. *And* he has motive. He is a kid with no job who needs money to survive.

"Madam," Toadius replied, "you've just described every rabble-rousing teenager in this museum."

"That's why I have this remote!" Van Eyck looked around

the room nervously. "You can never be too sure where teen-agers will be hiding."

"Yes, very good, Viktor," Toadius said, before giving the museum director a high-five.

"Are you saying this boy wasn't capable of stealing the ruby?" Jaclyn pressed.

"I never said he was incapable of stealing it—he appears to be a healthy young man. I said he didn't *try* to steal it." Toadius focused on the tool in his hand. After a moment that seemed to stretch on for an uncomfortably long time, he murmured, "Why the hammer?"

"Because he didn't have a key to open the case," Brownie said, finally finding his voice again. "He was the only one we found in the cage when we got here, and he's our only suspect!"

Toadius waved off the now flailing Brownie and turned his attention back to John. "Doctor . . ."

"Dude, I am not a doctor," John said.

Toadius's smile slipped. "My dear boy, I do appreciate a good joke, but now is not the time for humor."

John was losing his patience. "I already told them what I saw."

"And now I am asking you to tell me again," Toadius requested calmly.

"Fine. I snuck into the exhibit to look at the ruby after

the museum closed. In its reflection, I saw someone behind me, but before I could yell for help, I blacked out."

Toadius frowned. "That doesn't add up."

"That's what *I* said!" Brownie shouted, throwing his hands in the air.

"Now, what do we know about you?" Toadius continued, locking his gaze with John's. The inspector's brown eyes were almost hypnotic. "You are a twelve-year-old dropout, not because you struggled with your course material, but because of circumstances outside your control, which forced you to cease attending class. You like to read, but get headaches, so you can't do it for long periods of time. You are an insomniac. You are from Brooklyn. You are right-handed and quick-tempered, but you are loyal. You like punk rock music and love blueberry pie."

John gaped. "How do you know so much about me?"

"Simple. Only a preadolescent would part his hair in such a fashion. You are wearing a janitorial uniform and have dark rings under your eyes, indicating that you don't have a normal sleep cycle, but you are too young to be a worker, so I assume you've found a place to sleep here. You tie your shoes with a great bomber double loop, the same knot used by the Brooklyn Bombers, and a trend that only a kid from Brooklyn would know. You love to learn—that's why you picked the museum as your home. You learn from reading, but you are in desperate need of glasses, which is apparent from the way your eyes are straining to focus. Your fat lip is a yellowish color. I expect you were in a dustup a couple of days ago, likely because you have a temper, and being young and angry, you sometimes say things before thinking them through. The knuckles on your right hand are scraped, so I assume you are not a south paw. As for your musical preferences, unless I am mistaken, punk rock is still the music of the angry and defiant."

"And what about the blueberry pie?" Jaclyn Star asked, writing frantically.

"Who doesn't love blueberry pie?" Toadius returned his attention to John, his voice a few degrees gentler. "The only thing I don't know . . . is your name."

"I—I'm sorry. John Boarhog."

"Boarhog?" Toadius's expression softened for a moment.

"Enough with your parlor tricks, McGee," Brownie cut in. "What about my robbery?"

"You believe that the good doctor here tried to break into the exhibit and steal a ruby, but accidently set off the alarm and was knocked out before he knew what hit him?"

"Why do you keep calling him a doctor?" Brownie snapped.

"For the same reason I call you a detective," Toadius

replied, tapping the side of his nose. "It's all about potential, Doug. It's all about potential."

Brownie stepped up, his face close to Toadius's. It seemed for a second that the two men were about to brawl, but then a light bulb went off in Brownie's big square head. He licked his lips. "Okay, McGee, if you're so sure of yourself, you wouldn't mind a friendly wager."

"What do you have in mind? I do have a little cash on me," Toadius replied, reaching for his wallet.

"I don't want your money. I want your pin."

"I see. But you know as well as I, you have to earn this pin."

Brownie squared his shoulders, "I'm only one step away from getting my own, so if I'm right, you have to give me a recommendation."

John looked between the men as Toadius considered the proposition. *A recommendation for what?*

"All right," the inspector finally said. "And if you're wrong, you have to wear black wingtips for a week." John's eyes traveled down to Brownie's feet, which sported simple black loafers. What kind of bet was that? The longer he was in the room, the more he wondered if either of these men should be in charge of the case.

The two men stood with eyes locked for an uncomfortable moment, then reached out and shook hands.

"What in the blazes is going on here?" a man the size of a small refrigerator called out as he entered the exhibit hall, followed by a shorter, skinnier fellow, who was frantically trying to keep up with his companion's stride.

"Chief?" Brownie said, going pale. "What are you doing here?"

"I'm here to see if McGee has solved the case, of course." He turned to Toadius. "Inspector, it's good to see you again. Now, what happened here? Have you caught the guy who did it?"

"Yes," Brownie said quickly. "We caught him red-handed."

"Mr. Brownie is right. You did catch something red. . . . A red herring! *See?*" Toadius turned to address Detective Brownie. "It hurts when someone calls you by the wrong title."

John stifled a laugh.

"I'm sure that when we look at the security tapes, the film will show this brat trying to steal the ruby," Brownie insisted. "Mr. Van Eyck, what's taking so long?"

Van Eyck immediately snapped into action. He spoke into a walkie-talkie, listened for a response, and then smiled. "Follow me, gentlemen. Now remember, the rest of the museum is still open, so everyone, use your indoor voices and don't touch anything."

I've seen a lot of security rooms in my lifetime, but the

security room at the New York Museum of Natural History is by far the largest of them all. The entrance is located on the fourth floor, between the Hall of Ornithischian Dinosaurs and the Hall of Saurischian Dinosaurs.

Van Eyck walked up to a life-size model of a stegosaurus. He looked both ways, checking for anyone passing by. When he was certain the coast was clear, he reached down and pulled on one of the tail spikes. A hidden door opened in the wall.

"Quick, get in before a teenager sees us," Van Eyck urged, rushing everyone inside.

John peered around the room. For a moment, he thought he'd walked into a secret military base. A half-dozen people were watching what seemed to be over a hundred monitors, each showing a different part of the museum. One panel monitor the size of a small movie screen displayed the dinosaur room, where a pretty patron in a lavender dress could be seen perusing the exhibit. The entire security staff seemed mesmerized by the beautiful auburn-haired girl. Van Eyck coughed to get their attention. "Peter, did you pull up the video I asked you for?"

The man, who John assumed was Peter, turned to face the director. "Yes, sir. Bring it up on the main screen," he instructed one of the other guards.

The main screen flashed to the Egyptian exhibit. The

image was split into seven different windows, each showing a different angle of the crime scene.

"This is the footage from last night at approximately eleven fifty-nine p.m. As you can see, the night janitor is outside the exhibit. He punches in the code to the key box and enters the hall. Now, if we switch to a view inside the room . . ."

John watched as the video showed him moving through the light and up to the display case. The room was dim, illuminated with scattered pools of moonlight pouring though the skylights. On the screen, John disappeared and reappeared as he passed between beams, surveying the exhibit.

The John on screen stopped, staring into the shadows.

"What are you looking at there?" Toadius asked.

"The sarcophagus. It didn't have a display light focused on it. For a minute, she looked like someone I knew."

Toadius studied the footage. "I wonder why."

"Probably a trick of the light."

"A trick of the light, indeed," Toadius said, then winked.

Those in the room watched as John finally stopped right next to the jewel's case, just outside the perfect circle illuminating the Egypt's Fire. In the control room, John held his breath. Any minute now, the alarm would go off and the footage would prove that he hadn't stolen the ruby.

But then something happened that was straight out of a nightmare.

If you've ever been unfortunate enough to have had a nightmare, you know that it can be very scary, and it usually involves some sort of danger. For instance, one time I had a nightmare about a clown who tried to get me to eat a jar of peanut butter. I'm allergic to peanuts and therefore was in great danger. Luckily, when you have a nightmare, it's all make-believe, and you are, in fact, actually quite safe. In my case, when I awoke, my mother, who was not a clown, gave me some peanut-free hot cocoa, and we laughed about the absurdity of the bad dream until I was ready to go back to sleep.

That is also an important feature of nightmares: once you tell an adult about them, they can help you realize that the situation wasn't as scary as it seemed.

John, however, was *not* having a nightmare, and there were no adults to help him see that the circumstances weren't as scary as he believed them to be.

On the screen, John stepped out of the gloom, reached into his pocket, and pulled out the hammer Toadius had found at the crime scene. Drawing back his arm, he smashed the case, reached in with his left hand, grabbed the ruby, and hastily wrapped it in his handkerchief. In the background, the steel containment doors began to close.

One by one, the skylights went dark. Security-footage John slipped into the shadows, and right before the last security door shut, pink smoke began to pour out of the floor. After a minute, emergency security lights flickered on, illuminating the room, and the smoke dissipated, revealing the young boy passed out on the cold ground.

Brownie cheered. "I TOLD YOU, McGEE! I TOLD YOU!" he shouted, high-fiving some of the other officers while Ms. Star continued taking note. "Lock him up, boys!"

The cold metal cuffs stung John's wrists. He was no stranger to handcuffs, but this time they felt different.

"Check his pockets," Van Eyck demanded. One of the officers leaned in and pulled out the handkerchief-wrapped sandwich John had stowed away. Inside wasn't egg salad on white bread but the dazzling Egypt's Fire.

"No!" John insisted. "I swear I didn't take that! Please, Mr. Van Eyck! Inspector McGee!" Tears were running down his cheeks. "You have to believe me."

Toadius's gaze remained fixed on the screen. Van Eyck was too busy making sure the ruby hadn't been damaged. Ms. Star watched John, her blue eyes twinkling. As the officers led the boy away, the reporter gave him a little wave with her left hand.

John wished this day had never happened. He wished that

he'd never gone to see the ruby. Most of all, he wished someone would wake him from this nightmare.

But, if I could interject and give you one piece of advice, my dear reader, be careful what you wish for.

CHAPTER FOUR

*The time John met the world's greatest cat burglar
and worst stage magician.*

HAVING BEEN A GUEST MYSELF at the New York City County Jail, I can tell you that it isn't much fun. John had never been in jail before, but he had read many books about people stuck behind cold concrete walls and metal bars, wasting away until they became nothing but skin and bones.

Occasionally, John would get a peek of other criminals awaiting their fate.

It isn't customary to house a youth in a jail cell meant for adults. However, in an unfortunate mix-up, instead of the limestone blocks that had been ordered to build new facilities, two truckloads of juicy limes had been delivered to the prison, and since there wasn't exactly an influx of teens being arrested for high larceny jewel thefts, the two thousand tons of fruit were being stored in the juvenile detention cells. This caused two oddities: First, a young boy was now pacing a jail cell, shooting surreptitious looks at a gentleman with an eye patch and green whiskers, who had the words *El Diablo* tattooed in red ink on his left arm; and second, the cell, instead of wreaking of body odor, had a much more pleasant citrusy aroma.

John was even hungrier than usual, in part because he hadn't had more than a few bites of sandwich for over a day, but mostly because the cell smelled like a key lime pie.

He was pretty sure the authorities had locked him up and thrown away the key. The concrete box was bleak and dirty, its walls covered in graffiti—mostly names of other criminals who'd been there before, inspirational quotes, and bad jokes involving bodily functions. There were some interesting poems, such as:

I stole some wheels in Nashville,
A car of highest class.
I would have gotten away with it
If I'd thought to steal the gas.

And:

Tell my mother I'm sorry to hurt her.
Tell my dad it wasn't my fault.
But I needed a little more money,
So I took it from somebody's vault.

Normally, funny poems would have distracted John from his problems, but that night he couldn't stop thinking about the museum. The events of the night before were still hazy, but he did remember wanting to touch the Egypt's Fire. Maybe that's what the janitors had meant about the ruby being cursed. Maybe it had magical powers that caused a person to stop at nothing until they obtained it. John had read about an indigenous tribe in the Amazon called the Shuar that had once shrunken the heads of enemy warriors as part of a spiritual practice. He didn't believe in magic, but nonetheless found himself feeling his head to see if it was still a normal size.

After careful investigation, John decided his head wasn't any smaller than before this nightmare began, and his thoughts turned to that mysterious person who had snuck up behind him. He tried to remember what they'd looked like, but his head hurt.

Maybe prison won't be so bad, he thought. Maybe they had

a big library. He'd heard that some inmates even earned their degrees while locked up. Plus, he hadn't stolen the ruby, so maybe he'd get a lighter sentence. He tried hard to be positive. His mother had always said, "Johnny, we have a saying in this house. It always ends good. So, if it's not good, it's not the end."

"It must not be the end then, Mom," John whispered to himself.

The sound of his cell door opening startled him from his thoughts as the guard, a brick of a man, escorted in a very peculiar individual.

The new prisoner was wearing a giant black top hat with a purple band. He had a very long mustache that seemed to be shorter on one side below a crooked nose, which John assumed had been broken many times. The man's skin was dark, and his eyes were deep brown, like the Amazon River. He appeared mysterious—a traveler from a distant land, maybe Tucson, Arizona. Maybe he was a Shuar shaman, and had come to take John's head.

"What are you-a looking at?" the man asked in an Italian accent.

"Y-you can't have my head," John sputtered.

"What?" he sneered.

John's eyes darted around the cell, before settling on the small cot in the corner. He raced over and jumped on it. "*Bed*. You can't have my bed!"

"I don't want your bed. I'm-a, how do you say, not sleepy?"

"Tired?"

"No, that is not it." The man grunted as he sat down on an empty bench.

"So, what are you in for?" John finally summoned up the courage to ask. He was glad to at least have someone to talk to.

"In for?"

"Yeah, you know, why did they arrest you?" John noticed the man was fiddling with something in his hand. "Who are you?"

"Do you not know who I am?" the man said as if he were a swan and someone had mistaken him for a duck (and an ugly one at that).

"No." John shrugged. "I don't get out much."

"Why, I am the greatest thief this world has ever seen." The man leaned in closer to John. "I am THE GREAT GOATINEE-NEE-NEE-nee."

John laughed. "Sorry. Never heard of you."

"Good." The Goatinee's accent vanished. "Unlike in other professions, the greatest thieves are the ones no one talks about. You must be one with the wind, king of the shadows, the man who walks backward in the night."

John shuddered, thinking for a moment about his own situation. Whoever had framed him must really be the greatest thief of all time.

"And what about you? What did they-a, how do you say, get you for?" John noticed Goatinee's accent had reappeared as fast as it had gone away.

"I was framed."

"Good for you." The Great Goatinee nodded. "Never admit you committed the crime."

"No, I really didn't commit a crime." John was starting to get a little sick of trying to convince everyone he was innocent. "I was living at the New York Museum of Natural History. Someone framed me and made it look like I stole a ruby from one of the exhibits."

"The Egypt's Fire?"

The temperature in the cell seemed to drop several degrees.

"Yes." John jumped to his feet. "How did you know?"

"Please. I'm the greatest cat burglar ever to live. You think a billion-dollar ruby could come into my city and I wouldn't know about it? That was foolish of you. What would you do with a billion-dollar ruby? There is-a only one fence in town who would buy it, but you'd have to be a member of our union. And since I'm the chapter head, I know for a fact you are *not* in this union. The Thieves Guild would never induct a novice such as yourself. You could maybe try the henchmen program, but you don't seem like a kid who plays well with others."

"I already told you. I didn't steal the ruby. Someone planted it in my pocket."

"That doesn't make—what do you-a call it when it-a does not sound factual?"

"Sense?" John spat.

"You are not very good at this game." Goatinee adjusted his top hat. "How did the police know it was you?"

"There was security footage that showed me stealing it."

"Amateur." Goatinee shook his head. "You *always* look for security cameras first."

Now the thief was giving John advice?

"The tape was lying. I didn't steal the ruby. At least, I don't remember doing it."

"People lie; video cameras, not so much." Goatinee sniffed the air. "Do you smell limes?"

"I mean, I didn't do it. Someone else tricked me."

"Someone doesn't like you," the thief said matter-of-factly. "I know, because I don't like you, and I just met you."

"Great." John tried to fluff a well-used pillow on the cot. Pretending to sleep would be better than having to talk to this guy one moment longer.

"I mean, as first impressions go, I don't think this is a good one," the thief continued.

John huffed, laying his head on the pillow. "Yeah, well, the feeling is mutual."

"You're kind of rude, and you're in jail, so you probably can't be trusted."

"Okay, I think you made that clear."

"And you smell. I mean *bad*. Like a Red Sox catcher's mitt kind of bad. Like Jersey on a hot day—"

"OKAY!" John shouted. "I GET IT!"

The two sat in silence.

"I guess we both know why no one likes you," the Great Goatinee finally said, shaking his finger at the boy. "Tempers don't make friends."

"SHUT UP!"

John turned his back on his new cellmate, but every time he looked up, he'd see the Great Goatinee staring at him with a toothy grin and wide eyes, like he'd just passed gas and was waiting for someone to smell it.

Finally, John couldn't take it anymore.

"What?"

"Do you like the magic?" The Great Goatinee was shuffling a deck of playing cards that he seemed to have produced out of thin air.

"Not really." John rubbed at his head again.

"Okay, take a card."

John watched as the cardician tried to shuffle the cards, but ended up spilling them on the ground. Goatinee quickly grabbed them, hastily restacking the well-worn cards before fanning them out. Some were still faceup, some had different-colored backs, and John was pretty sure one of the cards was a piece of paper with the words *two hearts* written on it. He picked one anyway.

"Look at it, but don't-a tell me what it is."

John peeked at the card. It was the jack of hearts, but someone had drawn long hair and lipstick on the figure. The letter *J* had been scratched out, and *Q* had been scrawled in its place.

"Okay, put the-a card back into the deck."

John did as he was told.

"Now, I will attempt to look deep into your mind and read your thoughts." The Great Goatinee raised one of his eyebrows and stared with intense focus into John's eyes. He began to shuffle the deck, which he again fumbled, sending cards flying across the cell. Some of them went through the bars, out of the magician's reach. "Ignore those. They were not your card."

"Let's hope not."

"Okay, was this your card?" The magician pulled out the four of clubs.

"No."

"Of course not," Goatinee said, covering his mistake with a laugh. "I was joking. *This* is your real card."

The two of diamonds.

"Nope." John shook his head.

"Forget it," Goatinee said, tossing the deck across the cell. "Card tricks are for amateurs."

"This is just perfect! I can't wait to get out of here," John complained as he threw himself back on the cot.

"You want to escape? I can do that!"

John wiggled his fingers at the strange man mocking him. "What are you going to do? Use magic?"

"No." The Goatinee put his fingers to his temples and strained his eyes. "I will use the power of my mind!" He stretched out his hand and pointed to something hanging on the wall outside the cell. John spotted the object—a ring of keys hanging on a little hook.

"You're going to get the keys with your mind?"

"Be quiet, nonbeliever." Goatinee closed his eyes, concentrating. "I need complete silence."

John sighed. "Whatever."

But something caught the boy's eye. The keys began to jingle. Not just jingle, but move. As if the Great Goatinee had an invisible vacuum, the keys lifted into the air, barely even touching the hook.

"What on earth?" John couldn't believe his eyes.

"I am the Great Goat—"

But before the magician could finish his sentence, his hand began vibrating. Suddenly, an invisible force pulled the Goatinee toward the cell's bars. Out of control, the man slammed into the wall, his hand stuck to the metal bars.

It was then that John realized his cellmate didn't have mental powers. He had a powerful magnet under his sleeve. Yet another terrible trick of Goatinee's had failed.

"Could you help me?" the magician asked as he struggled to get free of the bars.

John lay back down on the cot. The soft glow of sunrise had begun to creep through the cell window. He closed his eyes, hoping he would fall asleep.

Fall he did, only not into Dreamland, but onto the cold cement floor. When the boy opened his eyes, Goatinee had somehow gotten free and was standing over him, holding the blanket from John's bed.

"Ouch! What are you doing?"

"Here." Goatinee shoved the blanket into John's hands. "Now, hold it up so you can't see me."

John shot up from the floor like a rabbit who'd just realized he'd forgotten his carrot cake was in the oven. "Just leave me alone."

"Okay." Goatinee thrust his hands in the air. "I get it. I also had trouble making friends when I was your age."

"I don't want to be your friend," John spat. "I want you to go away."

"I wasn't offering. Now, if you would be so kind as to hold up the blanket."

"I think we've had enough bad magic for one day."

"Humor me. Last trick. You'll like it. I promise."

"Fine, but this is the last one."

"The last one." Goatinee nodded, grinning. "Now, raise up the blanket and hold out your arms."

John, again, did as he was told. Facing the cot, he stretched out his arms as far as he could until the Great Goatinee was no longer visible.

"On the count of three, drop the blanket! Ready?"

"Ready," John replied, sounding more than a little bored.

"A-one and a-two and a-THREE!" Goatinee cried.

Taking his cue, John let the blanket fall.

John couldn't believe his eyes. The man had vanished! John waved his hand in front of his face to make sure his eyesight was working. The cell remained empty.

"Ahem."

John spun around. The magician stood outside the cell looking at him through the bars.

"How do you say . . . *TADA!*" The Great Goatinee's signature toothy smile stretched across his face.

"What? How did you do that?"

"Figlio, a magician never reveals his secrets. Oh, and check your left back pocket."

John suddenly felt woozy, the way he had the night before at the museum. Somehow, the magician had just teleported across the room. Without thinking about it, John reached into his pocket. Inside was a card. He pulled it out and blinked twice. The queen of hearts. Well, the Great Goatinee's handmade queen of hearts, anyway. His card.

"How did you—"

But the man was gone, and John was left gaping, alone in the cell.

CHAPTER FIVE

The time John had to make a choice.

THE ALTERED CARD MADE John wonder: What if someone disguised themselves to look like me and stole the ruby, just like the jack had been disguised to look like a queen?

"That doesn't make any sense," he muttered. "Think. Why would someone go through all the trouble of dressing up like me and knocking me out, just to leave the ruby in my pocket? *ARGHHHH!*"

He punched the wall, and a sharp pain shot up his arm, like someone had stuck needles into his hand. Everyone will get angry enough to punch a wall at some point. If I could give you a piece of advice, young reader, when you decide to punch something, let it be a pillow or a punching bag. Cement walls will always win in a fistfight.

John dropped to his knees. He wasn't sure what hurt more, his hand or the thought that he had been set up. But if he couldn't figure out *why*, he'd never figure out *who* had targeted him.

"Who's screaming?" the guard called out, turning to find John sitting alone in the cell. "Holy Toledo!" He grabbed for his walkie-talkie. "Huck, Goatinee did another one of his disappearing acts. Could you call the boys down at Precinct One and have them go over to the Grimly Diner to pick him up again?"

"Sure thing, Lou," a voice rattled back from the speaker. "Want me to ask them to send a uniform to pick up a couple of coffees while they're down there?"

"Yup. And doughnuts. I'm starving. Good thing Goatinee always goes to the same place."

"Yeah, magic must make him hungry, too." The guards seemed to find this amusing.

John thought that maybe they should be a little less cavalier about an escaped prisoner.

It took about an hour before John's hand started to feel better. He was super bored, but he'd collected most of the deck left from the Great Goatinee's trick and was midway through building a house of cards when the guard came back.

"John Boarhog?" The guard read his name off a list, and then looked around to see if anyone answered. "Are you John Boarhog?" the man finally asked after an awkward pause.

"Yes." John looked over his shoulder, half expecting to see the Great Goatinee sitting there.

The guard opened the cell door with a loud *creak* that rang out through the hallway. For a moment, John thought that maybe the cops had figured out he was innocent and were about to let him go. But only for a moment.

The guard pulled out a pair of handcuffs, told John to hold out his wrists, and then cuffed the boy. With a *snap*, John's dreams of freedom were once again squashed.

"This way," the guard said, motioning down the hall.

The corridor was darker than John would've liked. It seemed to go on for miles as he passed men of all shapes and sizes and cells filled with spiderwebs, graffiti, and eventually box upon box of limes.

The farther he walked, the darker the corridors became. Even the cells were scarier. These doors didn't have bars, just little slots through which food could be slid. John wondered if this was the part of the prison where they kept people who tried to steal billion-dollar rubies.

He'd once read a story about a man who was put in jail

and forgotten. The man had been innocent of his crimes, too, but in the story, he found out about a great treasure, escaped the prison, and then posed as a count to seek revenge on the people who'd framed him. It was a thrilling book, with sword fights and pirate gold. Maybe John could do the same thing. Maybe he could escape and figure out who'd framed him.

He was so busy imagining how he'd escape that he didn't realize where he was being led. By the time John had snapped out of his daydream, he had entered a courtroom.

He'd never been in a criminal courtroom before, but he'd seen them on TV and in movies, and was sure he'd read about them in his books. This chamber didn't seem like anything he'd seen or read about, though. There wasn't a jury and there weren't two sides with two lawyers giving each other dirty looks. There was just a single table in front of the judge's stand.

The guard guided John to the table. The boy scanned the gallery and recognized several faces. Mr. Van Eyck was sitting in the front row but wouldn't make eye contact. Jaclyn Star was a couple of rows behind him, still writing in her notebook. There were also some people he didn't recognize, but he couldn't help noticing: an older woman in a violet headscarf was in the back row, and a few rows before her sat a fat man in a tacky plum suit.

A worm of a lady sat at the table. Her tightly wrapped bun pulled her skin, giving her the appearance of a balloon that had been stretched over an avocado. When the woman saw John, she crinkled her nose like she'd smelled something very rotten.

"Mr. Boarhog," she croaked, her deep voice sounding out of place. "I'm Lynnea Vissé, a New York City public defender."

"You're my lawyer?" John asked.

"Yeah, kid. I'm not happy about it, either." She pointed to a chair. "Sit."

"What's going on?" John asked as he reluctantly did what he was told.

"You're awaiting bail."

"Bail?"

"Yes. The court will tell you how much it'll cost for you to go free until your trial."

"What if I can't pay the fee?" John, of course, didn't have any money.

"If you were an adult, you'd stay in jail. But as you're a minor, you'll probably be sent to live at the Jersey Home for Boys until your trial date." She wrinkled her nose again.

"The Jersey Home . . . what's that?"

"It's a home where criminal-minded boys live." She waved vaguely toward the large man sitting in the back of the courtroom. He had small, beady eyes and a mustache that reminded John of a walrus. He was sweating through the gaudy, plum-colored suit, and his hair was slicked back with oil. He looked at John as someone might look at a Christmas ham. "You'll work, eat, and sleep there."

"It sounds like a prison."

"Not a prison. A *home*."

Nothing could be further from the truth. The Jersey Home for Boys was more of a sweathouse than a home. Residents were kept busy making skinny jeans (which were sold to Brooklyn hipsters), were served only kale, and on Friday nights, forced to watch reality TV.

John glanced at the two large doors at the back of the room. Maybe he should run for it. He was fast, and there weren't many people in the court.

"All rise!" a bailiff announced. "The Honorable Judge Dench presiding."

Everyone stood as the judge entered the chamber. She sat down at her bench and took a minute to look over the file laid out before her. "You may be seated," she said, her stern-but-motherly tone echoing though the large room. She smiled at Van Eyck. He waved back sheepishly.

Judge Dench peered over her glasses at the boy. "Now, Mr. Boarhog, I have reviewed your case. Do you have anything to say before I set your bail?"

John wanted to tell her he was innocent, but Vissé gave him a look that suggested otherwise. "No, ma'am."

"You've been arrested for trying to steal a valuable jewel from the New York Museum of Natural History. My lord, that is a mouthful." She laughed to herself. "And you have nothing to say?"

"No, ma'am," John repeated.

She studied the boy for a moment, then shook her head. "And you, Ms. Vissé?"

"Being that my client is a minor and has no family to speak of, we ask that the court place him at the Jersey Home for Boys, where he will remain until his court date."

"Very well." The judge shook her head again. "If no one else has anything to say, the court will set bail at one hundred thousand dollars, and remand Mr. Boarhog to the Jersey Home for—"

"*NO!*" a voice called out. At first, John thought he'd accidentally spoken his thoughts aloud. Either his inner monologue had developed a rich baritone timbre, or someone else was calling from behind him.

"Wait!" the voice called again. This time John was sure it wasn't him. He turned to find the strange inspector from the museum running down the aisle.

"Inspector McGee." The judge eyed the man as if she were staring at a delicious dessert.

"Judi." Toadius winked at her, and she almost fell from her bench. "Apologies for my hasty entrance. I got lost. You know your tube in New York defies logic. So confusing."

"You mean *subway*, my dear inspector," Judi corrected.

"*Subway*. Quite." Toadius paused beside Ms. Star, who appeared to be writing away in her notebook with renewed enthusiasm. "Jackie," he said, tipping his hat.

Jaclyn Star snorted in disgust.

Toadius laughed, then recalled his reason for being in the courtroom. "There you are, my boy. I've been looking all over for you." He jumped over the rail, landing next to John. "Your Honor, I ask the court to take mercy on this poor lad," he continued, taking off his hat. "He is an idiot, yes. Impulsive, sure . . . but he isn't a bad kid. He has no direction. No parents. He's too smart for his own good and has no one to direct his cleverness toward productive pursuits. Sending this lad to the Jersey Home for Boys would be a terrible mistake. If you take a boy with his intelligence and lock him away with those who have chosen a path of destruction, it's like giving a duck lighter fluid and a map of southern France. It doesn't make sense and will only result in chaos."

"Are you suggesting I should simply let him go free?" Judge Dench asked.

"Well, of course not. He *is* the main suspect in an attempted billion-dollar ruby heist. Letting him back on the streets would be like giving a goose a driver's license and then asking him to drive the duck to southern France."

"Somebody should stop that duck!" a man yelled from the gallery.

"I pay taxes. I say let the duck go free!" a woman hollered.

"Order in the court!" Judge Dench shouted, banging her gavel on the stand. "The duck is clearly a danger to society and will remain in custody!" She narrowed her eyes at the people in the chamber. "I will not allow this court to turn into a circus. I'm in charge here. I make all the decisions, got it?"

Murmurs of agreement came from the spectators.

"Good. Now, Toadius, what do you then suggest we should do?"

"Find him a fair, but strict, guardian."

John balked. "What?"

"This boy needs rules, structure, and a shower." The inspector sniffed the air, then waved his hand beneath his nose. "Two showers!"

"Then it's settled." Judge Dench rapped her gavel. "John Boarhog, you are now the ward of Inspector Toadius McGee. Until your court case on August seventh of this year, you will remain with the inspector. You are not to leave his sight, and you will promise to uphold all laws as governed by the state of New York. Failing to do so will land you in prison."

"What?" Toadius yelped. "I didn't mean me!"

Judge Dench leaned back in her seat. "You are the perfect choice, Inspector. You're both fair and strict. And you're the most honest man I've ever come across—the boy needs that kind of role model in his life."

"I meant you and Viktor," Toadius insisted, waving franticly in the direction of the museum curator.

"Me and Viktor?" Judge Dench chuckled. "We're far too old to take in a new ward."

"Wait," John said. "Mr. Van Eyck is your *husband*? Isn't that a conflict of interest?" The boy looked to his lawyer for help, but she just shrugged.

"I am positive you would be the best choice," the judge insisted.

"Judge Dench, although I am grateful for your kind words, I simply do not have time to raise a boy."

"Make the time, Inspector McGee." By the judge's tone, this was her final word on the matter.

"But I'm working on a very important case," Toadius whined.

"Then take him along," she said with a wave. "Make him carry your umbrella or something."

"Your Honor, I simply cannot take on another assistant."

"Nonsense! Smithy and John will get along famously."

"Well, Smithy isn't with me anymore."

"Your Honor, may I say something?" John asked, trying to cut into the conversation.

Judge Dench furrowed her eyebrows. "Why, Toadius, what happened to Smithy?"

"He died."

"DIED!" John's eyes shot wide.

"Oh, yes. A horrible death." Toadius shuddered. "A giant squid got him. Eight arms and a sharp beak."

John shrank back.

"I'm afraid the beast split him quite in two," Toadius continued, shaking his head.

"How sad. That must've been awful for you," said Judge Dench, wiping her eyes.

"It was, my dear lady. Simply dreadful. Although, I suppose, not quite as dreadful as it was for Smithy."

"Your Honor, I think the Jersey Home for Boys sounds like a much safer route, don't you?" John pleaded, rising from his chair.

"Smithy's passing was bad, but not as bad as Davies's."

"What happened to Davies?" the judge asked.

"Cannibals!"

"No!" Judge Dench leaned in, eager to hear more. "Did they eat him?"

"EAT HIM?" John thought he was having a heart attack.

"No, no, not at all," Toadius said, shaking his head.

John wiped his brow. "Oh, good."

"Their alligators did. Munched him up, bones and all."

The boy went white from head to toe. "I need to sit down."

"That's why you should never smile at a crocodile."

"*Crocodile?* You said alligator!" John was almost in tears.

"Oh, that's right. Yes. Alligator. It was the crocodile that got Herman. Silly lad. Smiled too much."

"How many assistants have you *had*?" John asked, not really sure he wanted to know the answer.

Toadius did a quick count on his hand. "Seven."

"Seven?" John gulped. "Did—did they all die?"

"Don't be a Herman, my boy. Of course, they didn't *all* die." Toadius drew a paper sack from his breast pocket and handed it to John, motioning for him to breathe into it. "Thomas is still alive. Well, technically the machine does all the work, but he *is* alive."

John sank to his knees. "Your Honor, please don't put me in the hands of this madman."

"Stop being so dramatic," Judge Dench said, frowning. "I swear, kids these days are so overemotional. No, I think that the two of you will be good for each other."

"Tell that to Herman," John muttered as he begrudgingly rose.

"Toadius, either you take this young man as your ward, or he's back to the orphanage."

A loud clicking echoed across the room, as the large man in the tacky plum suit casually had made his way to the front row, his metal cane slamming the floor with each step.

"May I say something?"

"Who are you?" the judge asked.

Toadius shifted, putting himself between the man and John. "He is the proprietor of the Jersey Home for Boys."

"My name is Arthur Wormwood the Third," the man said, with a slight bow. "Obviously, this rapscallion of a lad is a danger to the public. Obviously, a simple orphanage can't deal with such a child. He's a thief, and he must learn the consequences of his actions. Young men these days simply don't have the work ethic that we had when we were children. Everything is handed to them, and they want instant gratification. Well, Your Honor, I, for one, will not stand for it. I'll welcome him as one of our boys and help him find the error of his ways." The man tightened his grip on his cane.

John noticed Toadius's grip tighten on his umbrella.

Judge Dench shook her head. "I guess, if the good inspector doesn't want the boy, then the only other option would be to release him into the care of Mr. Wormwood."

If you've ever heard of the phrase *the lesser of two evils*, then you probably know that John was in a very bad situation. He either would become gator bait for the most reckless detective of all time, or he'd be beaten to death while making hipster apparel. Neither seemed like a great option.

"Let the boy decide." Toadius's voice was wary, like he was warding off a bear who was very interested in his picnic basket.

Wormwood coughed. "If the boy were mature enough to make his own decisions, we would not be in this courtroom."

"There is one moment in every person's life when he must decide to choose his own destiny. Otherwise, he will never be anything more than a puppet." Toadius looked to the boy. "What will it be, lad?"

"I'll go with the inspector." John didn't recognize his own voice, but he knew this time the words had come from his own mouth.

Judge Dench peered down over her spectacles at the inspector. "And what about you, Toadius? What do you have to say?"

"I will be this boy's guardian," he said firmly, standing tall.

"Are you sure?" the judge asked. "You didn't seem very excited about the prospect a minute ago."

"The boy coming with me is the lesser of two evils. No matter what crime he may have committed, everyone deserves to be treated humanely." He gave Wormwood one last long stare. "Otherwise, we become the things we hunt."

Wormwood's upper lip twisted and his jaw clenched before his features settled into a forced smile. "No worries. He'll end up with me eventually. I can wait until August." Then the man turned and walked slowly out of the courtroom. "I'll see you soon, John. Enjoy your summer," he added as he slid out the back door.

Many of the other observers had left the room as well. The woman with the violet scarf must've slipped out earlier. Even Jaclyn Star had put her notepad away and was applying a bright shade of pink lipstick.

"You keep him out of trouble, Toadius," the judge instructed.

"How hard can it be?"

"A week from now, I don't want to read in the newspapers that the two of you were seen dangling from some tall building or spotted in the middle of a car chase through lower Manhattan."

"My dear judge, you know that I've sworn to uphold the law." Toadius crossed his heart. "I promise that I'll keep this boy safe."

"And you, John?" Judge Dench looked sternly at the boy. "Do you promise to stay with the inspector until your court date? If not, I'll have no choice but to send you to the Jersey Home for Boys."

"Anything's better than Jersey," John replied.

A surge of agreement swept across the courtroom.

"Then it's settled. John Randel Boarhog, you are now the ward of Inspector Toadius McGee," declared Judge Dench. "I'll see you on August seventh." She banged her gavel. "Court is adjourned."

The courtroom emptied until only the inspector and John remained. They looked at each other awkwardly. John wasn't thrilled to be shackled to this unpredictable man, but from what he could gather, Toadius was a very talented detective. Maybe John could convince the inspector to help him prove his innocence.

Toadius looked cautiously around the room before whispering, "Can you decipher code?"

"Are you talking to me?" John glanced around to confirm no one else had come in.

"Is there a mouse in your pocket?" Toadius tried to peek into the breast pocket of John's uniform, peering in as if something were about to jump out at him. "And if there is, can *he* decipher code?"

"What? No," John answered, pulling away.

"Oh." Toadius stared at the boy, disappointed. "My job would be so much easier if I could just find a mouse that could decipher codes. How do you feel about riddles?"

"I like them, I guess."

"And cheese? Do you like cheese?"

"I do . . . ?"

"Well, then, I suppose you'll have to do."

"So, now what?" John asked.

"Hmm, how about breakfast?" And with that, he was out the door.

"Inspector!" John called to Toadius, who was already halfway down the front steps of the courthouse. "Wait up!"

Toadius shook his head, continuing on his path. "Come along, Doctor. If we hurry, we can still make the early bird special."

"I'm *not* a doctor."

"Well, of course not. How can one be himself on an empty stomach?"

"No, I mean I don't have the qualifications."

"Nonsense. By the looks of your physique, I'd say you are very qualified for the early bird special." Toadius began to chuckle. "I do say, Doctor, you are very funny when you want to be. *Not qualified.* Ha!" Toadius walked faster.

"But where are we going?" John asked, hurrying to keep up.

"To Patty's Pancake Parlor, of course!" Toadius replied with a schoolboy grin. "I *am* really good at this guardian thing."

CHAPTER SIX

The time John learned the rules of being a detective.

HIDDEN IN MIDTOWN, ACROSS FROM Grand Central Station, sat Patty's Pancake Parlor. The local gem had seventy-eight different types of pancakes and fifty-seven different toppings, giving customers four thousand four hundred forty-six different ways to eat their pancakes.

On the parlor's east wall, in twinkling gold metallic letters, hung the words PATTY'S PANCAKE POSSE, below which was a list of twelve names. John was not surprised that Toadius's was one of them.

The rest of the parlor was covered with pancake

paraphenalia. Wall-to-wall were pictures of the world's largest pancakes, signed photos of various celebrities eating overflowing plates of pancakes, and even a huge pancake clock. All the tables and chairs were giant replicas of pancakes, and all the employees wore hats that looked like pancake stacks with pats of butter melting down the sides.

In short, there were a lot of pancakes.

Toadius passed the hostess and headed straight to a table.

"Inspector, shouldn't we wait to be seated?" John asked, following his new guardian.

Toadius plopped down in a booth. "This is my table."

Their server had black hair that matched her lipstick. "Hello, my name is Mindy," she said unenthusiastically. "Welcome to Patty's Pancake Parlor, home of four thousand four hundred forty-six different ways to eat a pancake. May I take your order?"

John imagined that working at a pancake parlor would be a fun job, but Mindy's sour expression made him think otherwise.

"Yes," Toadius said. "I'll have the blueberry pancakes with blueberry topping."

"And you?" Mindy didn't bother looking up from her notepad.

"Umm . . . I think I'll have the buttermilk pancakes with

maple pecan syrup." John flashed the waitress a smile. She didn't return it.

"Okay, whatever," Mindy muttered before walking away.

John noticed Toadius studying him.

"Is—is everything all right?"

"I thought you liked blueberry pancakes." Toadius seemed very wary of his new ward, like a dog when a stranger tries to pet it, or a stranger when a dog wants to pet them back.

"No. Too sour for me."

"Oh." Toadius looked down at his place mat. "So, you don't like blueberries?"

"Nope." John took a sip of his water, suddenly fascinated with the tabletop. "Have you had every combination this joint offers?" he finally asked.

"Yes, all four thousand four hundred forty-six."

"Aren't there more combinations than that, though?"

"Whatever do you mean?"

"Well, there are four thousand four hundred forty-six different ways to eat a pancake, but only if you choose one topping and one cake. If you wanted two toppings, or two different types of cake, there would be way more combinations."

When John glanced across the table, the inspector looked as if cold water had been dumped down his back. "*Two*

different toppings? You *are* a rebel. Whoever heard of ordering two different toppings?"

John thought it best not to push the subject, so he decided
to change it again. "Mr. McGee."

"Please call me Toadius," the inspector insisted.

"Toadius, can we talk about what happened at the
museum?" At that precise moment, John's stomach growled
quite loudly. The boy's cheeks went pink.

"You should never talk about a case on an empty stomach!" Toadius waved at Mindy, who was emerging from
the kitchen carrying a tray. "Lucky for us, Mindy's working
today, so we'll get our food fast. She is an excellent waitress,
as I'm sure you can already tell by just talking to her."

"Here you go," Mindy said, with the excitement of a
flat tire.

Toadius dug right in. "These blueberries are superb. Are
you sure you don't want to try them?"

"No, I'm good." John decided he might as well eat his
breakfast, too. It'd been a long time since he'd had a hot meal,
and the pancakes did smell delicious. He took a small bite,
then winced.

If you have ever felt guilty about something you've done,
you know that a knot sometimes forms in your stomach.
You can't concentrate on anything else because your brain is
clouded in a storm of confusion and fear. Your heart beats

so hard that you can't focus on the sounds around you. Things feel different, too. Settling in a comfortable chair suddenly feels like sitting on a cactus. But worst of all, your taste buds seem to change, and delicious dishes like buttermilk pancakes taste like sour iguana meat, maple syrup more like water from a dirty river.

John slid his plate away.

"Tastes like the Hudson, doesn't it?" Toadius raised his eyebrow.

"Worse," John muttered as he pushed the food around with his fork.

"Well, I told you to order the blueberry—"

"What's your deal with blueberries?"

"You can tell a lot about a man by his choice of toppings," Toadius replied, taking another bite.

"How can liking blueberries decide if you're a good or bad person?"

"It tells me as much about a person's morals as any other berry."

"Well, that makes everything clear," John snapped. "Why can't adults just give me a straightforward answer?"

"Because in the real world, John, there are no straightforward answers." Toadius folded his hands calmly on the table. "The only way to get the right answer is to ask the right question. You ask me how I can tell a good person from a bad person based on their preferred topping? The answer is you cannot, because good guys aren't the only ones who wear white hats and bad guys don't all have long mustaches."

This was not the aloof, singing detective John had first met. Toadius was sharp, focused, and determined. John sat back in his chair, gaping as the inspector continued his explanation.

"Someone who doesn't like blueberries either has never tried them or has a negative memory associated with the fruit. You don't like them, which is perfectly fine. But *how* you refuse them tells me a great deal about you. If you are gracious and kind about your dislike, I can assume that you'll be gracious and kind about any challenge you'll face. If you stick out your tongue or make a dramatic show of your distaste, I can tell you're someone who has been coddled or is inherently selfish. If I offer you a blueberry, and you say yes, then take one bite and thank me, I know you're polite. If you take the whole plate, I know that you'll put your own needs above others. It's not any particular answer but the reaction that I seek. Rule Number One of detective work: *In the silence of an interrogation, you will learn the most information.*

"The question you should be asking is, *what* is the reason why someone hates or loves blueberries? Blueberries are a seasonal berry. They're sour, but with the help of sugar, they make great syrup for pancakes and waffles. They're more expensive than other berries and stain fabrics easily. If you enjoy them, you either grew up with them, meaning you come from a family that could afford them or a family that doesn't care about materialistic things like stained shirts. Personally, I love blueberries because my mother loved them, and when I eat them, I'm transported to a better time when I didn't know the difference between good and evil." Toadius met John's eye, then slid his plate over and offered the boy his fork.

As the bite of blueberry pancake met John's tongue, he couldn't help but smile. These blueberries didn't taste at all sour. In fact, he liked them. He made to push the plate back to the inspector, but Toadius raised his hand.

"Thank you, but I'm full. Why don't you finish them? And while you do, we can talk about the case."

John inhaled a deep breath. "Well, sir, I want to start off by saying that I know you have no reason to believe me, and I know all the evidence points toward me, but I swear to you, I didn't try to steal that ruby."

"Yes, you did," Toadius said bluntly.

"No, I didn't. I'm innocent."

"Yes, I agree. You are."

"Wait! You think I'm innocent?" John felt the tension drain from his shoulders.

"Absolutely."

"But you just said I tried to steal the ruby."

Toadius nodded. "Yes."

"But I didn't."

"Yes, you did."

"It was an imposter."

"No, it wasn't. It was you."

John scratched his head. "But you said you believed that I'm innocent."

Toadius smiled. "And you are."

"How can I be innocent and guilty at the same time?"

"Because you were tricked. Hypnotized, probably."

"Hypnotized?" John couldn't believe his ears.

"Oh, yes. It's all the rage these days. I just don't understand why."

John was still confused. "Why it's all the rage?"

"No. Why someone would hypnotize you." Toadius considered the question. "I suppose whoever is truly responsible thought they could get you to steal the ruby and walk out the front door with it."

I thought you could only be hypnotized if you wanted to be."

"Exactly right. That is, unless you were drugged. There's a South American plant that, when mixed with mustard and sulfur, can put a man into a trance. You didn't eat any South American plants last night, did you?"

82

"Not that I remember. . . . So, once someone eats this plant, they'll do whatever they're told?"

"No, the plant only puts them into a suggestible state. Then a trained professional can use a pocket watch to hypnotize the individual and tell them what to do."

"Can you snap out of the trance? Or is it permanent?"

"Well, most people have some sort of safety word or phrase. Like *taco cat*, or *race car*. Really, any palindrome will work."

"And when they hear that phrase, they come out of their trance?"

"Yes. I'm also told a good bonk to the head will do the trick." The inspector took a sip of his tea.

"So, are you saying you think someone was trying to frame me?"

"Yes, but the question is, *why* were they trying to frame you?"

"Because they don't like me."

"That's ridiculous. Everyone likes you. I just met you, and I like you. More important, nobody knew you were in the museum. I suspect someone was trying to frame Bartholomew, the night janitor." Inspector McGee leaned down and pulled out a small card from his briefcase. "No, my dear boy. You were set up. And even though I don't know *why*, I do believe I know *who* is responsible."

"Who?"

"THE MAUVE MOTH!"

As if cued, the lights in Patty's Pancake Parlor began to flicker.

John looked around. Mindy was flipping the switch.

She waved. "Sorry. Wrong one."

"Who is the Mauve Moth?"

"The greatest criminal mind to ever live. He—"

"Or she," a voice interrupted. John turned to find Jaclyn Star standing behind him.

"Yes, you're right. We aren't sure of the mastermind's identity," Toadius admitted. "Still, the Mauve Moth has committed countless crimes all over the world."

Jaclyn Star pulled out a chair and made herself comfortable. "Toadius here has been trying to catch the Moth for . . . how long has it been now?"

The inspector didn't answer. The corners of his mouth drooped and the sparkle in his eye faded. John knew that look—it was the look of failure.

"His entire career," Jaclyn added after an uncomfortable silence. "You could say, he's an expert on the Moth."

"I'd hardly call myself an expert," Toadius cut in. "There isn't much to know about the Mauve Moth, except that he . . . she . . . they . . . like to steal artifacts of extraordinary value, always leaving a calling card with this symbol in the objects' place." Toadius pushed the card he'd taken from his briefcase across the table to John.

The boy studied the image printed on one side. "A purple butterfly?"

"No, not a purple butterfly," Toadius replied, narrowing his eyes. "A *mauve moth*."

John scratched his head. "I don't understand the difference between purple and mauve."

"Purple is the color of grapes, fuzzy dinosaurs, and, according to some recording artists, the rain." Toadius looked around. "Whereas mauve is the color of blushing cheeks, criminal masterminds, and apparently famed reporters' nail polish."

Ms. Star wiggled her fingers. "What can I say? I'm attracted to dangerous colors."

"Is that why you showed up at the museum?" John asked.

Toadius nodded. "The trail went cold in London last fall, but now it seems that the Mauve Moth has appeared again here in New York."

"Do you think you'll catch them this time?" Jaclyn asked as she flipped open her pad.

"Rule Number Twenty-Seven: *The clues will inevitably lead you to the right person*."

Jaclyn Star laughed. "Literally, in this case. Isn't that so, Inspector?"

"What my dear reporter friend is referencing is that the Mauve Moth leaves a card at every scene, complete with coded message."

"A coded message?" This new piece of information intrigued John. He was always up for a good riddle.

"Now you know why I asked if you're good at solving puzzles, Doctor," Toadius said, and gave an approving nod. "Each message contains a clue as to where the Moth will strike next."

"Why would the Moth tell us what he—"

Jaclyn cleared her throat.

"Or she," John corrected, "was going to steal? Doesn't that make it easier for us to find them?"

"And harder for them to steal their targets. But that, my dear boy, is the game the Moth likes to play." Toadius flipped the card over. On the back was a funny clue, written in red ink:

ADAM AND EVE'S FAVORITE LARGE FRUIT

IS WHERE I WILL FIND THE TREASURED LOOT.

AMONG THE ANIMALS NOW EXTINCT

I WILL STEAL THIS VALUABLE INK.

"What do you think, Doctor?" Toadius leaned forward.

John took a moment to examine the card and read the

riddle a few more times. "Well, we know that Adam and Eve liked apples." He pointed at the card, feeling clever. "We New Yorkers call the city 'the Big Apple.'"

"I figured that part out right away. The first part of the riddle, where the Moth reveals the location, tends to be quite easy to solve. The second part, the lines about what they're going to steal, is only clear after the Moth has stolen it." Toadius's eyes filled with dark despair, turning from his usually mischievous light brown to a dark umber. "One of these days, I'm going to solve the second part of the riddle *before* the Moth commits the crime."

John skimmed the card one more time. "All right, I get it. The second part is about the museum and the ruby."

"That is where you tried to steal it." Ms. Star, once again, was furiously writing in her notepad.

"I didn't steal anything." John pointed to the third line. "'The place where animals are extinct' means the museum, and the 'valuable ink' is the ink on this card, which is *ruby* red."

Toadius grinned. "See, Doctor, I knew you'd come in handy."

"Very good. Very good, indeed," Ms. Star said with a little clap.

"Well, I'm just glad the ruby is still safe in the museum, and not being passed around center stage at a Broadway show." John lifted another forkful to his mouth.

"What are you talking about?" the reporter asked, leaning forward.

"So, get this. Van Eyck had to hire a whole team, because some noob mixed up the shipment and some of the arti-facts got sent to this musical while the props from the show were shipped to the museum. It took them months to figure everything out."

The reporter drew her brows together. "Do you mean *Ask Me Why I Love Her?*"

"No. Asp *Me Why I Love Her. Asp*, as in the Egyptian snake," John explained. "It's a play on words."

Jaclyn wrinkled her nose. "You seem to know a lot about this."

"Well, it's one of the perks of secretly living in a museum."

"Please explain."

John chuckled. "Al, the security guard, loves to shoot the breeze. Plus, it's amazing what you hear when you're hiding above a bathroom."

Toadius leaned forward. "Whatever made you think to make a home up there?"

"Cathedral ceilings." John pointed up. "The fourth floor of the museum has cathedral ceilings. I read a book once about two kids who lived in a museum. They'd stand on the back of toilets so guards wouldn't see their feet under the stalls. One night, I was trying that out when I noticed the tiled roof above me and thought, *I bet there's enough room to hide up there.* It was perfect timing, too. Did you know it's very hard to sleep on the back of a toilet?"

"That's why the Gotcha 3000 never caught you before." Toadius smiled. "You'd hide in the crawl space at night. Genius."

"Why were you living in the museum in the first place?" Jaclyn asked.

John's smile faded.

"It's okay, Doctor," Toadius said, awkwardly patting his hand.

"Well, Mom always said if we were separated, we should meet on the steps of the museum. In a city like New York, getting lost is easy."

Jaclyn put her pen down. "So, when the orphanage got too rough, you went to a place where you felt safe?"

"Yeah, I hoped . . . Never mind, it's stupid." John wiped his face.

"Hope is never stupid." Toadius ducked his head so his eyes were level with John's. "You hoped she'd be standing there waiting for you. Is that it?"

"Yes."

"And when she wasn't, you just . . . stayed," Jaclyn added gently.

"It was very cold, and the night guard let me inside to get

warm. He was a nice man from Haiti. He said he'd let me stay until my mom came to get me. He didn't know she was, you know . . ." John swallowed hard.

"How long were you there?" Toadius asked.

"About six months."

"You poor thing," Jaclyn murmured. "You must've been very lonely."

"It wasn't so bad," John replied, making little circles in the syrup with his fork. "I like when exhibits get installed. There are always lots of boxes and plenty of packing stuff being thrown away. I could always find something to make furniture for my room."

"You made your own furniture?"

"Yeah. Out of boxes and recyclables."

Even Jaclyn began to tear up. "You had to dig through the trash?"

"The museum is big on sorting waste. It made it easy to find what I needed. I feel bad for the guy who has to clean up the crime scene. It'll take days to separate out all that glass."

Toadius's eyes narrowed. "What do you mean?"

"Well, by law they have to recycle clear glass," John explained.

"You sure know a lot about glass." Toadius sat back in his chair. "This is why I like to work with doctors!"

"First, still not a doctor. Second, hello, I'm a kid living in a museum. Do you know how many hours I spent digging through the trash? There are bins for everything: recyclables, metals, food, and other nasty goop. There was even one for frying pans. All the glass from the case has to be recycled. I noticed some pieces of colored glass on the floor, too. Those will need to be thrown away in a separate container."

"Oh. That's interesting. Interesting, indeed," Ms. Star said, gathering her things as she rose. "Well, boys, I'm off. I guess since the Moth didn't steal anything, I have to head back to the office and write yet another award-winning article. See you in the funny papers."

John watched her go, then turned back to Toadius. It took him a minute to realize the inspector was giving him a curious look. "What?"

Toadius moved the plates in front of John to the side and adjusted the place mat. "I need you to shake your head."

"Why?"

"You have something in your hair. Onto the mat, please. We don't want to lose any evidence."

With a sigh, and mostly to get the strange detective to stop staring at him, John did as he was told. Sure enough, pieces of glass (along with some unsavory items best not mentioned), fell out of his hair. "Wow, I do need a shower," he said, picking up a rather large piece of clear glass from the mat. "I could've really hurt myself."

"What did Ms. Star just say?"

"Umm . . . that she would see us in the funny papers?"

"No, before that."

"Oh, that she had to go write an award-winning article."

"No, just before that."

"She said that the Moth didn't steal anything."

Toadius was still as a statue. "The Moth didn't steal anything?" he repeated, still not moving a muscle.

"Yes. Those were her words."

Finally, Toadius reached over and plucked something up from the place mat. He shifted the shard of glass, catching the light and sending crimson sparkles skipping across the table. Then, as if his hair had suddenly caught on fire, the inspector leapt up and bolted out of the restaurant's front door.

It took a second for John to process what had just happened. Mindy was already clearing the plates as Toadius stopped, turned, and raced back to the table. Reaching into his pocket, he pulled out some bills, handed them to Mindy, grabbed his fork, took the last bite of his blueberry pancake, and turned again toward the street.

"Are you coming, Doctor?"

CHAPTER SEVEN

The time John discovered the dangers of egg salad sandwiches.

E VEN AT TWELVE, John had already done some dangerous things. Still, he was certain leaping into Toadius's car was by far the most dangerous, and John had grown up in Brooklyn. He had no idea where they were headed, and it didn't seem like Toadius planned on sharing their destination, why they were going there, and most important, whose car they were driving. In fact, the inspector hadn't said a word since he'd slipped behind the wheel, keeping his eyes focused on the road. And though Toadius will always be the greatest detective of all time, he will *never* be considered the greatest driver of all time.

Miraculously, the pair arrived at their destination in one piece. John's eyes had been shut so tightly during their wild ride, it took him a moment to recognize the stone building in front of him. They were back at the museum.

By the time John had climbed shakily out of the car, Toadius was halfway up the stairs. The inspector shouted for people to move aside as he ripped through the crowd.

John ran up the steps after him.

"Wait! You can't come in here!" a security guard yelled. He jabbed his thumb at a picture on the wall, a photograph of John. Across his face was a big red stamp: BANNED!

The boy didn't have time to explain, so he just kept running. The guard, of course, started chasing after him. And Toadius ran around chaotically, shouting and pushing visitors out of the way, as if he were being chased by a swarm of bees.

Viktor Van Eyck must have heard the inspector bellowing, because he came panting down the hall. "What is going on?"

"Toadius figured out who tried to steal the ruby," John replied as he booked it past Van Eyck, trying to keep up with the inspector.

Toadius's banshee cries echoed off the museum's stone walls. A banshee, as you may not know, is a ghost from Ireland. When you hear its woeful cry, it means you're almost certainly headed to your untimely demise.

"What on earth is that racket?" Van Eyck cried, joining the chase.

"It's the inspector!" John yelled back over his shoulder.

"Oh, good. I thought I was headed to my untimely demise!"

John followed the caterwauling past the dinosaur room, through the South Asia exhibit, finally stopping near a giant elephant sitting in the middle of the room.

Just as suddenly as they had started, the wails vanished, and with them, the illustrious Inspector McGee.

John found himself on the fourth floor outside Special Exhibit Room 4, where the Egyptian exhibit was still roped off with police tape.

He ducked under the barrier and came to a stop beside Toadius, who was standing like a statue, staring at the Egypt's Fire display. A man was installing new glass in the case. The ruby was not there. If John hadn't witnessed the disaster with his own eyes, he never would've believed there had been a robbery attempt the night before.

"There you are, Inspector," John rasped, trying to catch his breath.

"He didn't steal anything?" Toadius whispered to himself.

"Of course he didn't. The alarm sounded, and he was trapped." Van Eyck huffed and puffed as he made his way into the room.

"He didn't steal anything," Toadius repeated. This time it wasn't a question.

"No," John confirmed.

"Because?" Toadius turned his eyes to John. It felt like they were boring into his soul.

"I was set up."

"Why?" A gleam shined in the inspector's eyes.

"Because they wanted me to steal it?" John answered uncertainly.

"Doctor, I enjoy your jokes, but there is a time for humor and a time for crime solving. Now, why didn't the Mauve Moth steal this ruby, right then and there?"

"Because the Gotcha 3000 did its job." Van Eyck waved his remote control in the air like a fan at a football game wearing one of those giant foam fingers.

Toadius tilted his head. "Did it?"

John glanced at the empty spot where the famed ruby should have been. "It seems to have."

"And where is the ruby now?" the inspector asked Van Eyck.

"I have it in my personal safe."

"May I see it, please?" Toadius asked politely.

"Of course. Follow me, gentlemen."

The musky smell of old books mixed with the rich aroma of mahogany as John entered Mr. Van Eyck's office. John had never been inside this part of the museum before. An unlit fireplace sat between two large bookshelves. Above the mantle hung a giant portrait of either Theodore Roosevelt in desperate need of a shave or a giant bear with a monocle riding a horse. A deep leather chair was neatly tucked into a solid wood desk set in the middle of the room.

John noticed three framed photos sitting on Van Eyck's desk. The first was a snap of him and his wife, Judi, at what John assumed was their wedding. The second was a picture of Judi and a woman with long blond hair. And the third was a picture of a much younger Toadius McGee dressed in a bright red suit, Judi and Viktor on either side of him.

John tried, and failed, to hold back a snicker. "Is that you?" he asked the inspector.

"Oh my." Toadius blushed. "I am quite glad I outgrew that awkward phase."

"Yes, red was never your color," Van Eyck remarked. The old man pushed a button on his desk and a panel opened, revealing a small safe. "If you two would be kind enough to turn around, and no peeking!"

The detective and his ward shifted to face the door. After a minute, a red glow washed over the room. John snuck a peek over his shoulder and saw it, the Egypt's Fire. Even in the dim light of Van Eyck's office, the blood-colored jewel filled the room with its hypnotic radiance.

"May I see it?" Toadius asked, reaching out his hand. Van Eyck carefully placed the ruby in the inspector's hand but kept his eyes locked on it. "Has this jewel left your sight from when you got it back from the good doctor's pocket to the moment you placed it in your safe?"

"I am the only one who has handled the jewel," Van Eyck confirmed.

"Good." Toadius smiled, then lifted the Egypt's Fire into the air, and before John could shout, "No, Toadius!" he struck the ruby with the tip of his umbrella, shattering the stone into a million pieces.

"NO!" Viktor yelped. "NOT THE RUBY!"

"Not the ruby, indeed." Toadius rejoiced.

In 1822, a man named Carl Friedrich Christian Mohs was hired to figure out how strong different gems were. He ranked them on a scale from one to ten, with ten being the hardest. A ruby is ranked a nine. Glass is ranked at six. And apparently museum curators rank somewhere between a two and a three-point-five, because Viktor Van Eyck fell to his knees. His precious ruby lay shattered across the floor.

"It's glass," John said, taking in the scene.

"Well, of course it is, Doctor. Otherwise, it wouldn't have broken." Toadius picked up a shard and held it up to the light. "Rubies are the second-hardest mineral known to man. The first is diamonds, which are strong but rarely red.

Glass isn't strong, but can be red. And rubies are strong and red. So that means—"

"—that the real ruby was stolen. They knocked me out and planted a fake ruby in my pocket," John finished.

"My ruby!" Van Eyck burst into tears.

"No, not your ruby." Toadius handed the shard he'd been examining to John. "Do you recognize this?"

John held the fragment close to his face. "That looks like the piece of glass that was in my hair."

"Viktor." Toadius crouched down to help the whimpering man off the ground. "I need to see the videotapes again."

Van Eyck was scrambling around, trying to piece the fake ruby back together. "What's the use? It's gone. Nothing can make this better."

"Nonsense," Toadius chided. "Send one of your guards for ice cream."

John stumbled back. "What?"

"Ice cream. It always makes bad news feel better," Toadius explained as he tried to console the old man.

"Seriously?" John said, tilting his head.

"Can I have sprinkles?" Van Eyck asked with a sniffle.

"Yes." Toadius offered the museum director his hand. *"And* a cherry on top."

"Oh." Viktor smiled weakly. "I like cherries. They remind me of my mother."

And with that, the trio was off to watch the security footage once again.

THE SECURITY OFFICE seemed different. This time, the room didn't feel quite as big, dark, or scary, perhaps because during his first visit, John had been the prime suspect in a jewel theft, and in this second appearance, he was just interrupting someone's lunch.

Peter the security guard quickly stashed away his salad. Van Eyck cleared his throat and motioned to a sign on the wall by his head: NO FOOD OR DRINKS IN THE SECURITY ROOM.

"Hello, Peter. Could you please pull up the footage from the robbery?" Van Eyck commanded more than asked. The young man pressed a couple of buttons, and as before, the big monitor in the middle of the wall showed the night the ruby was stolen.

"Fast forward to after the gas was released," Toadius directed.

The smoke cleared, and there was John lying unconscious on the floor.

"See! He's stealing my ruby," Van Eyck cried, jumping up and down, pointing at the screen and nearly knocking over the guard who was walking up with his cherry-and-sprinkle-topped ice-cream cone.

The inspector pointed at the buttons. "Peter, please speed

this up, but keep the video rolling. I want to see all the footage until the guards get through to the containment unit."

What would've been roughly twenty minutes flew by in a couple of moments. The group watched the empty exhibit hall as nothing changed. At one point, a mouse ran across the floor. On the screen, the emergency lights looked more like a prison spotlight, perfectly focused on the sleeping body of John Boarhog. At last, John's body stirred a little, and then a moment later, the police barreled through the front door.

"See, no one was there but the boy," Van Eyck insisted.

"Wait. *There!*" Toadius jabbed his finger at the screen. "Pause that and zoom in."

With a couple of strokes, Peter froze the video and blew up the image. Scattered on the floor next to John were shards of red and clear glass.

John touched his head. "That's how I got red glass in my hair."

"Precisely, my boy. My ward for only one day and you're turning out to be a fine detective. Peter, could you please play that section one more time?"

As the tape rolled again, Toadius had Peter pause it just when John's hammer struck the glass case. Clear fragments fell to the floor.

"And would it be possible for you to pull up the footage from the day before?" the inspector asked.

The security guard pressed a couple of buttons, and the giant screen showed the exhibit again. A group of scientists worked to set up the Egyptian tomb. Toadius watched them for a minute. "Now, please show me the current video feed."

Once again, there was some clicking, and then the live feed filled the screen.

"There!" Toadius motioned wildly at the screen.

"What is it?" Van Eyck demanded.

Toadius smiled triumphantly. "A sarcophagus. Peter, is it possible to show us both feeds simultaneously?" Toadius tried to press the buttons, but when the guard growled like a dog protecting its food, Toadius patted the man on the head instead.

After a few more taps of the keyboard, two views of the room ran side by side. On the left, in the footage from the first day, the sarcophagus stood in the corner with its lid shut tight, but on the right, the lid was slightly ajar.

"It's open." Van Eyck's voice cracked.

"What does that mean?" John asked.

"I have no idea, but it's most likely not good. Let's go look inside and hope for the best, shall we?" And with that, John once again found himself chasing the inspector down the museum's marble halls.

When he finally caught up with Toadius in the Egyptian

exhibit, the inspector was already reaching forward to open the sarcophagus.

"*Wait!*" Van Eyck shouted as he raced into the room, panting. "Do *not* touch that sarcophagus. It's an ancient artifact on loan. I will *not* have you breaking any more of my museum today."

"But we need to see what's inside," Toadius protested, pouting like a preschooler who had been told he had to take a nap.

"I agree, but we need to do it gently, and using the proper tools. You can't go around breaking the rules anytime you want. Who do you think you are? A rabble-rousing teenager?"

"Can you open it?" John asked the museum director.

"I can try, but my strength isn't what it used to be." The curator gently pushed Toadius aside, reached into his pocket, pulled out a pair of violet rubber gloves, and put them on to keep the sarcophagus fingerprint free.

To everyone's surprise, the door opened very easily, and a foul, sulfuric smell wafted out of the container. John thought he was going to be sick. Everyone stumbled back a few steps except Van Eyck, who suddenly seemed ten years younger.

"I guess I was wrong," Van Eyck said, flexing his arms. "It barely felt like two pounds. But *pee-ew*."

Holding their noses, the trio peered into the dark. Inside they found an air tank, a janitor's uniform, and a very stinky half-eaten egg salad sandwich.

"What is all this?" Van Eyck asked as he wiped his brow.

"It, my good man," Toadius said, his eyes sparkling, "is the true hiding place of the real ruby thief—*THE MAUVE MOTH!*"

John gasped. "I *was* set up!"

"Don't act so surprised, Doctor." Toadius pointed to the air tank. "Someone was obviously hiding in this sarcophagus. I assume the Moth set up this trap days ago, waiting until our young janitor turned off the motion sensors, then snuck up behind the poor lad and knocked him out. And just as I thought." He reached in and nudged the offending sandwich. "What are the ingredients of an egg salad sandwich?"

"Eggs, mayonnaise, mustard, and relish," John answered, ticking them off on his fingers.

"Precisely. The plant used was the same one I mentioned at breakfast, a South American plant called the Tuta-Tuta. The right amount of the ground leaves mixed with sulfur and mustard will put anyone into a trance."

"The right amount?" John gulped.

"Too much will cause a man to fall asleep. Too little will give him wind. Eggs would cover the sulfur smell, and the

Tuta–Tuta is basically a cucumber, so it could be hidden easily within the relish."

"I do *not* approve of food or South American plants in my exhibits," Van Eyck said. "Unless, of course, the museum is hosting an exhibit about South American plants, which this is most certainly not."

"The Mauve Moth placed the egg salad sandwich in the refrigerator. Egg salad, as we all know, has been identified as the favorite sandwich of janitors, so it was probably meant for Bart. John found it, and being a hungry, growing boy, he happily took the bait. The Moth then waited in the shadows for the combination to take effect. Once John was fully under its spell, the Moth, safely ensconced in his hiding place, could suggest he steal the ruby. Hypnotized, he broke the glass, setting off the alarm. The containment doors took ten seconds to close before the gas was released. Using this air tank to breathe, the Moth slipped a fake ruby into John's pocket, before he slipped away with the genuine gem."

"Or her or them," John and Viktor said at once.

"The fake ruby, recovered from the bungled robbery attempt, was then placed back in its case, with none of us the wiser. That's why it shattered so easily when I smashed it. It was nothing more than colored glass."

"That's genius," John said.

"MY RUBY HAS BEEN STOLEN!" Van Eyck bellowed.

"No. Well, not yet," Toadius continued slowly. "You were never in possession of the ruby. The museum always had a fake."

Van Eyck turned even paler.

"And the red glass in my hair?"

"Pay attention, Doctor. The Moth smashed the ruby. Why would the criminal smash a ruby they were trying to steal?"

"They . . . figured out it was also a fake?" The moment the words were out of his mouth, John knew he'd come to the right conclusion.

"The thief must not have known the ruby you were planning to display was a fake. It takes a lot of time to plan the perfect crime. When the Moth finally got into the museum and touched the ruby, they would have known immediately it was not the genuine article. You don't become the world's greatest criminal mastermind stealing glass replicas. In a fit of anger, I suspect they angrily dashed the fake ruby to the ground, then escaped before the police arrived."

"If that's true," Van Eyck began, wringing his hands, "then where is my ruby now?"

John and Toadius exchanged a glance. It was as if they could read each other's minds.

"BROADWAY!"

CHAPTER EIGHT

The time John learned how to play a game of rock, paper, scissors.

FACT: BROADWAY DOES NOT REFER to a way that is very broad, but rather to a collection of city blocks filled with giant buildings in which people don funny clothes and hats to reenact stories for a live audience.

John stepped out of the inspector's car and was nearly knocked off his feet by a passerby. "You would think that with a name like *Broad*way, there would be more room for people to move around."

"Here we are, Doctor. *Asp Me Why I Love Her!*" Toadius said, waving his umbrella at one of the buildings. Banners hung along the facade, displaying larger-than-life pictures of mummies dancing around the Egypt's Fire. Being a lover of the arts, John had to admit it was a little exciting to get to see the inner workings of a Broadway production.

"So, what now?" John asked as he headed to the front door.

Toadius didn't respond. John was halfway inside when he noticed the detective was still staring at the marquee.

In case you don't know, a *marquee* is the sign outside a theater. It posts the name of the show, the name of the lead actress, and sometimes even the playwright's name.

"What's wrong?" John asked.

"Nothing." Toadius shook his head. "Be on the lookout for the Moth. They will no doubt be popping up where we least expect."

A line of people was being let into the theater. Toadius walked to the front, where an oily-faced individual was scanning tickets.

"Tickets, please," the usher spat, sending a glob of spittle at the inspector's perfectly pressed suit.

"Excuse me, my good man. I'm here on police business," Toadius said, flashing his badge. "I need to be escorted backstage."

"I'm sorry, *my good man*, but no one's allowed in the

theater without a ticket," the young person said rather rudely, scanning tickets from the next person in line.

"I don't think you understand. I'm tracking a thief, and at this very minute, they could be stealing a priceless ruby from your prop cabinet."

"I don't think *you* understand. You can't enter this theater unless you've purchased a ticket."

Toadius was losing his patience. "I am an officer of the law. You must let me pass."

"Listen, buddy, that might get you a free ticket to a show in Jersey, but this is the most epic theatrical performance of all time, and I don't care if you're the mayor of New York City. You can't get into this show without a ticket."

"So," John said, hoping to calm the situation, "where can we buy tickets?"

"Oh, good luck, kid. This show's sold out for months."

"If I can't get in without a ticket, and all the tickets are sold out, how am I supposed to stop a dangerous criminal from stealing the ruby?" Toadius demanded.

"Um, maybe try the TKTS booth? They open tomorrow at eleven."

"But the thief is in there now!"

"Yelling at me isn't going to make tomorrow come any faster, sir. Please leave before I have to call the police."

"I AM THE POLICE!" Toadius shouted, shoving his badge into the young man's face.

"Then you know you can't enter without a warrant." The ticket taker stuck his shiny nose in the air. "I know the law. I was Police Officer Number Four in an episode of *Bars and Cuffs*, and they base all their episodes on real life stories from the news. So, you see, I know exactly what it means to do *your* job."

"Toadius." John grabbed the inspector's arm. "Obviously, he isn't going to help us. We'll have to try again later."

"Yes, you will," the greasy usher said triumphantly.

"But we don't have time!"

John gestured to the alleyway. "There's more than one way to skin a cat."

More than one way to skin a cat, of course, is a brutal expression that means there are many ways to solve a problem. John loved cats, and he would never want to see any harm done to one. He did, however, have a better plan.

"Now, what is all this about skinning a cat?" The inspector's face was still red.

"What I meant was, there's another way to get in. We can use the stage door."

A stage door is a back entrance into a theater. Actors and other workers involved in the theatrical arts use these doors to get in and out of the building where a production is being staged, mainly because after a show, people like to stay behind and tell the actors how good (or bad) they thought they were.

"Jolly good, my boy." Toadius beamed. "I do believe our luck is changing."

"I wouldn't say that," a voice that could have come straight from the pages of a cleverly written detective story called from behind them.

The phrase *out of the frying pan and into the fire* is commonly used to mean that someone has narrowly avoided disaster only to find themselves in an even more troublesome situation. It didn't take long for John to realize that he and Toadius had stepped into the frying pan. The alleyway was a dead end. There was only one way to escape, and that was through a trio of men.

"What can I do for you gentlemen?" Toadius asked coolly, stepping between the men and his young ward.

"Cut the jokes, McGee," a short man in a red pinstriped suit snapped, pointing a knife at the detective. "The way I sees it, you got two options. You can either leave my city by yourself and don't come back, or you can leave this city with my help and don't come back."

"But that's only one choice," John muttered under his breath.

The man's smile curled under his pencil-thin mustache

as he raised the knife and began picking at his teeth with the blade.

"Hmm." Toadius considered the men for a moment. "I'll take option three, and place you all under arrest."

The three men laughed. Toadius raised his umbrella and pointed it at them as if it were a sword.

"There are three of us, and only two of you," said a lanky man with slicked-back hair, counting on his fingers. He, like the man in red, was wearing a suit. His was white, and it was hanging so loosely, he looked like a hastily wrapped wedding present.

"And one of you'ze is a li'l boy, and I ain't gonna fight a kid," the final man added. It was questionable, however, if you could call him a man at all. He towered over the others. Wiry suspenders crossed his sleeveless white undershirt, holding up dark-charcoal pants. A derby two sizes too small balanced on his egg-shaped head, completing the ensemble. "That doesn't seem very fair, does it, Slick?"

"Fridge is right," the lanky man in the white suit said. "Get out of here, kid. This don't concern you. Besides, McGee is mine."

Fridge flexed his giant arms. "Maybe we should pick straws to see who gets to off 'im."

"Rock, paper, scissors?" the man in the red suit suggested.

The other two men nodded their agreement.

If you have ever played rock, paper, scissors, then you know it's a game in which there are three different hand gestures to choose among. Rock beats scissors; scissors beats paper; and paper beats rock. It's a great way to figure out who gets to go first when playing a friendly game of basketball, but it's *not* very good if you have three stubborn thugs who are also quite predictable.

"Stop picking rock!" Red yelled at Fridge.

"Stop picking paper!" Fridge yelled at Slick.

"Stop picking scissors!" Slick yelled at Red.

The three men violently shook their hands at one another, but remained committed to their choices, until Toadius waved at them, politely interrupting. "Gentlemen? May I make a suggestion?"

"What is it, McGee?" Red barked, pointing his scissors at the inspector.

"Why don't you all fight together? Like a team?"

The three men stood motionless, their mouths gaping, eyeing Toadius the same way the inspector had puzzled over John when the boy had refused the offer of blueberry pancakes. After a moment, they huddled up to discuss the incredible option of working together. Every once in a while, one of the thugs would peek their head out to make sure Toadius was still waiting. Finally, Red spoke up. "Yeah, okay. Let's get him, boys."

"Toadius, what are you doing?" John tugged on the grown man's arm. "It's three to one!"

The sound of the orchestra warming up drifted into the alleyway, meaning the show was about to start.

"You're right, John. The odds aren't fair," Toadius replied, tipping his hat. "Would you gentlemen like to call a couple of your friends for backup?"

"That's not what I meant!" John blinked a couple of times to make sure he wasn't hallucinating. "How are you going to win a fight against three men?"

Toadius flashed his ward a wolfish grin. "Why, by playing rock, paper, scissors, my boy."

"You're going to fight them all? Are you out of your mind?"

"I don't need to fight them to beat them. Doctor, if you wouldn't mind." Toadius took off his jacket and handed it to the boy.

"This isn't a game," John pleaded. "They're gonna kill you!"

"Rule Number Twenty-Eight: *You can win any game if you know the rules.*" Toadius tilted his bowler hat to one side.

"All right, fellas. Let's show this shamus here how to get to Staten Island." Red gripped his knife and took a step toward Toadius. He lunged at the inspector, but Toadius moved out of the way with lightning-fast reflexes. Using the crook of his umbrella, he hooked the small gangster around his neck, and with a simple jerk, whipped Red around just in time for the Fridge to punch the knife-wielding man in the face. Red's eyes crossed, and he fell to the ground, unconscious.

"Rock beats scissors," Toadius said, before turning his attention to the other men.

John couldn't believe his eyes.

Slick and Fridge were just as awed, but shook off their shock, rounding on the inspector as one. Red's knife, which had been knocked clean out of his hands, had yet to hit the ground. It flew through the air, flipping three times like a high diver before, with an Olympic-style finish, sticking perfectly into the lanky man's foot.

"*Owwwww!*" Slick bellowed.

Taking advantage of the distraction, Toadius ran up the wall as if he were part spider, leapt over Fridge, and pulled Slick's hat down over his eyes, leaving him waving his arms wildly in the air, while hopping up and down to dislodge the knife.

There are advantages and disadvantages to being tall. A tall person can reach the highest shelf at the local library and can clearly see over the crowds of people who are running for their lives when a giant lizard monster attacks the city.

But though they are always asked to get books down off

high shelves, they are also constantly being asked to give updates on any lizard monster activity. Furthermore, those with long limbs can easily get them tangled around giant, fridge-like individuals, turning those lanky folks into giant ropes that drag their larger-than-average associates into metal trash cans in narrow alleyways, knocking them unconscious.

CRASH! The sound of Fridge's head hitting the trash can rang out in unison with a cymbal from the orchestra's overture.

"Paper beats rock."

"Toadius, the show is starting!" John called, motioning for the inspector to wrap it up. All great detectives know that *wrap it up* means to finish the fight so that they can stop a ruby from being stolen.

"One second!" Toadius flipped his umbrella into the air and caught the handle. In the interim, Slick had succeeded in freeing himself from his fallen comrade and yanked the knife from his foot. Fuming, he ran at the umbrella-wielding gumshoe. Toadius leveled his umbrella like a sword, thrusting it at the angry man. As the ferrule landed a direct hit on the tall man's belt buckle, the catch sprung open, and in the next instant, the white-suited thug's pants were around his ankles, revealing a very fetching pair of boxer shorts covered with giant hearts. Mortified, Slick tried to flee but tripped on his pants and joined his friends in their dreamlike state. To this day, John isn't sure whether the man hit his head or was just faking it to avoid further embarrassment.

"And finally," the inspector crowed victoriously, "Toadius beats Paper."

After quickly handcuffing the three men to a nearby railing, Toadius gave John a sharp nod.

The boy cracked open the stage door, and the pair jumped out of the frying pan and into the fire.

CHAPTER NINE

The time John met an actress named Pickles.

IN SPITE OF THE FACT that millions of people dream of becoming a world-famous actor, there are few in this world who can claim to know what it looks like behind the scenes of a Broadway play.

"How long till curtain up?" called an actor dressed in a mummy costume as he whizzed by Toadius, almost knocking the inspector to the ground.

A woman covered in peacock feathers ducked under a man on stilts. "Has anyone seen my heels?"

Half-dressed mummies and dancing girls with funny

peacock hats scurried down the hallway. Now, John was not a professional stage critic, but if the cast sang and danced half as well as they darted and dodged backstage, he predicted they'd win Tony Awards soon. The Tonys, of course, are the awards given to actors each year for the best performances, as well as being the best Italian restaurant north of 42nd Street.

"Well, this is an anthill, isn't it?" John said, but Toadius was halfway across the backstage crossover, leaving John in the wings. The inspector stepped and ducked, slid and dodged past each of the frantic performers as if he knew the steps to a difficult choreographed routine. He danced in front of an open door adorned with a big yellow star and, as if on cue, a bouquet smashed against the wall. With a flourish, Toadius reached out and caught one of the roses midair.

"Stop dillydallying, and let's go," he called.

"You don't belong here," a melodic voice whispered sweetly into the inspector's ear.

A philosopher named Plato believed that when a human is born, their soul is split into two parts. To find true happiness, they must search the rest of their life until the two halves are reunited. If you were to ask Toadius, he would say, "Romantic attraction is just a chemical reaction in the brain when an individual sees something that reminds them of a pleasing memory. A nice summer day or a blueberry pie would produce the same chemical reaction as kissing the so-called love of your life."

But the second Toadius saw her, I know he secretly agreed with Plato. I can say one thing for certain: everyone's lives changed forever the day Toadius McGee was reunited with a beautiful actress named Pickles.

CHAPTER TEN

The time when Toadius and John starred in a Broadway show.

"Someone smells of lilacs." Toadius's voice sounded distant.

The man's eyes glazed over, and a smile grew across his face as his arms slowly sank to his sides. In that split second, John witnessed a lifetime of memories flash across the inspector's eyes.

John took a cautious breath through his nose, but because he didn't know what lilacs smelled like, he wasn't sure what he was supposed to be smelling.

"Hello, Froggy," the mysterious figure's voice sang again.

"Polly?" Toadius went red.

Out of the shadows stepped one of the peacock dancers. She was, quite possibly, the most beautiful woman John had ever seen. Freckles dotted her pale skin, which was set off by the bright blue feathers of her costume. Her wild hair was the color of autumn leaves and her eyes, akin to the bluest of oceans. The mystery woman reached out and straightened the inspector's tie. Instinctively, he brushed the hair out of her eyes.

"What?" she asked. "Is there something in my teeth?"

"I'm sorry to stare." Toadius took off his hat. "You look exactly the same as the day I last saw you."

"If only that were true." She blushed. "So much time has passed. I was worried you wouldn't recognize me."

"I would sooner forget my own face," Toadius replied, handing her the rose he'd caught.

"Thank you. It's beautiful," she said as she pulled a damaged leaf from the stem.

Toadius motioned to the dressing-room door. "I do believe someone was aiming for my head. What are you doing here?"

"What else would I be doing here?" Polly smiled. "I'm acting."

"Of course. How silly of me." Toadius picked at his felt hat.

"It's my most difficult role. My finest work to date." The woman's eyes twinkled with delight.

"What happened to becoming an engineer?"

"It turns out engineering school has nothing to do with driving trains." She winked.

John, who had been standing awkwardly off to the side, finally cleared his throat.

"Oh my. Forgive my rudeness. Polly, this is my colleague, Doctor John Randel Boarhog. John, this is Pickles."

"I'm not a doctor," John said, reaching out his hand.

"And I'm not a pickle," Polly replied with a giggle.

Before John could say anything else, an ostentation of peacock dancers dashed in.

"Oh, it's my cue." Pickles put on a feathery hat. "It was nice meeting you, John. I have a feeling we'll see each other again." And as quickly as the actress had come back into Toadius's life, she was gone again.

The lights dimmed, and the first notes of the overture rang out. Most of the cast was already onstage frozen in their places. The curtain rose and, with that, the show began.

"Polly 'Pickles' Cronopolis." Toadius's smile stretched goofily across his face.

"Toadius, I need you to focus," John said.

"And she still smells of lilacs. She *is* remarkable."

"Inspector." John shook the man's arm. "I'm sure

Ms. Cronopolis is lovely, but we have bigger problems right now."

"And she's a professional actress."

"Great, and there's a professional criminal running around this theater. And the show already started."

Toadius's puppy-eyed gaze melted into an intense stare. "We must follow in Ms. Cronopolis's footsteps."

"What are you talking about?" John was so distracted with worrying about how they were supposed to find the ruby now that the show was in progress that he completely missed that his new guardian was forming a plan.

"When I first met Pickles, she was an amateur detective, and now she's a professional actress. I'm a professional detective. . . . Therefore, it's only fitting for me to become . . . an *amateur actor*." With a flourish, Toadius grabbed two costumes off a rack that was rolling by. He tossed one to John and flashed a smile that meant only one thing—*trouble*. "Come, Doctor. *The show must go on!*"

Now, I'm not sure if you've ever had the pleasure of being in a theatrical performance, but it's harder than it looks. Even if John had not been covered from head to toe in mummy rags, he still wouldn't have been able to keep up. With the blinding stage lights and strips of cloth falling over his eyes, he could barely make out the faces of the patrons in the first row.

As John stumbled toward the front of the stage, a mummy passed by him. And then another. John was soon swept into a mummified conga line. The peacocks all lined up in a row, and then one at a time morphed into Egyptian princesses. For a man of the inspector's size, Toadius blended in quite well with the other princesses. In fact, if it weren't for his bright-blue bowler hat, John might not have recognized him at all.

The inspector tipped his hat, then disappeared into the chorus of mummies.

"John?" The boy shifted his rags to find Pickles staring into his face. Mascara made her lashes look a mile long. "Aren't you a little short to be a mummy?"

He smiled awkwardly.

She laughed, dipping John in her arms. "What are you doing?"

"Trying to stop someone from stealing a giant ruby."

She grabbed John's hands and began to dance with him. "Is the inspector with you?"

He would have answered, but just then, a group of mummies surrounded Pickles and began wrapping her in bandages, before whisking her away.

One by one, all the princesses were similarly covered, and the entire stage was filled with dancing mummies. Even so, John could tell the Egyptian princesses from the regular mummies by the shiny jeweled belts they wore. A bandaged Toadius still wearing his bowler hat passed John, riding what appeared to be a unicycle with Egyptian markings.

This staging decision was of course ridiculous, as the unicycle was not invented until the mid-1800s. If there's one thing I can't stand, it's a lack of dedication to facts and historical accuracy, be it in theater, film, or cable news.

Just then, something caught John's eye—a purple butterfly.

One of the mummies had a purple butterfly . . . no . . . a *mauve moth* on a sash around its waist.

"It's them," John called, pointing.

But it was too late. The next moment, the Moth disappeared within the chorus of ragged monsters.

John thought he saw Toadius's hat for a second, and tried to dance toward him.

The music stopped abruptly, and the stage went dark. John froze. The sudden eerie silence that had fallen over the theater sent shivers creeping up John's spine, chilling him to the bone. He held his breath waiting for something to happen.

Then a spotlight struck the stage. A hole opened in the floor, and rising out of it, like a phoenix being reborn, was the most beautiful ruby in the entire world—the Egypt's Fire.

The magnificent ruby rested on a golden pedestal. As a beam of light from the rafters lit up the gem, John was transported back to the night at the museum that had drawn him into this mess. If he could retrieve the real ruby, then he could prove that he hadn't tried to steal it, and that the Moth had indeed planted the fake on him. In short, he could get his life back.

It was now or never. He had to get to the ruby before the Moth.

The music started up softly but began to crescendo.

John reached out for the stone. His fingers were inches away when light once again flooded the stage. A number of new dancers flew in from the wings, and now the stage was covered with more peacocks, Egyptian soldiers, and mummies. As the music escalated to a frenzy, someone else grabbed the ruby. John lunged for the mummy, but just as he reached the performer, she tossed the stone to another mummy. The mummies began to pass the priceless gem back and forth as the music, the feverish steps of the dance, and the beating of John's heart surged.

Toadius had the stone. *FLASH!* Then a peacock. *BANG!* Now another mummy . . . then a soldier . . . Cleopatra? *FLASH!* It was in the mouth of a T. rex . . . one more mummy! *FLASH!* John rubbed his eyes, then scanned the stage for the ruby.

A pair of hands held the precious stone. Purple-gloved hands.

The Mauve Moth had the ruby.

John frantically searched the stage for Toadius, but the inspector was literally tied up in his mummy costume. The fate of the rare gem rested in the hands of a twelve-year-old from Brooklyn. John took a deep breath as the inspector's words rang out in his ears: *There is one moment in every person's life when they must decide to choose their own destiny. Otherwise, they will never be anything more than a puppet.*

"I'm not a puppet!" John yelled as he leapt into action.

A careful account of the next few minutes would later serve to secure John's name in the history books. His attempt to capture the ruby would become known as the greatest dance sequence ever performed on a stage. John didn't know what had come over his body, but at that moment, he was a bona fide Broadway star.

He took three steps forward and then two steps back, avoiding a mummy on a unicycle, before spinning around like a whirling dervish to rid himself of his mummy costume. The crowd roared. He did a quick tumble and then a cartwheel to get past the Egyptian princess mummies, a slide step and two hand claps to get the Moth's attention, and finally a mighty jazz hand to knock the ruby out of the notorious thief's grasp.

The Moth pushed John back and the boy hit the stage hard, sending the ruby hurtling through the air. The Moth was just about to grab the stone when an umbrella opened, knocking the criminal to the ground. Toadius had finally escaped his mummified constraints. John rolled over onto his feet and jumped for the ruby, which bounced offstage and careened toward the orchestra pit. With a hard push, he slid toward the edge of the stage. Screams came from the audience as the boy lost control.

John closed his eyes, preparing himself for the fall, when he was unexpectedly jerked back. Toadius had grabbed onto the boy's ankles.

Once his ward was safely back on the solid stage, the inspector shook John by the shoulders, staring at him hard. "Doctor! Did you get the stone?"

"I did!" John thrust the ruby high into the air.

"Well done, my boy." Toadius beamed with joy. "Very well done, indeed."

His smile stiffened as something caught his eye. John's joy shifted to worry. He searched the stage, trying to spot what Toadius had seen.

A mummy standing right offstage in the wings took a small bow. On their belt was the same symbol John had seen earlier—a mauve moth. A final flash lit the stage, and in the next instant, the mummy was gone into the night.

The audience burst into roaring applause. As they rose to their feet, whistling and cheering, and the cast swept him into their bows, a sense of dread rose in John's chest.

What did the Moth have in store for him next?

CHAPTER ELEVEN

The time John found his place in the world.

*H*EART OF THE CITY is a term used by people to describe two things. The first is an area located directly in the middle of a city. The second describes a place where people love to spend time. The spot does not necessarily have to meet both of those criteria, but it just so happens that in New York City they do, and that magical place is called Times Square.

Times Square is known for three things: Broadway plays, New Year's Eve celebrations, and dazzlingly illuminated buildings. Every structure in Times Square is usually lit up in a rainbow of neon so bright that even at midnight, it feels like daytime. On the night in question, John sat on a bench outside the theater as Toadius finished up with the police officers who had arrived on the scene.

Even though they had successfully saved the ruby, John felt strangely disappointed. With the precious stone returned, he assumed his name would be cleared, but the events of the evening still weighed on his mind. For the last twenty-four hours, all John had wanted was to put this unpleasantness behind him. Now that it was going to happen, he realized he didn't want to go back to the museum—if that was even a possibility.

Ever since his mother had died, he'd been tossed from foster home to foster home, from orphanage to orphanage. He just wanted to find his place. The museum was the closest thing to happiness he'd had since his mother's passing, yet to be honest it had become more like hiding than truly living. At first, being framed for the theft of the ruby was the worst thing that John could have imagined, but now he knew differently. Now, the worst thing in the world would to be to go back to where he'd started.

John thought about the inspector's words. *Well done, my boy. Very well done, indeed.*

He hadn't felt this good about himself in a long time.

Since he'd gotten to know the inspector a little better, he wanted to continue working with him. But in his heart, John knew that wasn't going to happen. The next morning, Judge Judi would rule that John was innocent, and Toadius would be relieved of his guardian duties. By the next night, John would be forced back into the foster care system, and he would never see his new friend again.

The inspector must have noticed John's lack of enthusiasm. He settled down next to the lad and put his hand on his shoulder. "Why are you so sad, Doctor? You received a standing ovation tonight. That's the best an actor can hope for. You really were impressive. It took quite the athletic ability to dive for the ruby as you did. If you ever decide not to be a doctor, you should think about joining the Brooklyn Bombers. They could use a good shortstop, and you certainly have the speed for it."

"I'm not a doctor," John said grimly.

"No, I'd say you're more like a rain cloud." Toadius leaned back, taking a second to admire the city lights.

"I guess I can clear my name, then," John muttered, kicking a piece of trash resting underneath the bench.

Toadius pointed to a sign across the way. "I wonder who replaces the bulbs when one burns out?"

"I don't know." John didn't want to talk about bulbs. He

wanted to talk about his life. He'd had his first big adventure, and in that moment, he selfishly wanted the night to never end.

"It's amazing to me how many mysteries remain yet to be solved in this world."

"Who changes light bulbs isn't a mystery, Toadius." John huffed. "When a light bulb burns out, it's someone's job to replace it."

"Well, we don't know who that individual is, so to us, it *is* a mystery. After all, one man's answer is another man's mystery." Toadius motioned to an individual setting up a ladder, and watched as the guy slowly climbed, unscrewed the old bulb, and put a new one in its place. "See. He's the one. And so that mystery is solved."

"Oh, that's good news. I was going to be up all night worrying," John said, rolling his eyes.

"Yes, once I lay awake for a week trying to solve a bank robbery involving two men and a penguin. Turned out the penguin had a twin. I truly hadn't seen that one coming."

They were silent for a moment. "Toadius, thanks for helping me clear my name."

"It was nothing. Rule Number Thirty-Five: *One must always follow the case until it is finished. No matter what the cost.*"

"Are there any mysteries that you haven't been able to solve?"

"Yes. Other than the identity of the Mauve Moth, there have been three great mysteries I have yet to personally unlock. What happens after one dies? How many licks does it take to get to the center of a Tootsie Pop? And, finally, women."

"Women?" John also knew very little about women.

"They are a sticky caramel puzzle, dipped in a mystery, covered in a thick candy shell of confusion."

"Are you describing Tootsie Pops or women?"

"Exactly." The sparkle of Toadius's pin glistened in the glow of Times Square.

"What is S.O.S.?" John asked.

"S.O.S.? The Society of Sleuths. It's the premiere league of detectives and investigators. Only the greatest crime solvers are invited to join."

"Is that what Brownie was talking about in the museum?"

"Doug Brownie has been applying for years, poor fellow."

"How long have you been a member?"

"Oh, ages. I was just a couple of years older than you when I was accepted." Toadius pulled out a packet from his pocket. "Gum?"

"Wait, kids can be members of the S.O.S.?" John sat up straighter.

"Anyone can as long as they meet the requirements."

John tried not to sound too excited. "What are they?"

"There are three things a candidate must do. First, solve a major crime. That's a given. Next, they must be written up in the trades. I assume that's why Ms. Star was at the museum. She's the star reporter for *Confidential Informer*, and anyone who is anyone reads it."

"And the third thing?"

"The last and final requirement is the hardest of them all." Toadius leaned in. "You have to have a sponsor."

"A sponsor?"

"An active member of the society must sponsor any new member."

"And that's difficult?"

"Very. Rule Number Nineteen: *Your name is only as good as your word.*" Toadius settled back on the bench. "It's unwise to sponsor just anyone. Once you put your name on something, you're banking your whole career on it."

"How many members are there in the group?" John asked.

"Hmm, I don't know." Toadius thought for a second, and then pulled out a small notebook—also adorned with the S.O.S. logo—and scribbled something down. "I guess there are five mysteries I haven't solved."

John peeked at Toadius's notes. Sure enough, in bold blue ink were the words *Moth, Death, Tootsies, Pickles,* and now *Members of S.O.S.* The inspector shut the cover, then sighed.

"Why, isn't Ms. Cronopolis your girl?" John asked.

Toadius's smile faded. "I'm afraid, as the old saying goes, that ship has sailed, my dear boy."

"I don't know what that means."

Toadius shook his head. "It means that Polly Cronopolis and I are over."

"What happened?"

"You are asking me to tell you the sorrowful history of Ms. Cronopolis and me?" Toadius crossed his arms.

"Um, yeah."

"As your mentor, I feel it is my duty to give you some advice. A man who is willing to tell the details of his past romantic affairs is no man at all. And if you truly care about someone, then it is your duty to protect their honor by not soiling their good name. One should never reduce a relationship from a life-altering experience to a trophy collecting dust on your shelf."

"So, what you're saying is . . . you've kissed her." John snickered.

"What I'm saying is whether I've had the pleasure of kissing someone or not, it would spoil the moment if I told all my pals about it. When you kiss someone, you are sharing a single moment in time with them and only them. It doesn't mean anything if you go around sharing it with everyone else. The other person has given you a piece of them—a moment of their lives—and it's bad form to share that with someone else. Do you understand?"

"Yes, sir." John nodded.

"Good lad," Toadius said, giving John a light bump with his shoulder. The pair took in the view for a moment. Even though Times Square is always busy, it seemed for a second, they were the only two people in the city.

John finally broke the silence. "I'm going to miss you, Toadius," he whispered.

The inspector looked perplexed. "Am I going somewhere?"

"No. . . . It's just—" But John fell silent when a glint of red caught his eye. He watched, horrified, as the inspector pulled the Egypt's Fire out of his pocket. "Please tell me that's one of the props from the show."

Toadius grinned. "What would be the point of having a fake?"

"That belongs in the museum. I thought you gave it to the police."

"No, I'm going to keep it."

"What? No. *Why?*" John's eyes darted around, making sure they weren't being watched.

"So that we can catch the Moth, of course. If we return the stone to the museum, it will only be a couple of days before the Moth steals it again. No, we'll have Mr. Van Eyck put another fake ruby in its place for the time being." With that, Toadius slipped the gem back into his pocket.

"*We?*" John thought his ears were playing tricks on him.

"Yes, *we*. Now that we've recovered the ruby, I'm sure Mr. Van Eyck will be in your debt for returning it. Why, he'll probably even offer you a job. Maybe the museum will take on another night janitor. You probably want to learn how to sweep floors at the museum. I would, too, if I were your age. Nothing beats a good sweeping, and I'm sure someone of your stature would find the mundane task of tracking down an international criminal mastermind to be terribly dull. It's a shame, too, because I really need a good assistant. But alas, there's gum to be scraped off the bottom of tables, and you probably wouldn't want to be dragged all over the world learning to break up forgery rings and—"

John threw his arms around Toadius.

"I take this as a sign you'd like to continue with the case," Toadius choked out, trying to pry the young man's grip from around his neck.

"Yes! I mean ALL THE YESES!"

"I'm glad to hear that, Doctor, because honestly the only true way to clear your name is to catch the thief who did commit the theft. Now, I won't lie to you. If you're going to be my assistant, there are likely many dangers ahead.

You'll have to listen very carefully and do exactly what I ask of you."

"Yes, sir."

"Don't call me sir."

"Inspector, I will *not* let you down!" John said with a salute.

"Good, then I need you to do something for me immediately."

"Sure. Anything."

Toadius waved his hand in front of his face. "I need you to take a shower. You smell horrible."

If you have ever had the unfortunate privilege of weathering a hurricane, you know its center is called the eye. When the eye passes over your house, a calm appears to settle on the world. Many people mistake this calm for the end of the storm. I am afraid to report that John was one of these people, for although it felt like his journey was about to end, he was in fact smack-dab in the middle of the mayhem.

CHAPTER TWELVE

The time when John came up with a plan.

S OULS CAN BE REJUVENATED in many ways. Some people meditate on the top of mountains. Others drink a nice, hot cup of tea. For me, a vacation to a tropical island and a banana split do the trick.

John's cure-all was as powerful as any sorcerer's spell. A hot shower and a good night's rest, and he woke up feeling like a new man. He climbed from his bed to find a new set of clothes waiting for him, including a brown tweed suit and a cabbie cap. A cabbie cap is also known as a long-shoreman's cap, a cloth cap, a scally cap, a Wigens cap, an ivy cap, a golf cap, a duffer cap, a duckbill cap, a driving cap, a bicycle cap, a jeff cap, an Irish cap, or a paddy cap. For the sake of the story, I'll stick to a cabbie cap, because you've probably seen one being worn by a man driving a taxicab. John wasn't really into hats, and often felt he looked ridiculous in them, but for some reason he liked the way this one made him feel. Its round top seemed to bring out his square jawline.

John was so busy admiring his new duds, he didn't hear the inspector enter the room.

"My mentor used to say, 'The hat makes the man.'"

"Is that one of the detective rules?" John asked, as he tried a slight tilt to see if it looked better.

"No, but you never can tell. Maybe it's part of some tailor's code. Come along now, Doctor. Lots and lots to do. We must come up with a plan to catch the Moth, which will require devising one of the greatest thief traps of all time." Toadius took off out the door at a brisk pace.

John raced to catch up. "Where do we start?"

"The only place where we can find the necessary tools to pull off the greatest thief trap of all time."

"HELLO, MY NAME IS MINDY. Welcome to Patty's Pancake Parlor, home of four thousand four hundred forty-six

different ways to eat a pancake. May I take your order?"
Mindy's delivery was less than cheery.

Once again, John found himself crammed into a booth,
which looked like a giant pancake, surrounded by a crowd of
happy diners enjoying their breakfast. Conversation and the
clinks and *tinks* of silverware scraping against plates swirled
around the restaurant thicker than any maple syrup, while
the smells of frying bacon and freshly brewed coffee wafted
through the air.

"Good morning, Mindy. How are the parental units?"
Toadius asked.

"They're at their timeshare in Cabo. Capitalist scum," she
muttered as an afterthought.

"Down with the man. I'd like the blueberry pancakes—"

"With blueberry topping," Mindy drawled, rolling her
eyes. She turned to John. "And you?"

"The same."

Toadius gave his new assistant a nod of approval.

"It's about time you came around, pipsqueak," Mindy
said. "I was starting to wonder if you were a good person or
not." With that, she collected their menus and made her way
to the kitchen.

"So, what's our first move?" John asked, eager to help
Toadius with his plan.

"Well, we have to come up with a trap to get the Moth to come out of hiding," Toadius explained as he unwrapped his silverware and neatly tucked the napkin into his shirt collar. "Do you know how to trap a moth?"

"Once, the museum had a ginormous mouse. The janitors tried to get it with those catch-and-release traps. They put a piece of cheese inside as bait every night, but every morning, the cheese was gone. The mouse was too smart. I was worried that the maintenance guys might decide to search above the ceiling tiles, so one day I decided to help."

"And how did you catch the cunning rodent?"

"I didn't," John said, grinning. "I let someone else catch him for me. I brought in another mouse."

Toadius was intrigued. "I don't follow. How did bringing in another mouse help? Seems to me you'd have two mice eating all your cheese."

"Exactly," John said. "There were two mice and only one piece of cheese, so the first mouse had to get to the cheese before the other one did. Without the entire night to plan, he rushed, and that made him sloppy. He made a mistake and was caught in my cage."

Toadius shook his head. "I don't see why another thief attempting to steal the ruby would help in our case. As we all know, the early bird gets the worm, but it's the second mouse that gets the cheese."

"I wasn't suggesting we find another thief. I was just suggesting we set it up so the ruby resurfaces out of the blue. What if we announced it was going to be put on display somewhere for a very short time? We might be able to trick the Moth into moving too quickly." John paused while Toadius considered the idea. "We just need to make sure the Moth doesn't have enough time to plan everything out. If they have to come up with something on the fly, maybe they'll slip up and we catch them in the act."

"Very good thinking," Toadius said as he took off his hat and began to run through scenarios in his mind. "We can't just display the ruby. That would be too obvious, and we'd have to guard it twenty-four seven, which puts us at a disadvantage. The museum must get it back once we are done with our sting."

"We could threaten to destroy it?" John offered.

"A *billion-dollar* ruby? No, the Moth is too clever to think we would actually follow through."

The two were silent, lost in their own thoughts, as their pancakes were delivered.

"Why does the Moth want the ruby so badly?" John asked. "Maybe if we figure out the Moth's motivation, it gives us a clue how to trap them."

"Why does any criminal steal something?" Toadius asked. "To obtain the object for their private collection? To use it for some nefarious purpose? Or the oldest reason in the book: to make money?"

"Why is the ruby worth so much, anyway? Because it's so big? Or does it have magical powers?"

"I would wager size over anything supernatural," Toadius said, chuckling, "but you do bring up a good point. The ruby is worth a billion dollars. It's not exactly the sort of gem you would sell at your local antique store."

"There's only one fence in town who can move that kind of merchandise, and you have to be part of the Thieves Guild to get a meeting with him," John mused, before popping a bite of his blueberry pancake into his mouth.

"Wait. What did you say?" Toadius asked, his fork pausing in mid-air.

John shook his head. "There's only one dude who'd be able to buy the ruby and you have to be part of something called the Thieves Guild to get to him?"

"How do you know about the Thieves Guild?" Toadius demanded.

"The night I spent in jail, some magician told me about it." John shrugged, then took another forkful of pancake.

Toadius's eyes darkened. "Describe this magician. Did he have a bad Italian accent? Did he wear an oversize top hat? Did he have trouble finding the right words to use in a sentence, and then when you tried to help, he sneered at you and said, 'No . . . that's not it'?"

"Yeah, that's the guy."

"THE GREAT GOATINEE-NEE-NEE-nee." The lights flickered. "Hey, Mindy, leave that switch alone," Toadius barked.

"You know him?" John asked.

"The greatest cat burglar and worst stage magician to ever live? Yes, of course I know him. We must go to the jail at once. There's no time to waste."

"No good. He isn't there." John started shoveling the rest of the pancake stack in his mouth, hoping to finish his breakfast before the inspector raced off.

"Let me guess. He used the 'hold this blanket while I escape an unbelievably difficult location' trick?"

"That's exactly what he did!"

Toadius frowned. "Then he's long gone. And, unfortunately, the Great Goatinee is not easily found."

"That's not true. I know exactly where to find him." John stuffed a last huge bite in his mouth. "He's at the Grimly Diner!"

CHAPTER THIRTEEN

The time when John found out he was royalty.

EVERY CITY HAS A SPECIAL PLACE where the locals go to eat—a spot with the best brewed coffee and the freshest apple pie.

The Grimly Diner was *not* that place. The Grimly Diner didn't have fresh *anything*. It was dirty, rundown, and the exact opposite of Patty's Pancake Parlor. Old booths lined the walls. An elderly lady in a faded waitress uniform served burnt coffee to a group of Brooklyn Bombers fans, who were yelling at a small screen attached to the wall. A cook with a meat-stained apron working in the back glared over a metal counter, snarling at each order ticket as it was passed to him. It was a quintessentially New York diner save one thing: the makeshift stage next to the front door.

And on the day in question, a handmade sign on that stage announced: "THE GREAT GOATINEE. NEXT SHOW: NOON."

"Two Earl Grey teas," Toadius said, without even glancing at the menu. "Earl Grey is the best for a rainy day, don't you think?"

John looked outside at the sunny sidewalk. "If you say so."

"Why didn't you tell me you knew the Great Goatinee earlier?" Toadius asked, eyeing John like he might be an imposter.

"Why are you looking at me like that?"

"I'm trying to figure out if you engage in deception under an assumed name or identity."

"Of course I don't. Unless you count dressing up as a mummy, but that wasn't really my idea, was it?"

"Certainly not. It was mine, and a most brilliant one, too."

"We can agree to disagree on that one. Anyway, I'm me."

"And who else would you be? I say, Doctor, I do love a good riddle, but now's not the time. The show is about to begin."

John focused his attention on the makeshift stage, which, upon closer inspection, was nothing more than a pile of wooden crates haphazardly nailed together and painted black. A frayed red curtain that was likely the home of a few spiders hung from an old shower rod.

"I don't really know Goatinee. He was my cellmate for about fifteen minutes."

"And yet, you were able to collect crucial information from him. Doctor, you are a natural detective."

A natural? John liked the sound of that. Detective Boarhog had a nice ring to it. "Do you think Goatinee can tell us how the Moth pulled off the first heist?"

"No, but he could give you some advice on stealing a kitten if you like." Toadius pushed a steaming cup in front of John.

The boy took a sip of his Earl Grey, gagged, and then politely spit it back into the cup. "I hope the Great Goatinee's show is better than this dishwater."

"It's not. Shh! He's starting." Toadius clapped. "Oh, and the tea here is hideous."

"If he isn't any good, why are you so excited to see him?" John asked.

"Magic is like pizza. Even when it's bad, it's still a little good. I only wish Ms. Cronopolis could have joined us. She's always been fond of bad magicians."

"You should've invited her."

"With a talent like hers, I'm sure she has a day full of

dance classes." Toadius put some sugar in John's tea. "That should help."

"Why would she need dance lessons? She was fabulous."

"That's because she takes lessons continuously. Just because you studied something once, doesn't mean you should let your craft get rusty. Rule Number Twenty-Three: *The day you stop learning is the day you stop living.* Plus, this establishment is no place for a dignified actor."

Someone coughed nearby, and John turned to see Jaclyn Star in the next booth, scribbling in her notepad.

"Sorry, I didn't see you there," Toadius said, tipping his hat.

"You can't get the best stories without sipping bitter tea." Jaclyn's blue eyes sparkled.

"Pipe down, you two," John scolded, and the two adults quieted as the lights dimmed.

A strange Russian violin tune crept from the wall's speakers, and then two smoke machines—one of them working better than the other—began pumping fog into the diner. The lights flickered, though John didn't think that was on purpose. There was a loud *bang*, then a large puff of smoke, and when it cleared, a magician stood in the middle of the stage. His top hat was far too big for his head. It slipped over his eyes, and he started dancing around the stage in something akin to an amateur clown act. The magician tripped, his foot accidentally connecting with the broken fog machine, sparking it back to life. He coughed violently while white smoke filled the stage.

Toadius applauded loudly as the Great Goatinee tried to regain his focus.

The magician turned his back to the audience, and a mystical and eerie voice echoed out of the speakers. "Ladies and gentlemen, from the far edges of the earth, I am pleased to present the greatest magician to ever live. Be still, be awed, be . . . um . . . awed again, by THE GREAT GOATINEE-NEE-NEE-ɴᴇᴇ."

He swirled around to begin his act, realizing too late that the voice-maker was still on. As he fumbled with the microphone attached to his top hat, the entire ragged headpiece tumbled to the stage floor and a shriek of feedback cut through the room.

"For my first trick," Goatinee said, his face quite pink, "I will amaze you with a mystical ability I learned in the course of my travels. The squeamish may want to cover their eyes. This sight is not for the weak of heart."

Goatinee stared at the audience as the music changed to a semi-haunting, yet out of tune, flute solo. He then began what I can only describe as the worst performance of magic that has ever been or ever will be performed in history. It was so horrible that it would be criminal to recount the details. I will spare you the hour and twenty-seven minutes John and Toadius were forced to endure. I will not tell you about the botched card tricks and shoddy sleight of hand. I will not bore you with descriptions of the man fumbling with several little red balls and three silver cups. And I will not keep you up all night chronicling a rabbit-out-of-a-hat trick that included neither a rabbit nor a hat. I will skip over all the horrible details, dear reader, and simply say: *it was bad*.

At last, mercifully, the Great Goatinee raised his arms and shot fireballs from his hands in his grand finale. It would've been quite impressive if the diner's sprinkler system hadn't engaged.

Water poured from the ceiling and chaos ensued as members of the audience scattered, trying to flee the now soggy restaurant. Jaclyn Star squealed as she ran out of the building. Goatinee sprinted around the room, splashing through puddles, pleading for people to stay.

Toadius just sat in the booth laughing. "Well, I think I've seen enough." He took a sip of his tea, dumped the water out of his hat, and carefully settled it back on his head. "Come, Doctor, we have questions that need answers." He reached out and, fast as lightning, grabbed the collar of the Great Goatinee as the second-rate magician looped past the dingy booth.

"It's-a *you!*" the Great Goatinee shrieked as if he'd seen the boogeyman.

"Nice show," Toadius replied evenly.

"You're just saying that."

"No, really. I like the new act."

"The old-a one seemed to be getting stale."

"They do that." Toadius motioned for John to follow, then dragged Goatinee to a back room. The walls were covered in magic trick diagrams and posters of great magicians. A wooden stool with a paper sign that said THE GREAT GOATINEE stood next to a large, cracked mirror in the corner of the room. Beside it sat a small metal desk lined with top hats and vases full of dead flowers.

Toadius shut the door behind them and dragged a chair under the handle to be sure they wouldn't be disturbed. "Why are you alone?" the inspector asked the magician.

"I won't tell you anything, Pagliacci," Goatinee spat. "I am not a rat."

Toadius looked at the pathetic magician for a moment, then sat down in the chair. "You were ousted." Toadius chuckled. "You've been kicked out of the Thieves Guild."

The Great Goatinee went pale as his eyes darted around the room, looking anywhere except at Toadius. "No, I wasn't." He sniffled.

"Then where are your henchman?"

"Henchmen?"

"Yes, Kamin. The three union-appointed henchmen that by union laws are required to assist a full-time member of the guild. Where are they?"

"Okay, okay." Goatinee burst into tears. "They said I was getting old. That stealing cats wasn't a real crime. *Not a real crime!* I am-a the very best cat burglar in generations, and what do those sorry swindlers do? They cast me aside. Do you know how hard it is for a man to start over at my age? I helped the guild get to where it is, and now I am-a forced to pickpocket strangers in a smelly diner. Oh, no!" He began to sob. *"I have a day job!"*

Toadius patted him on the back. "You still have it."

"No, I don't."

"I saw your performance. It was inspiring. With a little bit of help, you could be a great magician."

"Do you really think so?" Goatinee wiped his eyes with a handkerchief he pulled out of his sleeve. It, of course, was attached to another handkerchief, and the magician kept wiping until a ridiculously long strand had accumulated on the floor.

Toadius gave Goatinee an encouraging smile. "Have you thought about taking some classes? If you like, I can write you a letter of recommendation to NYU's prestigious School of Prestidigitation."

"I would like that, how do you say, very much?"

"A lot," John suggested.

"No, that's not it."

Toadius reached out his hand. "You do realize you'll have to give back all the customers' wallets."

"I don't-a know what-a you are-a talking about."

"Doctor, the Great Goatinee is the world's greatest cat burglar and worst stage magician. He uses his bad magic to stage petty robberies."

"You have to make-a the living somehow. The economy, it is, ah, how do you say, not good?" Goatinee shrugged.

"Horrible," John said.

He shook his head. "No, that's not it."

"You mean to say that you purposely set off the fire alarm to cause panic and then pickpocketed the panicking audience members in the chaos?" John was ashamed to admit it, but it was an impressive plan.

"Well, no." Goatinee blushed. "I mean-a, well, I wanna be a stage magician, like the Penn and the Teller. But finding a master trick maker who doesn't like to speak, they are so, how do you say, hard to discover?"

"Find," John answered.

"No, that's not it," Goatinee said, shaking his head. "You know, someone should really steal you a nice thesaurus."

"A thesaurus?"

"It's a *book* with *words* in it." Goatinee stuck his nose in the air. "Kids these days just don't have the vocabulary they should."

John crossed his arms. "Whatever, dude."

"*Whatever, dude,*" Goatinee mimicked. "You could have said *fellow, buddy, chap,* or if you were attempting to insult me, you could have chosen *blockhead, dolt, cretin, dimwit, numbskull,* or my favorite, *nincompoop.* But by all means, go with the uninspired *dude.*"

Toadius clapped his hands together, interrupting the unexpected vocabulary lecture. "Dr. Boarhog, please go through this man's pockets."

"Stop! Fine, Inspector. You win." Goatinee reached into his wet top hat. One by one, he pulled out pieces of jewelry, watches, and wallets, piling the loot onto the table in front of him. "What do you want?" The magician pouted. "I'm sure you're not here about a couple of wallets."

"We need to find a fence who will buy the Egypt's Fire from us," Toadius explained, drawing out the ruby and setting it on the table.

Goatinee turned away. "I cannot help you."

"Why not?" Toadius asked.

"Well, first, you are a cop, and I don't like cops. Second, you ruined my magic show. And third, you are not part of the guild. There are rules, you know." Goatinee crossed his arms over his chest, glaring across the small room.

"Come now," Toadius said, leaning in. "You and I both know there is no honor among thieves."

"True, but there *is* organization," Goatinee replied as he continued to empty the rest of his pockets.

John noticed his locket in the pile of loot. Instinctively, he reached up and felt his chest where the locket should have been. It had never occurred to John that he could lose the only piece of his mother he had left. He started to breathe heavily, sweat beaded on his forehead, and his heart was pounding so hard, the sound of the two men talking seemed muffled.

He dove across the table, lunging for the locket, but his arm was caught mid-grab by the Goatinee, who, in addition to being the world's best cat burglar, had catlike reflexes.

"What are you doing?"

"That's mine!" John cried.

"I seriously doubt that," Goatinee said, as he snatched the necklace from the boy's grasp.

"Toadius, that's my locket!" John pleaded.

"Give it back to the boy," Toadius said in a tone that indicated he would not be repeating himself. "It belongs to him."

"I assure you, sir, that the owner of this locket is deceased." The magician gently ran a finger over the metal heart as if he were saying hello to an old friend. His sorrowful gaze turned back to the inspector. "This does not belong to the boy. He is a liar, and I will not help you."

"That belonged to my mother!" John shouted. "Give it back to me!"

Goatinee looked up sharply. "Mother?"

"Yes, her name was Sar—"

"Cerise." Goatinee's accent had vanished completely. "Her name was Cerise Viceroy."

"No," John snapped. "Her name was Sarah Boarhog, and she gave me that before she died. If you open it, you'll see a picture of her."

The Great Goatinee's hand shook as he carefully pulled open the locket. He let out a squeak, and tears again began to flow from his eyes. Then he hugged the boy close as if John were his own long-lost son.

"Let go of me!" John demanded as he struggled to pull away.

"Forgive an old man," Goatinee murmured after loudly blowing his nose. "To be in the same room with a boy such as yourself. I mean, wow, right here in my lair. The son of Cerise Viceroy. Did you know Viceroy had a son?" he asked, turning to the inspector.

Toadius eyed John with that same *Are-you-sure-you're-not-an-imposter* look. "No, I did not."

The fight drained from John's body. "Why do you keep calling her Cerise?"

"Because that's her name." Goatinee opened a drawer in the desk and pulled out an old photo album. He flipped the dusty cover to reveal a picture of a group of circus people outside a large tent. A clown stood next to a woman with a beard. Next to her were three small, hairy-chested men balanced like a furry totem pole.

In the middle of the photograph, arms outstretched, was a man wearing a large top hat, and directly to his right was the Great Goatinee. There was no mistaking him, even though he was much younger—even back then, he sported his crumpled hat and misshapen mustache.

There were two girls joined at the hip, a woman with a snake, and a bear. A mountain of a man flexed his massive arm, on which was balanced a woman John didn't think he'd ever see again. *It was his mother.*

"My mom was in the circus?"

"Oh, yes, we all were," Goatinee said. "Cerise joined up when I was seventeen. I had such a big crush on her. She was, how do you say, the most beautiful woman in the world?"

"Pickles," Toadius murmured.

"I would've given anything to catch your mother's eye, but I wasn't her type." The Great Goatinee furrowed his brow. "Cerise became the greatest thief I have ever known. In fact, she was the one who came up with the guild. You should've seen the crime world back then: no honor, everyone stealing from one another. Just no organization at all. Then Cerise suggests, 'Let's unionize. We'll have better wages, a health plan, paid vacations.' . . . I even got dental." Goatinee flashed a bright white grin.

"Mom was a thief?"

"Not just a thief. *The queen of thieves.*"

John couldn't believe what he was hearing. "But you just said she was part of a circus."

"Yes, the circus. Where do you think poor people learn the trade? Not everyone's rich enough to go into politics." Goatinee laughed. "You know, you have your mother's sense of humor."

This couldn't be happening. John was certain there was absolutely no way his mother was a criminal. She was the smartest, kindest person he'd ever known.

If you have ever heard the phrase *to pull the rug out from under someone*, you probably have a sense of how John felt in that moment. *Having the rug pulled out from under you* means that someone's surprised you with information that is unpleasant and hurtful, as though you were standing on a nice Oriental carpet and someone gave it a good yank, sending you crashing to the hard floor.

Sarah Boarhog had a secret, and John had just found

out about it. At first he was upset and hurt, but the sadness quickly dissolved as rage took its place.

"Is that how she died?" John didn't realize he was shouting. *"During some robbery?"*

"You don't know?" Goatinee said gently, trying to calm the boy down.

"DID YOU HAVE SOMETHING TO DO WITH MY MOM'S DEATH?" John threw himself at the magician, and they tumbled to the ground. He swung out wildly, but before any harm could come to Goatinee, two strong arms wrapped around the boy and pulled him back. Toadius held onto his flailing ward as John tried to fight his way free. As the anger ebbed away almost as quickly as it had washed over him, he turned, sobbing in the inspector's arms.

Toadius couldn't make out what the boy was saying, but sometimes in our lives, we don't need people to understand the words. All we need is someone to be there with us.

"My dear, dear boy," Goatinee said quietly as he slowly rose from the ground. He reached out and handed the locket back to John, who wiped his face on the sleeve of his new suit. "Your mother was the most important person in my life. When I found out she had died, I died a little myself. I remember the day as if it were yesterday, even though it was thirteen years ago. I can remember the last words she said to me. 'Kamin, we have a rule in this house. It's always ends good—'"

" '—so, if it isn't good, it's not the end,' " John finished.

Toadius gaped at the magician. "Did you say thirteen years ago?"

"I know. Hard to believe so much time has passed." Goatinee sniffled.

John scratched his head. "Are you saying Cerise Viceroy died thirteen years ago?"

"Just about. It was in a car accident. She'd been visiting family in Colorado and was driving to meet up with the circus when she ran into a horrible snowstorm. Drove right off a mountain pass. They never even found a body."

John felt a chill shoot down his spine. "Then Cerise Viceroy couldn't be my mom. She died two years ago."

"No, that can't be right," insisted Goatinee, shaking his head. "I am-a telling you, the woman in that picture died thirteen years ago."

"And I'm telling *you* that she didn't."

"I think both of you are correct," Toadius said before the two started fighting again. "I think Cerise died twice."

The Great Goatinee sank into his chair. "How can someone die twice?"

"She faked it," John whispered. "Thirteen years ago, Mom must've faked her own death."

"Why would she do that? We were family." Goatinee touched the picture of the circus people gently.

"She must've had a reason," John said. "Maybe she found out she was going to have me, and she decided she didn't want her son to grow up in a life of crime."

"Maybe." Goatinee wiped his eyes. "Well, no matter. If you are the son of Cerise Viceroy, then as far as I'm concerned, you're family." Goatinee shot up, clicked his heels together, pulled his shoulders back, and crossed his arms at the wrists. Then, he wrapped his thumbs together and flapped his fingers as if making a bird with his hands. "I swear by the darkness of the night, by the keepers of secrets and the stealers of dreams, if you ever are in need of assistance, THE GREAT GOATINEE-NEE-NEE-NEE"—he paused for dramatic effect, then bowed—"will always be where you need him."

John crossed his arms. "Well, that's lucky, because I need your help."

"What! Already? I mean, give a guy a chance to take a breath. Kids these days with their need for instant gratification. I blame TV. Rots your brain, you know."

John glared at him. "Are you going to help or not?"

The magician sighed. "I would, but I cannot set up the meeting."

"But you just said—"

"I know what I said, but only a member of the guild can set up a meeting with the fence you are looking for."

"Then give us the name of someone who's in the guild," John insisted.

"Fine, I will help you. But I give you this warning: Be careful searching for things that hide in the shadows, for they are in the shadows for a reason."

"The name, please," John said, narrowing his eyes.

"Shim-Sham." The Great Goatinee frowned. "You want to find a snitch named Shim-Sham."

CHAPTER FOURTEEN

The time John met a monkey.

N OVICE DETECTIVES LEARN EARLY on that there are many techniques that can be employed to solve a crime. Some are taught to use high-tech equipment, while others apply the lessons they learned while out on the street. Some work with informants or a network of spies, while there are those who prefer to go solo, searching for clues by themselves. Still others have been known to dress in funny human-size bat costumes and use all the aforementioned methods while striking fear in the hearts of criminals across the city.

Toadius did not, out of habit, dress like a giant bat, though he was known to use all varieties of methods to catch a thief. So far in this case, he'd employed the use of high-tech equipment, relied on hard-won life lessons, followed clues, and even dressed up like a mummy. Yet none of these methods were as impressive as the skill that the inspector was about to draw on.

"Shim-Sham . . . *Of course* it would be Shim-Sham." Toadius was walking at a furious pace, and John was rushing a step or two behind, desperately trying to keep up.

"Who is this Shim-Sham? And how do you know him?"

"Shim-Sham is a beady-eyed scoundrel who would sell his own mother if the price was right. He is the worst kind of scum. He has no convictions and does whatever suits his personal whims. I should've thought of him earlier. If there is anything dirty going on in this city, you can bet Shim-Sham has his filthy paws in it."

"Could you . . . slow . . . down?" John said, panting. "If this guy is as dangerous as you say, we probably should stop and make a plan."

"We simply don't have the time." Toadius surveyed the park. "Keep your eyes open. He should be around here somewhere."

"What exactly does he look like?"

"Short, fuzzy face, beady eyes. Be careful. He's dangerous."

The pair rushed around a corner. "Aha!" Toadius declared, pointing. "Just as I thought!"

Ahead, John saw a short, Italian-looking man with a big, fuzzy mustache. He had brown, beady eyes, and his toothless grin did indeed conjure the impression of someone seedy. The man had a small monkey on a leash and was grinding away on an out-of-tune hand organ. The monkey was dressed in a red vest adorned with brass buttons and sported a matching hat. He danced about before the man, holding out his hat to passersby, collecting coins and dollars for his master.

The entertainers had drawn a good-sized crowd. As Toadius and John got closer, the group parted to reveal the monkey dancing around the beautiful, redheaded actress John had met the night before.

"It's Pickles," John said.

"Why, yes it is." Toadius's eyes glinted.

The monkey, at this point, had succeeded in climbing up her leg and torso, and was now perched on her shoulder clapping a silly rhythm. She bounced and twirled to the monkey's rhythm. It was quite a sight, and if John hadn't been so out of breath, he probably would have laughed along with the rest of the crowd.

Toadius, however, was not laughing. He pulled out his badge. "All right, show's over!" Pickles stopped dancing, and the rest of the onlookers drifted away. "That's right. Keep moving. Nothing to see here."

The organ grinder and his monkey started to slip away, too.

"Not you, Shim-Sham!" Toadius commanded.

John stepped in the way of the organ grinder to make sure he didn't try to run.

"Doctor," Toadius said, a look of confusion on his face. "Let Mario by. We don't have time for entertainment right now."

Mario shrugged as he passed the boy and continued on his way.

Toadius tipped his hat at Ms. Cronopolis. "All right, Shim-Sham. The gig is up."

"Miss Cronopolis is Shim-Sham?" John said, his eyes wide.

"What? No! Ms. Cronopolis is an actress. Shim-Sham is Shim-Sham." Toadius rested the back of his hand across John's forehead to check for a fever. "Are you sure you're not overtired?"

"Wait. Let me get this straight. We're looking for a *monkey*?" John glanced at the fuzzy creature. He leered back and held out his hat expectantly.

"You didn't think it was the organ grinder, did you?" Toadius chortled. "Doctor, you never cease to make me laugh. Why, everyone knows that the most trusted people in the city are police officers, clergymen, and organ grinders."

"What about monkeys?" Pickles asked as she scratched Shim-Sham behind his ears.

"Most of them." Toadius looked skeptically at Shim-Sham like the jury was still out. "I have only ever heard tell of two evil monkeys. One scaled the Empire State Building in 1933, and the other one is—"

"Eek, eek," Shim-Sham interrupted.

"Yes, you're right, Shim-Sham. This is a boring conversation. We're not here for a history lesson."

"You—you can understand Monkey?" John sputtered.

"Not as well as he understands English."

"Eek, eek," Shim-Sham said before sticking his tongue out at the boy.

"No need for name calling," Toadius scolded. "He only meant that Monkey is much harder to understand than English. More people speak English than Monkey, as you well know."

"And most of the people who can speak Monkey are criminals," Pickles added.

The monkey shrugged. "Eek, eek."

"Oh, yes, of course. We aren't here to chitchat. We need your expertise." Toadius knelt next to the fluffy informant.

"Eek, eek." Shim-Sham pulled a ridiculously large knife out of his pocket and brandished it like a sword.

"No, we don't need anyone killed," Toadius said sternly.

"Eek, eek." Reluctantly, Shim-Sham put his sword away, looking disappointed.

"What we want is for you to set a meeting with your fence," Toadius explained.

"Eek, eek." Shim-Sham cackled.

Toadius laughed loudly before awkwardly realizing John and Pickles were staring at him. "Sorry. I told Shim-Sham we wanted to meet his fence, and he replied, 'I don't have a fence. I don't even own a yard.' Get it? Like a fence that lines a yard. Quite funny, really. I, however, was referring to a person who deals in illegal merchandise. I was told you would know who is a big-enough player to be interested in purchasing the Egypt's Fire."

"Eek, eek!"

"Yes, the billion-dollar ruby, not an actual fire." Toadius looked around to be sure they weren't being watched, then carefully showed the ruby to the monkey.

"Eek, eek," Shim-Sham said as he poked at the stone.

"No, you can*not* have it. We are trying to catch a thief."

"EEK, EEK!" The monkey pulled out his knife again.

"Not *you*!" Toadius shouted, jumping back.

"Eek, eek?" Shim-Shim asked in a disapproving tone.

"No, of course I'm not. I am an inspector. Being a member of the Thieves Guild would rather defeat the purpose, don't you agree?" In the next instant, Toadius had grabbed hold of John and pushed him toward the monkey. "I'm not a member, but he is."

Shim-Sam looked surprised. "Eek, eek."

"I am?" If it were possible, John looked even more surprised.

"Well, not a card-carrying member. But you are a legacy."

"A what?"

"A legacy. It means that you are the child of a member," Pickles explained.

"John's mother was in the guild," Toadius continued, nodding toward the boy, "and as I recall, a Thieves Guild membership never expires."

"Eek, eek." Shim-Sham frowned as he studied John for a minute.

"Show him who your mother is," Toadius said, waving his ward forward. John opened the locket.

Shim-Sham's pupils grew so large, John thought for a moment that maybe the monkey had been hypnotized. His furry little body swayed back and forth. "Eek, eek." The tiny thief gulped.

"*Hey*, don't talk like that in front of the boy!" Toadius gave Shim-Sham a stern look, but the monkey didn't respond. He was staring directly at John.

There will be a moment in your life when time seems

to stop. For example, when you are about to be hit by a car or share your first kiss. For some, this phenomenon occurs when they taste their first bite of banana cream pie. For John, time slowed the instant Shim-Sham saw John's mom's face. The boy didn't have to say a word to the monkey to know that the fuzzy criminal had known his mother well. But that part wasn't life-changing enough to stop time. It wasn't even surprising. Cerise Viceroy, John had recently discovered, was the queen of thieves, and Toadius had said Shim-Sham had his hand in every criminal activity in the city. What made John's world slow to a snail's crawl was that, for some reason, he knew Shim-Sham's heart had just broken into a million pieces. John had felt that way the day he'd learned his mother had died. And in that instant, standing in the middle of the park, he knew with complete certainty Shim-Sham had not only known his mother but loved her deeply.

The monkey took a large breath, then turned around. And just like the Great Goatinee, he clicked his heels together and waved his hands like a bird. "Eek, eek," he said with a bow.

"I need your help. I need to clear my name, and the only way that's going to happen is to find this fence so they can help us figure out who's trying to frame me."

The monkey turned his attention to the inspector, took off his hat, and held it out to Toadius. "Eek, eek."

"Money? How much money?"

"What is he saying?" John asked.

"He wants to know how much I'm going to pay him for the information." Toadius shook his fist. "I cannot believe I'm being extorted by a monkey."

"Please, Inspector," John pleaded.

Toadius reached into his pocket, then glared at the monkey. "Give it back this instant, Shim-Sham."

The monkey laughed and shrugged. "Eek, eek?"

"My wallet," Toadius said through clenched teeth. "It's in your pocket."

"Eek, eek," the monkey muttered, reaching into his vest. John marveled that the monkey had been able to fit the leather case in an opening so small.

"I am not cheap! I paid you a large sum for your information on that car theft ring in Brooklyn," Toadius replied as he cracked open the wallet to make sure all his money was still there.

"Eek, eek."

"I know rent has gone up. Landlords, now those guys are the real criminals." Toadius pulled out a twenty-dollar bill. "What do you think?"

"Eek, eek," Shim-Sham said, smiling up at Ms. Cronopolis.

"I mean about the fence. Can you get us a meeting?"

"Eek, eek!" The monkey nodded.

"What did he say?" John asked.

"He said he can set up a meeting with his fence, but it would have to be in a public place," Pickles answered, putting her hands on her hips.

"Eek, eek," Shim-Sham said reluctantly.

"That's a perfect spot," Toadius agreed. "He's suggested we meet at the Blue Moose."

"The Blue what?" John asked.

"Moose. It's a jazz club down on the pier," Pickles explained with a smile. "I'm singing there tomorrow. What are the odds?" Her blue eyes sparkled.

"Eek, eek," Shim-Sham answered.

"He said one million, four hundred fifty-two thousand, six hundred forty-nine to one," Toadius translated.

"What a clever little monkey." Pickles reached into her purse and pulled out a banana. Shim-Sham snatched it out of her hand and bowed graciously.

"You sure have a way with animals," Toadius noted, sounding impressed.

She blushed. "I volunteer at the Central Park Zoo every other Thursday."

"You're an amateur zoologist as well?" John asked.

"It's one of my many interests." She winked.

"Well, then it's settled. Tomorrow night. That gives us twenty-four hours to come up with a plan." Toadius's eyes gleamed in anticipation.

"Thank you, Shim-Sham," John said, shaking the monkey's paw.

Shim-Sham hoisted himself up Toadius's jacket and onto his shoulder, then whispered something in the inspector's ear. Toadius glanced at John. The man and the monkey both watched the boy warily for a moment, and then Shim-Sham jumped down. The inspector reached into his breast pocket, pulling out an envelope, and the monkey snatched it before scurrying off into the park.

"What was that about?" John asked.

"Rule Number Two: *Information is the most valuable currency in the world.*"

John frowned. "What information did you give him?"

"Nothing to be concerned about," Toadius replied, rubbing his right earlobe. "Now, who's hungry?"

CHAPTER FIFTEEN

The time John learned the first rule of being a criminal.

D INNER AT PATTY'S PANCAKE PARLOR was not much different from lunch or breakfast. In fact, if it hadn't been dark
outside, John would have sworn they'd just left the restaurant.

"Welcome to Patty's Pancake Parlor," a singsong voice
called from across the space, as a short woman with bug-like
eyes and cotton-candy hair waved at them.

"Patty!" Toadius waved back. "I thought you were on
vacation."

"I was. Just got home. Bruno took me to the most romantic place on earth."

Pickles squealed. "Paris?"

"Better than that, my dear," Patty said, throwing her hands in the air.

"Venice?" John guessed.

"No. I hate water," Patty replied as she glided over to them. John realized the old lady was on roller skates.

"Lanark County?" Toadius offered as he tossed his hat on a coatrack before hugging the pancake parlor proprietor. She wrapped her arms around his neck, and her feet dangled in the air, roller skates and all.

"Yes! You *are* the world's greatest detective."

"Well, Lanark County is the maple syrup capital of the world," the inspector replied, grinning. "And I see Bruno is wearing a new shirt."

John noticed an old man with a large white mustache sitting at the counter. Sure enough, he had on a white T-shirt with a graphic of a giant maple leaf high-fiving a waffle.

"How goes it, Bruno?" Toadius called.

"Life's like an elevator." Bruno tipped his hat. "It has its ups and downs. . . . "

"But it's always moving somewhere." Toadius chuckled.

"You kids sit down and let ol' Patty treat you to some real flapjacks," the old woman instructed as she skated toward a swinging door, which John imagined was the entrance to the kitchen.

Toadius motioned for Pickles to go first. She smiled politely and took a seat while John slid into the booth on the other side.

Pickles batted her eyes at Toadius. "So, what's the plan, Gumshoe?"

"Can we trust Shim-Sham?" John asked.

"*Trust*," Toadius echoed thoughtfully. "How does one define *trust*?"

John folded his arms on the table. "*Trust*. Noun. Belief that someone or something is reliable, good, honest, effective."

"If that's the case, then no," Toadius replied as he handed a menu to Pickles.

"*No!* Then why did you pay him?" At this point, John was beginning to wonder if his temporary guardian could be relied on to make good choices.

"So he would introduce us to the fence, of course."

"But can we trust him to get the meeting?" Pickles asked.

"Yes." Toadius gave a sharp nod.

"Then can we trust him not to betray us?" Pickles smiled.

"I hope not." Toadius picked up a menu. "I'm counting on the fact he *will* betray us."

John frowned. "We should be the ones setting the trap, Toadius, not the ones walking into it."

"We are setting the trap." Toadius paused. "I didn't tell you the plan, did I?"

"No, you didn't," Pickles replied, arching an eyebrow.

"Oh, it's very brilliant. It was all the good doctor's idea."

"What doctor?" John asked.

"What doctor?" Toadius sputtered. "Funny *and* humble. Good show, my boy."

"I'm *not* a doctor." Did Toadius listen to a single thing he said?

Toadius motioned the others to lean in closer. "Here is the plan," he whispered. "Shim-Sham is arranging a meeting with his fence. The fence will want to meet in a public place."

"Why the Blue Moose?" John asked. "Wouldn't a park be easier?"

"The downside of being a fence is that your clientele is made up almost entirely of criminals, which makes you very untrusting of people," Pickles explained. "The more people around, the less likely someone is to make trouble. If the fence meets us in public, they probably won't attack us and take the money *and* the stolen object. Criminal Rule Number One: *The more eyes on you, the less you can steal.*"

"Right you are, my dear." Toadius smiled. "But we want to be in public, too. The more people there, the better chance we have that the Moth will make an appearance."

"That doesn't sound like a good thing at all." John was starting to think this wasn't such a great plan.

"It is, I assure you. We want the Moth to think they have a chance to steal the real ruby once and for all. If we tried to broker the deal in some back alley, the Moth wouldn't show, or they'd send a thug to try and nab it from us. Besides, we both know from recent experience what happens when you hang out in alleyways. It's not always the safest pastime."

"How are you so sure the Moth will show up?" Pickles asked.

"Because, at this very moment, Shim-Sham is telling the Moth where the ruby is going to be," Toadius said matter-of-factly.

"And how do you know that?" Pickles asked.

"When Shim-Sham gave me back my wallet, it was full of money. He wouldn't have done that if he were in need of funds. He had already been paid, I presume by the Moth, before we got there."

The inspector looked at his two friends, who were both still staring at him, silent and confused. "Come, you two. Think about it. I'm a police officer. Why on earth would a criminal help an officer of the law put his contacts in jail? We have been set up. Rather poorly, I might add."

"But what about the oath he took?" John asked, his face turning red.

"What oath?"

John mimicked the complex choreography both the Great Goatinee and Shim-Sham had performed when they'd vowed to protect him.

"Oh, please. There is no honor among thieves. That mangy monkey was trying to win you over to get you to go along with his plan."

"You really think he would sell me out?"

"I certainly hope so. The only thing you can count on when it comes to Shim-Sham is that you can't count on Shim-Sham. But I assure you, my boy, that is a *good* thing. The Moth believes we're walking into a trap. You will take the ruby and meet the fence. I, being a popular and well-known law enforcement professional, am too recognizable. But I will disguise myself and keep close by—but not too close. Pickles will be on the stage singing, so she'll have the best view of the club. She can signal when she sees the Moth."

"How will she know who the Moth is?" John asked.

"Mauve," Toadius proclaimed. "No matter what alias the Moth assumes, they will be wearing mauve. Look for gloves, hats, flowers . . . anything that is mauve."

"That shouldn't be too hard to spot." Pickles smiled.

"John, you are the most important part of this plan. The second the fence verifies the stone you have is the real ruby, the Moth will strike. All you need to do is make sure you hold on to the ruby. I will take care of the rest."

"I think I can do that," John replied, though his voice wavered. In truth, he wasn't so sure that he could.

"Don't worry. I'll be there the whole time. By this hour tomorrow night, you will have finally cleared your name and I will have finally caught the Mauve Moth!"

"Are you absolutely sure that symbol isn't a purple butterfly?" Pickles asked, batting her eyes at Toadius.

"No, it's a mauve moth," Toadius insisted.

"How do you know?"

"Because if you look at the symbol"—Toadius drew out the card with the clue from his inside jacket pocket—"you will clearly see it is a moth."

Pickles studied the note. "I don't want to argue, but it looks like a butterfly to me."

"I have a book in my library at home that contains pictures of all the moths and butterflies in the world. This one is the Colomychus talis or the distinguished colymychus moth," Toadius said, pointing at the image's wings.

"Distinguished? Oh, my. Maybe you can show me this book," Pickles suggested. "I have tons of questions about butterflies. Particularly the ones that seem to live in my stomach lately."

"Does this happen often?" Toadius asked, concerned.

She gave a little shrug. "Only when I'm onstage or when I'm with you."

Now it was Toadius's turn to go pink.

John cleared his throat rather conspicuously. "I hate to interrupt you two, but don't we have a Moth to catch?"

"We absolutely do." Toadius put out his hand, holding it over the middle of the table. Pickles placed her hand atop his. "What to do you say, John? Will you help me catch a thief?"

John placed his hand on top of Pickles's.

"What do we say?" Pickles asked.

"*Pancakes* on three?" Toadius suggested.

John looked at his new friends. For the first time in a long while, he felt like everything was going to work out in his favor.

"Pancakes!" the three yelled together, throwing up their hands to seal their pact.

"*Pancakes!*" Patty wheeled around the corner and skidded to a stop at their table. John couldn't believe how many plates the old lady could carry. "Let's see. We have blueberry, raspberry, maple, and lemon. There are some cherry and banana. This one's called Chocolate Chip Heaven. We have one glass of freshly squeezed OJ, one hot apple cider, an Earl Grey tea, and three glasses of water."

"Thanks, Patty," John said, eager to dig into the feast.

"Are you kidding me? It's the least I can do for my

favorite boy." She pinched Toadius's cheek. "He's a real hero."

"You and Patty have a lot in common, John," Toadius said as he stabbed a pancake and placed it on his plate.

"You're an international bank robber?" Patty asked the boy.

"No!" John said, surprised. "Are you?"

"I was, but that was years ago. Back when I had the time to squeeze into those tight cat burglar outfits. *Meow.*"

"When she finally got caught, instead of going to jail, she was recruited by the FBI," Toadius explained.

Patty nodded. "Then I turned my bank-robbing ways into bank-robber-catching ways. But that was back in a simpler time."

"And now you own a pancake parlor," John said.

"Oh, I've done tons of things. Pancake parlor proprietor, professional roller-derby racer, jewel thief, tour guide, country singer—"

"Don't forget general!" Bruno barked from across the room.

"You were a *general*?" John couldn't see how this little old lady could've ever served in the military.

"Well, someone had to step up to the plate. Panama wasn't going to free itself," Patty replied as she gave John a salute.

Toadius put his hand gently on top of the old woman's. "Patty has been everywhere and seen everything."

"Not everything. Still haven't gone to the moon," Patty said, before rolling off to the kitchen. "But August is right around the corner!"

CHAPTER SIXTEEN

The time John stayed up past his bedtime.

S OMEHOW, THE IDEA OF grabbing a quick dinner rapidly turned into a seven-course pancake celebration. Every time John thought there couldn't be more, Patty would roll in and drop off another round of toppings or new batches of flapjacks. Everyone shared. Pickles even took the time to cut up each new dish into bite-size portions.

"You'll like this one, Froggy," she said as she raised a fork to Toadius's lips.

"I couldn't possibly eat another bite. I don't think my belt can take it."

"Toadius McGee too full for a blueberry pancake? My word, what is this world coming to?"

"My dear, this world is a wondrous mecca of light and love, but I know when to say when, even when it involves blueberry pancakes." He pushed his plate toward John. "Doctor, do you want any more?"

"I think if I eat another bite I'll explode," John replied, placing his napkin on the table.

BEEP! BEEP! Pickles hastily reached for her watch and pressed a button to turn off the alarm. "I hate for this evening to end," she said, touching Toadius's hand, "but as every good actress knows, eventually everyone must take a bow and let the curtain fall."

"Yes, quite. We should pay our tab and get some rest. We have a very big day ahead of us tomorrow." Toadius pulled out his wallet and started fishing out some bills.

"Why don't you walk Ms. Pickles home? I'll stay here and help Patty clean up," John offered.

"But how will you get back to the flat?"

"Toadius, I've lived on my own for two years. I think I can walk a couple of blocks without too much trouble."

"It would be nice to walk off some of these pancakes." Pickles hadn't moved her hand from Toadius's.

"An encore?" Toadius swallowed hard. "If you don't mind the company."

"I think it would be lovely."

"Then it's settled. I'll go pay the bill. I'll be right back." He fumbled getting out of the booth, tripping on his own feet, and almost tumbled to the ground. Pickles and John laughed as he regained his balance and faced them, tipping his hat.

When he was out of earshot, John turned to Pickles. "So?"

"So?"

"So, what's up with you and the inspector?"

"It's complicated."

"So, what you're saying is you like him," John pressed.

"What isn't there to like?"

"No, I mean, you *like* like him." It didn't take a master detective to figure that out.

"Mr. Boarhog, I don't know what you mean."

"You know he's in love with you, and I think you feel the same way about him."

She blushed again. "If only that were enough." She touched the boy's face. "I'm glad you're in his life now. He needs someone to keep him honest."

John was about to ask her what she meant—the inspector was the most honest person he'd ever known—but just then, Toadius returned from paying the check.

"What are you two conspiring about?"

John panicked. "My locket. How important it is to me."

"Ah, yes. That reminds me." Toadius pulled out his wallet,

withdrew a picture, and handed it to John—a miniature of the boy's mugshot. "When the Great Goatinee was reminiscing over his time with your mother, I noticed the damaged photo on the other side. I thought this might fill the spot."

"Thank you," John said.

"Here, allow me." Pickles reached for the locket and carefully pressed the new photo inside. Her lips curled in a small smile. "I used to have one of these."

Toadius cleared his throat. "Um, shall we?" he asked, offering Pickles his arm.

"We shall," she replied as she swept up and took it. "John, it was wonderful seeing you again."

"Same here," he said, giving her a hug.

"Until tomorrow." She smiled.

"Doctor." Toadius clapped John on the shoulder, then led Pickles out of the parlor.

John watched the couple leave, still not sure why they didn't just tell each other how they felt. *Grown-ups are impossible to understand.*

Patty wheeled up to the table and started to stack dishes.

"Can I help?" John offered. He felt bad that the older woman was going to have to clean up such a big mess all by herself.

"Oh, no. I can handle this," Patty said, patting the boy on his head.

"Please, it's the least I can do," John said as he started stacking plates.

"That is very sweet of you."

After helping clear the table, washing the dishes, and putting away food in a giant refrigerator, John was stacking clean plates in the pantry when a thought occurred to him. "Patty, can I ask you a question?"

"Sure, kid. Lay it on me."

"You were a bank robber, right?"

"One of the best."

"Did you know a woman named Cerise Viceroy?" His heart started to beat faster.

"Can't say that I did. Was she a bank robber, too?"

"She was a thief." John frowned. He knew it had been a long shot, but if there was one thing he'd learned so far, it was that the criminal world was very small.

"It was all a long time ago," the old woman said, as she sat to take off her roller skates. "Why do you ask?"

"Just wondering. What made you change jobs so often? Was it the adventure?"

"No," Patty said. "It was fear."

"Fear? How could you be a bank robber, a general, and a roller-derby champion if you were afraid?"

"Not the fear of doing. The fear of missing out."

"Missing out on what?"

"Happiness. Every time I'd get a job, I'd see someone else doing something else and think, *I'd be so much happier if I were them*. I was convinced that everyone else was happier than I was. But after a while, I came to realize that no one is happy all the time. And what you do isn't what makes you happy. It's who you do it with. Would you mind?" Patty pointed to two large garbage bags.

"Do you regret trying so many different jobs?" John asked as he tied up the last bag of garbage.

"No, but I wouldn't trade my Bruno for anything. Or my seven kids, or twenty-three grandkids. . . . Well, maybe Mindy, but we're hoping it's just a phase."

"Mindy? You mean the waitress is your granddaughter?"

"All my kids and grandkids work here. We're a family business. That's why this is my favorite job of all. It's where my family is . . . and they are my heart. Now, while you throw away those bags in the bin in the alley, I'll wrap up some pancakes for you to take home."

CHAPTER SEVENTEEN

The time John lost his locket.

H ALFWAY OUT THE DOOR, John realized he'd forgotten his jacket. The chilly air stung his face as he stepped into the alleyway. It was strangely quiet back there. He almost forgot he was in the Big Apple.

There will be times in your life when you step into a new place or make eye contact with a stranger, and something won't feel right. You may think it's too quiet or the person is too friendly. That feeling is called *intuition*. Once, I was invited to a surprise birthday party for a friend who lived in Alaska. When I arrived, there was a massive cave where the event was to take place. It was cold and dark, the air was still, and my intuition told me I was not safe. Luckily, the polar bear who had taken up residence in that cave was vegan, or this story would never have been told.

John wasn't hiding in a cave, of course, and the chance of a polar bear making its home in a New York City alley was unlikely at best. But John's intuition told him something was off. Unfortunately, John had not yet heard my story about the polar bear, and thus made the poor choice to ignore his feelings. When he heard someone speak behind him, he realized his mistake . . . but it was too late.

"Turn around," demanded a whiny voice that sounded a lot like nails on a chalkboard.

John slowly circled around until he was facing a ginger-haired boy, with freckled skin and a crooked nose, dressed in dirty clothes. The boy looked to be about John's age and height, but he was much skinnier. Normally, John wouldn't have been afraid of someone matching this description, but this crooked-nosed teen was holding a nasty-looking lead pipe.

"You got any money?" the teen demanded, his voice cracking on the final word.

"No."

"Turn out your pockets."

"No," John repeated, digging his heels into the asphalt.

"*No?*" The teen smacked the pipe menacingly against his

palm. "You'll give me your money if you knows what's good for you."

John took a step toward the kitchen door but didn't get far. Another boy slipped out of the shadows. This one was taller and had darker skin and two different-colored shoes— one red, one blue. John changed direction, but was met by a third foe. This kid was so large, he made the other two look like toddlers. John guessed by his patchy blond facial hair that the third goon was a couple of years older—and possibly a Viking.

"Look, guys, I don't want any trouble. And I don't have any money."

"*I don't have any money*," Crooked-Nose repeated in a mocking voice.

"Well, too bad, because you have to pay the toll." John noticed that Patchy-Face also had some kind of pipe or stick in his hand—it was hard to tell in the shadows. The kid pointed whatever the object was at John's locket.

"You can't have that," John said matter-of-factly.

"I'm pretty sure we can." Mismatched-Kicks laughed. "There are three of us, and only one of you."

John raised his fisted hands. He didn't want to fight, but he wasn't going to lose his mother's locket, either. Why couldn't she have given him a samurai sword? Or a jet pack? "Like I said, you can't have it. Leave me alone."

"Okay, don't get all crybaby on me. I was only joshing."
The crooked-nosed kid smiled. And then, without any warning, he struck John in the stomach with his pipe.

The air rushed out of John's lungs. He gasped, but he couldn't find his breath.

The crooked-nosed kid loomed over him. Leering, he crouched down and snatched the locket off John's neck. "Thank you," the boy said. "Nighty night." The thug raised his pipe up into the air and readied his aim.

"What's going on here?" a deep voice called from the other end of the alleyway. John's heart skipped a beat as a shadowy figure walked toward them. John felt a wave of relief wash over him—until he heard the familiar clicking of a metal cane, and out of the gloom, he caught a glimpse of an ugly plum suit. This was no ally—it was none other than Mr. Wormwood, the proprietor of the Jersey Home for Boys.

"Boys?" Even from several feet away, John could smell Wormwood's sardine-and-cauliflower breath. "What's going on here?"

"Nothing, Mr. Wormwood," the crooked-nosed boy said.

"Nothing? Danny, what did I tell you about lying to me?" Spittle sprayed from his mouth. His eyes flashed, and Danny flinched.

"He stole my locket," John spat out.

"No, I didn't," the crooked-nosed boy cried. "He's lying!"

"Enough out of you both." Wormwood sneered. "Give me the trinket."

The crooked-nosed boy dropped the necklace into Wormwood's outstretched hand.

John took a breath and reached out for the locket.

"I suggest you get going, Boarhog. I'd hate to see something bad happen to you before you come to stay with us." With that, Wormwood pocketed the necklace and turned back down the alley.

"Hey! Give that back!" John demanded.

"Give what back?" Wormwood flashed his teeth wolfishly.

A cold chill raced down the back of John's neck.

"I have no idea what you're talking about, but I really have no more time to waste," Wormwood said, beginning to turn again.

John summoned his last ounce of courage. "Give my locket back, or I'll call the police!"

"Well, we don't want that, do we?" Wormwood replied. "Boys, your curfew is two a.m. Don't be late." The man stepped casually back into the shadows. "It's too bad, John. You would've made an excellent addition to our family."

The crooked-nosed boy smiled and cracked his knuckles.

There was only one way John was going to get out of that alley alive. His lungs still stung and his eyes were watering from pain, but slowly he stood up and raised his fists.

"Look, boys. We got ourselves a fighter," Mismatched-Kicks jeered.

The others laughed.

Crooked-Nose pointed his pipe at John. "Like my friend said before, there are three of us and one of you. You really think you can take us all?"

"Rule Number Twenty-Eight." John lunged at the crooked-nosed kid, grabbed the pipe, and pulled on it, yanking the other boy in close, a perfect opportunity to land a punch on the kid's jaw. The crooked-nosed boy flew back, landing with a giant thud. And John was still holding his pipe.

Patchy-Face leered and bull-rushed John, knocking the pipe out of his hand. John went sliding across the alley, slamming into a group of trash cans. He quickly stood, trying to gauge his surroundings. Patchy-Face laughed, scraping his foot on the ground, preparing for another charge. John grabbed a trash-can lid, prepared to use it as a shield, but the force of the massive teen knocked him off his feet again. Mismatched-Kicks took the opening and landed a kick in the ribs.

John again struggled to get up, but the two other boys were too much. They landed blow after blow, and every time John tried to rise, the bigger boy would throw him back to the ground. John cowered, covering his head. He could see between his attackers' legs that Crooked-Nose had regained consciousness and was moving slowly toward them, brandishing his reclaimed pipe.

"Stop it!" Crooked-Nose called to his friends. The other two paused, confused.

John rolled over on his back, heaving to catch his breath.

Crooked-Nose stood over him. "Who's the tough guy now?"

John was too winded to speak.

"That's what I thought," the teen spat as he raised his pipe. But just before he struck, a rope flew from the shadows and lassoed the young man's arm.

Crooked-Nose gaped at his hand, and in the next instant, he was pulled into the shadows like a fish on a hook.

There were no screams. No sound. In fact, the alley was eerily quiet. The other two boys stood frozen, half in fear, half in anticipation. A shape shifted in the dim light, and the boys instinctively readied themselves for battle. Then out of the shadows rolled Crooked-Nose's pipe, exactly as if a monster had spit out his bones. The pipe slowed and stopped next to the biggest kid's boot. He eyed it, then turned to his associate, but once again, before he could open his mouth, his friend with the mismatched kicks was lassoed and yanked into the darkness.

Patchy-Face let out a battle cry and charged into the shadows. John could hear sounds of a struggle. And then the alley again fell silent.

John managed to roll onto his side, but he was too weak to push himself up off the ground. Fading in and out of consciousness, he was too spent to shift when someone stepped out from the shadows, but he got a good look at the person's boots. Familiar boots. He'd seen them before when he was little and hid in his mother's closet.

I know those boots.

That's the last thought he had, as he watched his mother's shoes retreating into the darkness before his vision blurred and he blacked out.

JOHN SHOT UP IN HIS BED, sweat pouring down his forehead, his chest heaving. His gaze darted around the room, and it took a minute before he realized he was back in Toadius's apartment.

"TOADIUS!" John yelled as loud as he could.

"I'm right here, my boy!" The inspector leapt out of an armchair in the corner, tossing off his blanket. A cup of tea and a half-eaten sandwich were sitting on a small, makeshift table nearby.

"Toadius! My mom—she's still alive! I saw her. I just saw her!"

"Slow down," Toadius murmured, trying to quiet the boy. "Let me see your head."

"My head? You're not listening to me. I saw a woman in the alley. Don't you get it? She rescued me. It was my mom. She must've faked her death a second time."

"John, please." Toadius placed his hand on his ward's shoulder. "You need to calm down.

"NO!" John pushed the inspector aside. "MY MOTHER IS ALIVE!"

"It was a dream," Toadius tried to explain soothingly.

"*It wasn't a dream!*" John's head started to pound. He reached up and felt a bandage wrapped tightly around it. Looking past Toadius to the mirror hanging on the far wall, he saw a dark bruise forming under his right eye. "What happened?"

"By the looks of it, you were either in a fight with three hooligans or trampled by a herd of buffalo."

John remembered his necklace and reached for his neck instinctively. "My locket. He stole my locket."

"Who did? Was it the buffalo?"

"Wormwood." John tried to get out of bed, but Toadius gently pushed him back down. "He and three of his boys. Toadius, they took it."

"Don't worry. We'll get it back," a melodic voice said from the doorway. John turned to find Polly standing there.

"What are you doing here?" John asked, then turned to Toadius. "What is she doing here?"

"I called her. Although I pride myself on being the greatest detective of all time, I am *not* the greatest doctor of all time," Toadius admitted.

"She's not a doctor." At that moment, John realized he was in his pajamas and quickly pulled the sheets up.

"True," Polly said politely, pointedly ignoring the boy's pink cheeks, "but I am an expert at patching up hooligans."

"That she is." Toadius locked eyes with her, but only for a second.

"Let me have a look, John Boarhog," she said, unwrapping his head. "I think Toadius went a little overboard with the bandages."

"Well, you can never be too careful when it comes to head injuries," Toadius protested. "They are quite serious, and often the danger isn't apparent until it's too late."

"It looks like he's going to have a black eye for a day or two, but I think he'll survive," Polly said, shooting Toadius a *Don't talk about it in front of the kid* look.

"That's good, because I don't want to have a black eye when we find my mom."

"I just put a kettle on the stove. How about I get you boys some tea?"

"That would be lovely." Toadius watched Polly as she

slipped from the room. Once again, John tried to get out of bed, but Toadius stopped him easily. "Where do you think you're going?"

"I need to get dressed. We have to go find her."

"You're in no shape to be going anywhere," Toadius said sternly.

"I need you to listen to me," John insisted. "My mother is still alive. She was in that alley."

"John, I'm sorry, but that's not the truth."

"How do you know?"

"Because you're describing a phenomenon known as memory confabulation, in which the brain fills in the missing pieces of a partial memory but with incorrect information." Toadius frowned. "When we want something very badly, we fit the pieces together and ignore the evidence that may suggest what we're recalling is inaccurate. I'm so sorry, John, but I don't think your mother is still alive."

"I know what I saw! If there's even a tiny chance she's alive—"

"Then I would move mountains to find her for you." Toadius's voice grew softer. "I'll make you a deal. If you eat something and get some rest, then tomorrow we will go find the fence together."

"And my mom?" John's eyes were bright with desperation.

"We'll talk about that in the morning."

John tried to sit up again. "I want to talk about it now."

"You need to rest."

"No, I need to find my mom."

"People don't come back from the dead," Toadius snapped. He immediately looked like he'd regretted his words, but he pressed on. After all, some truths are hard to hear, but we need to hear them all the same. "No matter how much you hope or wish," the inspector said more gently, "no matter how badly you want it not to be true, when someone dies, then they are dead. Deceased. Gone. Finished. *Dead*. And no matter how many leads you follow, and no matter how many cases you solve, it will never bring them back."

Toadius froze, staring past John as if he'd seen a ghost. John turned to see what the inspector was looking at. Pickles had silently reentered the room and was standing behind Toadius. He must've seen her reflection in the mirror. By the look on her face, John guessed she had heard everything the inspector had said.

Without another word, Toadius rose from his chair and walked out of the room. John jumped up to follow him, but Pickles reached out her hand.

"Where's he going?"

"Just give him some space." Pickles patted the boy's

shoulder. "He's a tiger right now, and it's best that you don't chase tigers."

"Is he mad at me?" John asked, still confused about what had just happened.

"No, he's mad at himself."

"Why?"

"Because Toadius McGee has been chasing ghosts since he was your age." Polly sighed as she set a cup of tea on the bedside table next to John. "And ghosts can't be caught."

"We could go after him," John said.

"I think you should rest. Toadius is a very capable man. Once he cools off, he'll come home." She smiled. "I'll stay with you until he's back. With you injured, and Toadius off, someone needs to be guarding the ruby."

"But Toadius has the ruby." A cold chill washed over the boy. "If he's ambushed, we'll all be in trouble. You have to go find him! Please."

Pickles fussed with John's pillows. "Okay," she said reluctantly after a moment. "I'll find him. You stay here." She tucked John in and turned off the light.

"Polly?" he whispered.

"Yes, John?"

"Who was it?" The words tumbled out before he had a chance to stop them.

Pickles glanced over her shoulder. "Who was who?"

"Who was the person Toadius lost?"

Polly's expression said more than any words ever could. John had seen that face before. He'd felt that pain. "Was it his dad?"

"No," Polly whispered. "He was my father."

"What happened?"

"That's a very long story. One I'd rather never tell again."

"I understand."

Polly touched John's hand gently. "I bet you do."

"I'm sorry for your loss."

"Oh, I didn't lose him. He was taken from me." Her ocean-blue eyes darkened, like clouds gathering before a storm.

"Does it get easier?" John finally asked.

"Easier?"

"Your dad's death. Did you ever get over it?"

"No, I'm sorry to say. I'm afraid you never completely get over a death like that. But you learn to go on. Having someone you love taken from you is like losing an arm. You can go on living without an arm. You can learn how to function without it—maybe even almost as well as before you lost it. But it will always be missing from your life." She carefully smoothed the hair back from John's forehead.

"I don't know what to do without her," John whispered. His ribs still hurt from the fight.

Pickles smiled sadly. "You just need a compass."

"A compass?"

"No matter which direction you're facing, or how lost you feel, with a compass, you'll always know where north is. And if you know that, you can't truly be lost." She tapped John's hand. "You need a compass."

"I'm not sure how being able to find north will help."

"I don't mean an actual compass. You need to find something you love and trust in it when you're feeling uncertain. You can't lose your way if you let your heart guide you. It may not always keep you safe, but it will always bring you home."

"Is that why you and Toadius found each other again?" John asked.

"You are too clever, Mr. Boarhog," Pickles said, tousling the boy's hair. He winced as she accidentally brushed the egg-shaped bruise on his head. "Oh! I'm so sorry."

"It's okay." John laughed, trying to pretend his head didn't hurt. "Do you think Toadius will be all right?"

"You're really worried about him, aren't you?"

"That's what family does, right? They worry about each other." John put his hand on hers. "Whether he admits it or not, he needs us."

Pickles leaned in and gently kissed John's forehead, before handing him some ice and looking him directly in the eye.

"Rest now, my clever boy. I'll find Toadius, but you need to get your sleep. Promise me you'll stay put?"

John nodded reluctantly.

Pickles rose and walked to the door, but she stopped and turned back to him. "I'm glad we found each other, too." She flashed him a dazzling smile, then slipped out into the hall and closed the door. Settling back into his pillows, John couldn't help but smile back.

He heard the thump of the door as Pickles left the apartment. He tried to go back to sleep—tried to keep his promise—but his mind kept replaying the episode in the alleyway, the rescue, and then his talk with Pickles. His mom had always been his true north. Pickles was right about that.

The more he thought, the more uncomfortable the bed became.

John had once read about a princess who couldn't sleep. A queen put a pea under her mattress, and it bothered the princess so much that she was kept awake all night. The next day, she confronted the queen and found out it had all been a test. John knew that the princess wasn't real, but he couldn't help but feel maybe he, too, was being tested.

Maybe his mother hadn't left him after all. Maybe she was out there watching him, testing to see if he could stand on his own. Maybe she'd set up this entire strange adventure so that he'd find himself. He was certain she didn't want him to take up a life of crime. If she had, she wouldn't have faked her death the first time. She wanted him to be an inspector. Yes, that was it. This was a quest to right her wrongs. And John knew a lot about quests. He'd read dozens of books about knights and dragons.

John sighed, trying to find a comfortable position. His mother had always said that if they got separated, they'd meet on the steps of the museum. Could she have arranged it so he'd live at the museum?

John shook his head. That seemed unlikely. The only way she would have known all this was going to happen is if she were a psychic. She was a master thief, not a fortune teller.

She was a master thief.

A master thief!

John sat straight up. A master thief could've planned it all, and there was only one master thief in town: *the Mauve Moth*. John leapt out of bed and ran down the hall, ignoring his promise to Pickles, his pounding head, and his protesting body.

Ripping open the door to the study, he ran to Toadius's large bookshelf, remembering what the inspector had said at the diner. He searched for the book on butterflies and moths, finally spotting it on the top shelf. With a grunt, he gritted his teeth and stretched to pull the book down. Flipping it open, he skimmed the pages looking for purple butterflies.

Sure enough, on page thirty-seven, was a spread filled with exactly what he was looking for.

His hands began to shake, and he felt a bit lightheaded.

Right in the middle of the page was a beautiful purple butterfly. And next to it read the words "*Purpura Limenitis archippus.* Also known as the Cerise Viceroy."

CHAPTER EIGHTEEN

The time John got a partner.

I LOVE RIGATONI. It has always been my favorite type of pasta. My grandmother used to make a rigatoni and banana soufflé that was simply heavenly. I've tried to recreate the recipe on many occasions, but it never comes out quite right, probably because Gram-Gram never told me the secret ingredient. If only she had, I could've enjoyed rigatoni banana soufflé whenever I wanted. Instead, I spent most of my childhood using every tactic I could think of to get that recipe.

One day, I snuck into Gram-Gram's recipe box and found

it. But upon further examination, I learned something horrible: All those years, Gram-Gram *did* have a secret. She didn't cook at all. The four-star chef had simply been ordering takeout and transferring it into one of her casserole dishes. If you're like me, you may have a hard time accepting people after finding out they aren't who they say they are.

John stared at the book, his thoughts racing. Not only was his mother alive, but she was also the very criminal he was chasing. How could he tell Toadius? The inspector was determined to see her in jail. Worse, she was about to walk into a trap, and he, her very own son, was the bait. Had Toadius known this all along? Is that why the inspector had been so kind to him? John suddenly didn't know whom to trust. What he did know was that he had to find out if his mother really was the Mauve Moth, and the only way to solve that riddle was to confront the Moth face-to-face.

John was so lost in his thoughts, he didn't notice the person standing behind him.

"What are you looking at?"

John spun around, readying himself for another fight, but instead of a new menace, he saw only a very sheepish Toadius McGee.

"Toadius!" John slammed the book closed. "I was just . . ."

"Researching. A very admirable skill for a detective." The

inspector took off his hat and settled into one of the giant leather chairs. "Would you kindly sit down for a moment, John? I owe you an apology . . . and an explanation."

John took the seat across from Toadius, and as he did, he noticed there was something different about the inspector. His normal playful smile had turned upside down. His eyes had gone dark, and his shoulders slumped as if he were carrying the weight of the world.

"I'm sorry for my outburst. I wasn't upset with you. I just understand how terrible it feels to want someone to be back in your life, while at the same time knowing that desire will never come to pass." Toadius paused, taking a deep breath. "I wasn't always a detective. I was born in Colorado. My father was a musician and my mother a librarian. I was their only child, and then they died. Car accident."

"You were an orphan, too?"

"I was. Which is why I believe I have a sense of what you're going through. To this day, I sometimes lie awake at night thinking about what my life would've been like if they were still alive."

The silence stretched between them.

"When did you move to England?" John finally asked.

"When I was ten. I was adopted by a woman named Delores Kay Powell. Delores is very much alive. She teaches

Year Eight in England. *Year Eight* is what you call the seventh grade here. She was the one who introduced me to crime solving."

"She sounds great," John said, distracted as his gaze wandered back to the butterfly book.

"She is. If I were a braver man, I would've become a middle school English teacher, like Madam Powell."

"Being a detective isn't brave?"

"Not compared to being a middle school English teacher. They have the toughest, most rewarding job in the world. And Delores was the toughest. I'd gotten in with a group of hooligans." Toadius leaned in, lowering his voice to a whisper. "A hooligan, as you probably know, is a troublemaker."

John rolled his eyes. "Tell me something I don't know."

"Well, my group of hooligans was a rowdy lot. When we broke the windows of an abandoned building and got arrested, Delores said, 'Toadius, there are two types of people in the world: those who want to make tornadoes and those who want to make rainbows. The rainbows attract gold and sharply dressed leprechauns. The tornadoes attract sorrow and shoe-obsessed witch hunters.' Then she introduced me to the man who would become my mentor, Professor Gavin Cronopolis. He wrote the single most important book about modern crime solving."

"What is it called?" John asked.

"*The Single Most Important Book about Modern Crime Solving*. I must've read it a thousand times. It changed my life. As an avid reader, you know the power of a good book."

"I'd love to read it."

"You should. I think I have a copy on the shelf here." Toadius stood, surveying one of the bookcases.

"That's very nice of you, but why don't you finish your story first," John said too quickly.

Toadius smiled and settled back down. "Very well. You see, Dr. Gavin introduced me to my first two loves. The first was crime fighting. Dr. Gavin was a master detective—the world's greatest. He was amazing. He didn't need reference books or super computers. He remembered *everything*. He could read something once and explain it to you as if he'd studied it for a million years and memorize all the details of a crime scene without so much as a glance at the photos. He was, by far, the greatest man I have ever known. He took me under his wing and taught me the Thirty-Seven Rules of Crime Fighting. It was the best time of my life, and if you had asked me back then if I could be happier, I would've laughed in your face. That, of course, was until he introduced me to his daughter, Polly."

"Polly was your second love."

"Polly came second, but she has, and will always be, my greatest love. We met the winter of my second year at university. She was studying at an all-girl's college here in the United States, and she only came home at holidays. I normally spent my holidays with Delores, so we never met until one very special New Year's Eve. I remember it like it was yesterday. From the moment I saw her, I knew I loved her, and not in some silly, schoolboy crush kind of way. Polly locked eyes with me and for a moment, time stopped. The problem, of course, was that Polly already had a boyfriend. His name was Jacob Gatsby, no relation to Jay Gatsby. He had been the quarterback of the Notre Dame football team, no relation to Paris. And frankly, he was a bully. To make a long story short, one broken heel, two black eyes, and a punch bowl's worth of carpet stains later, Polly and I ended up together."

"Did Gavin forbid it?" John mostly knew about romance from books, and it seemed to him that the fathers in stories were always forbidding true love.

"No, he supported it wholeheartedly." Toadius laughed. "Actually, to this day I have a theory that the only reason I was invited to the party was so that Polly would finally see Jacob for what he really was. That, and I think Gavin hated the carpet in the living room. I mean, who sets up a punch station in a room with white carpeting?"

"What happened?"

"Gavin had his own master criminal he'd been hunting—a

man simply known as Cicada. If you think the Mauve Moth is bad, then you cannot imagine how dangerous Cicada was. I wanted to help catch this criminal, but Gavin forbade it. He instead relied on the one person I hated most—Jacob Gatsby. Gatsby had just graduated and was an up-and-coming star in the FBI. I was jealous of Gatsby and all the attention he was getting from Gavin. *I* had always been Gavin's right-hand man, and to be suddenly shut out was unbearable. I took it upon myself to bring Cicada to justice. And so, I used my contacts from my hooligan days and got myself a job in his criminal organization."

"You went undercover?" John had moved so close to the edge of his seat that he almost fell off.

"Yes. I worked my way up through the ranks, and one day I got word that Cicada, himself, would like to meet with me. It was my opportunity to unmask the master criminal. Gavin caught wind of my plans and came to save me. That's when it happened. It remains the worst thing that's ever occurred in my entire life."

"He was killed?"

"Yes," Toadius said quietly. "He lost his life trying to save mine. He died because I was a fool. The whole time I was working under Cicada, it was a trap. They knew from the moment I entered the organization that I was part of the S.O.S. If only I'd listened to Gavin, we all would still be alive. *I* was meant to be in the tent where we found Gavin's body. The only piece of evidence left behind was this symbol." Toadius drew out the Mauve Moth's calling card. "I never found Cicada again. It was as if he had never existed."

"And that's why you're after the Mauve Moth?"

"Cicada might have been the one who gave the orders, but the Moth was the one who finished the job. The Mauve Moth is the only link that remains to Cicada. If I can catch the Moth, I can find the man who murdered my mentor. I will not rest until Cicada and the Moth are behind bars."

John sat in silence, the sentence echoing in his head. Could it be true? Was his mom one of Cicada's agents? Maybe that was why she'd faked her death—maybe she was hiding from Cicada.

"How do you know the Moth is working for Cicada?" John asked carefully.

"Because all Cicada's agents have pseudonyms associated with insects."

"Pseudonyms?"

"It means a fictitious name. Cicada used insects so that we would know that he was behind the crimes they committed. Most criminals live for two things: money and notoriety."

"And his agents would do anything he told them to?"

"If they wanted to stay alive, then yes, I suppose they would."

"So, they would kill for him?" John took a deep breath, not sure he was ready for the answer.

"Doctor, I assure you that you are perfectly safe." Toadius reached out and put his hand on the boy's shoulder.

"Rule Number Two," John whispered.

"What about it?"

"You said that the world's most valuable currency is information." John crossed his arms as he eyed his guardian. "I need to have all the information if we're going to continue as partners."

Toadius stood up and walked over to his desk. He pulled out a file, considered for a moment, and then handed it to John. The file was old. The folder, itself, was stained, like it had once been used as a coaster, and the papers inside had started yellowing. GAVIN CRONOPOLIS was stamped on the front in little letters.

"What's this?" John asked.

"It's all the evidence I have on Gavin's death and the Moth." Toadius walked to the doorway. "I will never lie to you, John. But I must warn you that what you find in there may not be what you are searching for."

There was a pause as John contemplated the file in his hands. "Good night," he finally said.

"Good night," Toadius echoed. Frowning, he left the room.

CHAPTER NINETEEN

The time John learned the truth about his mother.

S LOWLY, JOHN OPENED the file and immediately felt like a
bucket of ice had been dumped down his back. The first
page was an advertisement for a circus. He recognized the
tent from the picture the Great Goatinee had shown him.

His mother's circus. Looking at the image, John was
reminded of another book he'd read long ago. This one was
about a girl who followed a white rabbit down a hole and ended
up in a magical, but very dangerous, wonderland. And now,
John was about to go down his own rabbit hole—discovering
things he wasn't sure he wanted to know.

The next series of pages were notes about the crime scene. John wasn't a forensic scientist and didn't really understand what some of the words meant, but he gathered that Gavin Cronopolis had been shot in the chest.

There were photos along with the forensic report. John tried not to look at them. Next was a series of criminal mug-shots. He found the Great Goatinee's and stopped to laugh when he read that the man with an obsession for synonyms was originally from Canada. John didn't know much about Canada, but he was pretty sure Goatinee's accent was *not* Canadian.

John flipped through a couple of the other criminal pro-files, before he came to the one he was looking for: *Cerise Viceroy. Age: 19. Location: Unknown.*

His mom had a long rap sheet, mostly petty theft. There weren't as many notes on her as on the others in the file, though stamped on the front page of her report in big red letters was the word *DECEASED*.

The date of her death was listed as one day before Gavin was killed. Which meant she had faked her death before Gavin died. John felt a sense of relief. She couldn't have been the killer. If he showed Toadius what he'd found, maybe the inspector would believe him.

He smiled as he flipped through some old photos of the circus people. There were pictures of his mom. She was grinning ear to ear, mid-performance. In one photograph, she stood with a man who wore a big black top hat and had a neat brown mustache. There was one of the Great Goatinee with a big puff of black smoke surrounding him as the audience pointed and laughed. John couldn't help chuckling, too, until he saw a familiar face. The clown had a furry monkey on his shoulder, and that monkey was the informant Shim-Sham.

"That dirty ape—"

But his words were snuffed out as his focus shifted to the clown in the picture. The figure was so familiar. John squinted, bringing the photo closer, and his eyes went wide. *Toadius McGee!*

John shouldn't have been surprised. Toadius had said he'd infiltrated Cicada's organization. But what really made John pause was the other person in the picture—his mother. Toadius had known his *mother*. The thought hadn't crossed his mind until that moment. He froze.

"She was a wonderful woman."

John looked up. Toadius stood in the doorway.

"You—you knew her."

"I did."

"Why didn't you tell me?"

"Because if I did, you'd only ask more questions, and when you didn't get the answers you wanted, you would have tried to find them on your own. It wasn't until I met you, John, that I understood why Gavin didn't want me to go after Cicada. Whether you like it or not, you were not ready for that responsibility."

"And now?" John rubbed angrily at his eyes.

"Now you have a partner. Why don't you tell me what you found in my *Book of Butterflies and Moths*?"

John felt his cheeks burn. "You knew I'd seen the book."

"Of course I did. You *are* very clever, John, but you are also very young. The young never put away their references properly." Toadius walked to the desk and flipped the book open to page thirty-seven. "I assume you saw the purple butterfly with your mother's name?"

John nodded.

"Don't worry yourself that your mother is the Mauve Moth, John. Believe me, she is not. I went down that rabbit hole many years ago."

"Do you think my mom could still be alive?"

"Honestly, I don't know." Toadius shook his head. "I want to believe for your sake, but if she were alive, I believe she would've contacted you by now. I find it is very hard to leave someone you love behind. In any case, she's not the Mauve Moth."

"How do you know? How can you be so sure?"

"I've tracked the Mauve Moth from Saint Petersburg to

Timbuktu, but my hunt has stretched far longer than two years. If Sarah Boarhog were the Mauve Moth, then how could she have been in New York City with you and in Paris with me? No, I am certain that whoever is behind the mask, it is not your mother."

John looked between the symbol of the Mauve Moth and the picture of the purple butterfly. . . . He desperately wanted them to be the same, but he had to admit now that they were not.

Maybe Cicada was blackmailing her. Maybe he'd figured out she'd faked her death, and now he was forcing her to help him.

"I don't know what to do." John sniffled. "I miss her so much, but the more I think about her, the more it hurts. The more it hurts, the more I need her. I'm alone, and I'll never see her again. That just makes me miss her even more."

"That, Doctor, is what is called a paradox," Toadius said calmly.

"A paradox?" John tried to control his tears.

"A situation, person, or thing that combines contradictory features or qualities. The memories of your mother are so happy, thinking about them makes you sad. The sadder you get, the more you miss her, but the more you miss her, the more you think about how much you love her, which in turn, makes you sadder still. It is an endless cycle. A paradox."

"How do I stop it?"

"Short of breaking the paradox and resetting time as we know it, I'm afraid I don't have an answer." Toadius handed the boy his handkerchief. "I can't promise you that your mother is alive. I can't promise you that we'll find out anything about her death. I can, however, promise that you'll always be welcome here, and you'll never be alone again."

John wiped his eyes and wrapped his arms around Toadius. "We'd better get some sleep," he said. "We still have a Moth to catch."

CHAPTER TWENTY

The time John was betrayed.

R<small>EGARDLESS OF WHAT CITY</small> you're in, there's a place where criminals go to make deals, drink sugary beverages, and listen to soft, soothing jazz music. In New York, that place is the Blue Moose Jazz and Root Beer Club, the city's best-kept secret speakeasy.

A *speakeasy* is a business that seems normal to the public. It may appear to be a bookstore or flower shop or ice-cream parlor. If you entered such an establishment, you'd probably see nothing unusual about it. Behind the scenes, however, in the basement or back room, an entirely different business would be taking place—one wrapped up in illegal activities, like gambling or drinking alcohol or eating sushi. To gain access to this part of the business would usually require knowing about a secret door, a special knock, or a particularly clever password. In the case of the Blue Moose, you'd enter the ice-cream parlor and to get into the jazz club in the back, you'd have to say a secret password to the person at the counter.

Very often the secret phrases were found hidden in books. In many cases, the first letter of each chapter would spell out the password. For instance, the first letter of each chapter in this book spells out a secret message. But though the phrase might get you a discount at your local aquarium, it would *not* get you into the Blue Moose.

The exact phrase needed to enter the Blue Moose was *root beer float,* which would hardly be an unusual order in an ice-cream parlor. The problem was that root beer floats were also the shop's specialty, so almost everyone entering the establishment wanted one. Soon, the root beer floats were making much more money than the illegal alcohol, so eventually the Blue Moose stopped serving alcohol altogether.

Now, just because the Blue Moose stopped selling illegal booze years ago, doesn't mean that criminals, mobsters, and bootleggers stopped coming to the club. It's a well-known fact that most criminals love root beer. The Blue Moose made it easy for them to conduct business while sipping on a nice, sweet drink topped with the finest ice cream.

Toadius, being the World's Greatest Detective, couldn't just walk into a place like the Blue Moose without being recognized as a cop, so he'd changed out of his signature blue suit, bowler hat, and red tie into a pinstripe suit and donned a fedora. He'd even drawn on a pencil-thin mustache with eyeliner. John wore an eye patch to cover his black eye and a puffy pirate shirt. He'd used wax to slick back his hair, and walked with a limp.

As they approached the ice-cream parlor/jazz club, John caught a glimpse of his reflection in a window outside.

"What do you think?" Toadius asked.

"I think we look awesome." John grinned. "Although, I wish these had pockets."

"Ah, yes, I am sorry about that, but the only pants I could find that would fit you were made for ladies," the inspector explained.

"Why don't women's pants have pockets?" John asked.

"What an excellent mystery to solve." Toadius pulled out his S.O.S. notebook and quickly made a note. "As soon as we catch the Moth, we will find out the answer together." With that, Toadius turned his attention to the door and rapped firmly. A small slot opened, and a pair of dark eyes stared back at them.

"What's the password?" A deep voice matched the dark eyes.

"Root beer float," Toadius whispered.

A second later, the door opened. "Now, Doctor, keep a lookout for any people wearing purple," Toadius said in a low voice as they passed through into the jazz club. And then they realized their mistake. *Everyone* in the room was dressed in purple: the waiters, the customers—even the tables were covered in purple tablecloths.

John had never seen so much purple in one place. "I have a bad feeling about this."

Although ownership of the Blue Moose had changed hands many times, the decor had remained the same. It was like being transported back to the 1920s. Ivory art deco pillars lined the walls, and a large stage stood at one end with a towering proscenium. A beautiful red-velvet curtain hung in front of the stage. To the side, a chalkboard sign announced: UP NEXT . . . POLLY CRONOPOLIS. Sitting at the tables was the oddest mix of human specimens. Old banker tycoons with their pretty young companions. A table of rowdy hockey players sharing a root beer toast. Maverick Johnston, the pitcher for the Brooklyn Bombers, was showing off his numerous World Series rings to Hollywood starlet Gina Malone. Master Igon Malik III, famed artist, was explaining his ice sculpture *The Friendly Gent,* a life-size depiction of a man reaching out to shake hands.

The New York City Chief of Police and his assistant sat across from a woman who must've been the chief's wife. Unlike the chief, who was taking up most of the table, she was a small, round woman with bright red cheeks.

John was so focused on perfecting his limp and scanning for the Moth, he wasn't paying attention and ran straight into a wall. He winced, grabbing his bruised ribs, and the ruby slipped from his fingers, tumbling to the floor. Reaching down to pick it up, he realized the wall had feet.

John slowly looked up, meeting the eyes of a giant of a man, who sneered back at him as brown, fizzy liquid dripped down the front of his shirt.

"I'm so sorry," John said quickly. "I wasn't paying attention to where I was going."

"You'd better get out if you know what's good for you," the Wall growled.

But before John could respond, Toadius stepped between them. "That was rude, sir. My friend here was good enough to apologize, and a gentleman would accept that apology."

"I'm not a gentleman," the Wall rumbled. "I'm a pugilist."

A *pugilist* is not someone who is fond of small dogs with flat faces, but rather is the term commonly used for a professional boxer.

"My name is Scotty Moose," the Wall continued. "This is

my club. And I ain't never seen you around here before. Are you a copper?"

John gulped. Any minute now, Scotty Moose would out them, and they'd be surrounded by every criminal in New York City. So he was surprised when Toadius grinned and brightly asked, "Then Tall Andy is your partner?"

"He is. What's it to you?" Scotty raised his fists.

"Well, years ago I helped Tall Andy find his missing puggle."

"Mr. Flatface?" A tear formed in Scotty's eye. He bent down so his gaze was level with that of the inspector. "Are you saying you are the great detective *Toadius McGee?*" The boxer whispered so as not to bring unwanted attention. Within seconds, Scotty Moose had lifted Toadius off the ground, hugging him tightly. "My Andy was so happy." Toadius, however, was probably not, as he had gone a sickly pale color. "If there's anything you *ever* need, Scotty Moose will make it yours."

"There . . . is . . . one . . . thing . . . ," Toadius squeaked out.

"Name it!"

"Would . . . you . . . kindly . . . let . . . me . . . down?"

"Oh." Scotty Moose released Toadius, and the inspector fell to the floor like a ton of bricks. He stayed there for a moment, gasping for air as the color slowly returned to his face.

Scotty smiled down sheepishly. "Sorry."

"No trouble," Toadius said with a cough.

"Let's get you a seat up front," Scotty suggested, scooping Toadius up and ushering him through the crowd. "And the root beer's on me tonight. Get it? *The root beer's* on *me*," he said, waving at his soaked shirt. For a brute of a man, John noted, Scotty Moose sure had a great sense of humor.

Toadius nodded toward an empty table in the rear corner. "Actually, if you don't mind, we'd prefer to sit in the back. That way we can take in the whole room."

"Yes, sir." Scotty Moose bellowed to a waiter, "JERRY, CLEAR THAT TABLE!"

Jerry tripped over himself, rushing to remove the used glasses and wipe down the surface.

Toadius scanned the room as they headed toward the back. "Let's take a seat and watch for the Moth. They could be anyone here."

A waitress approached them wearing a mauve vest with a matching mauve hat. "How do ya do?" She leaned over the table. "My name's Esther. I'll be your server this evening. The gentleman at the bar sends his regards."

"Which gentleman?" John asked politely.

"That one," she said as she set down a tray holding two bananas on mauve plates.

Shim-Sham waved to them from across the room.

"Thank him for us," Toadius said, peeling one of the bananas. "That's a very nice outfit you have on."

"Thanks, hon." She winked.

"Why is everyone dressed in purple tonight?" John asked.

"It's not purple, sweetie." She struck a pose. "It's mauve."

"Oh, my mistake. Why is everyone dressed in mauve?"

"You must be new." She touched Toadius's shoulder and gave it a little push. "It's Mauve Monday. Tall Andy likes to have color-themed days: Mauve Mondays, Turquoise Tuesdays, White Wednesdays, Thistle Thursdays—that's gray, don't cha know—Fire Fridays, Silver Saturdays, and last but not least, Green Sundays."

"*Green Sundays?*" John asked.

"Scotty Moose is Irish," Esther replied in a serious tone.

"We're from out of town," Toadius said to break the awkward silence. "We've been traveling so much, we lost track of the days. We thought it was Thursday." He motioned to his clothes, which were grayer in color.

"Totally understandable, doll." Esther placed menus on the table. "I'll see if I can find a couple of purple flowers for your lapel. Don't worry, shug. The show's about to start."

And as if on cue, the music began, the lights dimmed, and the curtain slowly opened.

Lying on a piano in a sequined dress was none other than the beautiful and talented Polly "Pickles" Cronopolis.

Her dress was a deep mauve, and she had a matching mauve feather boa draped around her shoulders. She sat up and softly sang into the microphone.

While Toadius clapped loudly and whistled, John glanced back to the bar. Shim-Sham caught his eye, then pointed to a table across the room. In a booth in the back corner, a shady fellow sat, covered in shadow. John could only tell it was a man because the figure was wearing a large top hat.

John tapped Toadius on the shoulder and lifted his chin toward the booth. "There is our fence."

"Well, I suppose it's time." Toadius signaled to Pickles, and she shifted her gaze to the booth without missing a note before she gave a small nod back to Toadius, then descended into the audience as though this were all part of the performance.

"You're up, Doctor," Toadius said, locking eyes with the boy. "All you have to do is take the ruby to the gentleman. Show it to him, but *do not* let him hold it. I'll be right behind you."

John bit his lip. "What if something goes wrong?"

"Then go to Plan B."

"What's Plan B?" John asked.

"Run away as fast as you can. Go somewhere safe and wait for me to find you." Toadius shook the boy's hand. "It has been a pleasure fighting crime with you, Doctor."

And with that, the inspector disappeared into the crowd jostling to get a better view of Ms. Pickles.

John rose from his seat and slowly walked across the club toward the fence. This was it. Any minute now, the Moth would make their move.

John crept closer to the table. The audience was getting larger, people craning their necks and bumping against one other. Everyone in the club wanted to see Pickles. John couldn't even spot her anymore.

Just when John was starting to panic, he spotted Pickles climbing back onto the stage. She caught John's eye and smiled at him.

John weaved through the crowd, watching for a familiar face. He swore he kept glimpsing his mother in the swarm of patrons, but each time he got close, the woman was always too tall or too short or too blond. The only thing they all had in common was that they weren't her. Was she there, watching from the shadows? Now almost at the fence's table, he squeezed the ruby.

The shadowy figure had not shifted from his spot. John took another step toward his table and then stopped. He was suddenly afraid—but not because of what he saw before him. Rather, it was because of what he didn't see.

There wasn't anyone there. Where the fence was meant to be was a propped-up broom with a top hat placed at just the right tilt to look like it sat atop a person's head. He and Toadius hadn't set a trap; they'd walked right into one.

Panicked, John turned to the stage and called out, "IT'S A TRICK!" But the moment the words left his mouth, he knew he was too late. Pickles's joy turned to confusion as a trapdoor opened beneath her feet. The young actress let out a piercing scream before she fell away into a dark pit.

"*POLLY!*" the undisguisable voice of Toadius McGee cried out from somewhere in the sea of spectators. John scanned the room, trying to find him, but the inspector spotted John first. A sense of dread rose as Toadius tried to make his way across the club to his ward, but the crowd was too thick. "*JOHN!*" Toadius yelled above the panic. "*PLAN B!*"

John heard the words of his mentor, but his body betrayed him. Instead of running to the door, he headed deeper into the chaos. After only a couple of steps, the lights suddenly went out. Shrieks and shouts echoed off the club's walls, and John felt more lost than ever.

Many things occurred in that blackout. I cannot be certain of my accuracy, but I do believe the following happened in this exact order:

There was a *crash*. A gunshot. Another crash, this time accompanied by glass shattering. The chief of police bellowed, "Turn on the lights!" A wet *splat*—John wiped something slimy from his cheek. Two more crashes. A shrill

BAAAAAH! And finally, a maniacal laugh that made chills race down John's spine.

He was struck from behind and tumbled to the ground. As he did, the ruby was knocked out of his hand and launched across the floor. And then, just as quickly as the lights had gone out, the club was blindingly aglow.

After blinking for a moment, John took in the scene. The room was a complete mess, and now he could see why. The first crash had been the hockey team—the players were brave on the ice, but apparently afraid of the dark. The seven large men had flipped their table over and were cowering together behind their makeshift fort. A gangster had fired his gun in the chaos, which had caused a chandelier to fall, smashing the table next to the chief's table. The chief's wife lay unconscious on the floor next to the ice sculpture. As it turned out, she was not afraid of the dark, but *very* afraid of the ice. While shuffling around searching for a light switch in the dark, she'd accidentally made contact with the sculpture's freezing hand and fainted, out cold. The next two crashes had actually been just one poor table, which had suffered the wrath of Scotty Moose's pugilistic tendencies.

The goat's scream had come from the chief's assistant, who was not in fact a goat, but would be very good at impersonating one professionally. He was not brave in the dark. The tiny man continued his high-pitched wail until

Toadius walked up to him, grabbed a glass of root beer sitting on a nearby table, and splashed him in the face.

"Thank you," the assistant said, wiping foam from his eyes.

Toadius didn't reply. Instead, he scanned the room for John. "Where's Pickles?"

Esther the waitress handed Toadius a small bowl of pickles. "Here you go, hon."

Toadius looked at the bowl, then to the waitress, then back to the bowl. "I meant the actress and singer, Polly 'Pickles' Cronopolis."

"Oh, then why didn't you say so," Esther said, taking the bowl back. He stopped her for a moment, grabbing a handful of sour dills, then turned back to the chaos.

"What in the blazes is going on?" the chief demanded, fanning his swooning wife with a cocktail napkin.

Scotty Moose hollered, "*Jerry, call the police!*"

That did it. The patrons of the jazz club scattered, like a light switch had been flipped in a closet filled with cockroaches. Thinking fast, Toadius rushed to help John off the floor before he was trampled by the fleeing criminals.

John couldn't meet the inspector's eye. "The ruby . . . I lost it."

"It's all right. We'll get it back," Toadius said, checking the boy to make sure he hadn't been injured.

"Nobody move! You are all under arrest!" Brownie busted

through the front door, his badge held high for all to see. A half dozen police officers flooded into the room behind him. "Clean this place up, boys!" he yelled as he tripped one of the criminals. An officer rushed in to handcuff the fallen foe.

The chief of police spotted Toadius. Sweeping up his wife and throwing her over his shoulder, he ran to the inspector's side. "McGee? What the blazes is going on here?" he demanded, unceremoniously dumping his wife into Brownie's unready arms. "You, help my wife."

"Sir," Toadius called to the chief, "there's been a kidnapping." He turned to the trapdoor. "The Mauve Moth is behind this. I'm certain of it."

"The Moth?" the chief replied, furrowing his brow. "What are you talking about?"

"The Moth kidnapped Pickles and stole the ruby," John explained to the policeman, his voice frantic.

"Toadius, what is this boy talking about? What ruby?"

"The Egypt's Fire. We set a trap for the Mauve Moth."

"You did *what*?"

Toadius reached out his hand. "Sir, if you'd let me explain—"

"ENOUGH, McGEE!" the chief roared. "You're fired!"

"What?"

"FIRED! KAPUT! FINISHED! DONE! You *stole* a billion-dollar ruby to use as bait to catch a mythical criminal, and then you lost it! Your policing days are over. Someone, arrest this man."

Most of the officers were busy chasing around criminals and celebrities, trying to stop them from fleeing the club. Brownie, however, stopped dead in his tracks, pushing another officer out of the way so he wouldn't miss a word.

"You don't understand. The ruby was—"

"Tell it to the judge, McGee." Brownie almost tripped over himself trying to be the one who got to handcuff his rival.

"Chief, you have to listen to me," Toadius pleaded.

"I'm done listening to you. You've destroyed this wonderful jazz club, you endangered a minor while performing an unsanctioned police sting, you got an innocent girl kidnapped, and worst of all, you made my Boopie pass out." The chief's face was now an unnatural shade of red. "You can't take the law into your own hands, McGee. You were once the greatest detective of all time, but the city and I can no longer afford your antics. Give me your badge."

Toadius reached into his pocket and pulled it out, looking at the shiny metal object for a moment before placing it into the chief's hand.

"Looks like your tomfoolery finally caught up with you, McGee." Brownie took his cuffs and rather harshly restrained the ex-inspector. "Looks like we both are gonna end up in next week's copy of *Confidential Informer*."

John couldn't believe what was happening. "What about Ms. Cronopolis?" he demanded.

"We'll put our best men on it," the chief said. "Oh, and McGee, you won't be needing this anymore." The chief reached up and pulled the S.O.S. pin off Toadius's lapel. John waited for the inspector to protest or struggle, but the once-vibrant inspector just hung his head, defeated.

That's when John noticed something on the chief's left wrist. It looked like a tattoo of a bug.

"What's that?" John asked, pointing at the mark.

The chief pulled his sleeve down. "Drop the kid off at the Jersey Home for Boys," he barked.

"*NO!*" John screamed as he wiggled loose of an officer's grip. He remembered what Toadius had said earlier that evening. It was time for Plan B. A surge of adrenaline rushed through his body, and suddenly he couldn't feel the aching of his still-bruised ribs. He didn't hesitate. He took a deep breath and ran.

I've seen some amazing football games in my life, but to this day I have never witnessed such skill as John Boarhog demonstrated that evening at the Blue Moose, dodging New York's finest. He ducked under the first officer in his path, then spun around the second. As a third officer grabbed at him, John deftly unbuckled the officer's belt, sending the poor man's pants pooling around his ankles, transforming the six-foot-tall policeman into a six-foot-long barricade. Two more officers tumbled to the ground. Exasperated by his officers' ineptness, the chief threw out his arms to secure the boy, but John scaled the man like a ladder, leapt up, and grabbed onto a chandelier. He flew through the air with the greatest of ease, that daring young man on the flying . . . chandelier?

"Leave him alone!" Toadius hollered as he bodychecked the chief to the ground. The inspector tried to get back up, but his hands were still handcuffed, and he hit the floor face-first, knocking himself out cold.

"NO ONE HURTS MY FRIEND!" Scotty Moose roared like a bear. The boxer jumped over the bar and punched the officer in the face. The man was out like a light. At that point, half the cops in the club were trying to catch John while the other half were trying to hold off Scotty Moose.

John vaulted from the chandelier, landing in the rafters. The officers had resorted to throwing root beer bottles at him, trying to knock him down like a carnival game.

John heard a familiar chittering above his head. There,

perched on an open windowsill, was Shim-Sham. The monkey hissed at the boy.

"Thanks," John said as he dove through the small opening.

"Eek, eek," the monkey taunted, sticking his tongue out at the cops below. An officer hurled a bottle, hitting Shim-Sham square in the noggin. The monkey spun in a circle then dropped. Right onto Scotty Moose's large cranium. The boxer's eyes rolled up into his head as he, too, found himself in the Land of Dreams.

By then, John was on the roof, free. His heart racing, he ran to the edge of the building. Looking down at the freezing water of the Hudson River stretching below him, he came to a terrible conclusion: There was nowhere to go.

Behind him, he heard a crash, followed by Brownie kicking the door to the roof open. The next thing John knew, police officers were spilling out of the access point, shouting at him to back away from the edge.

"There's nowhere to go, kid!" Brownie shouted. "Put your hands up and get down on your knees!"

John looked back over his shoulder at the detective. He could jump.

"I mean it, Boarhog. It's over!" Brownie's desperate hollers echoed off the rooftops.

John took a deep breath, closed his eyes, and leapt.

CHAPTER TWENTY-ONE

The time John had too many uncles.

E VERY DECISION YOU MAKE in your life will have consequences. Sometimes, those consequences will be positive.
For instance, if you were to decide to serve chocolate cake at your
birthday party, the consequence would be that after you blew out
your candles, you would then get to eat a scrumptious dessert.
But some consequences can be much less pleasant. For instance,
if you jumped off a building into the ice-cold Hudson River to
escape police capture, the consequences could consist of a wide
range of things, from ruining your pirate costume to getting
water up your nose, to freezing to death in a watery grave.

The key to sound decision making is to think about your choices and what the consequence of each path might be. This is not always as easy as picking chocolate cake. Sometimes you come across situations where no matter what your decision, the outcome will be bad.

As John waited for the icy river to overtake him, he couldn't help but think of warmer days: the last summer when he'd seen his mother; the warmth of his handmade hammock above the bathroom at the museum; sitting at dinner with Toadius eating blueberry pancakes. The cozy memories swirled in his head as he prepared for the shocking cold future below.

But he didn't feel any water—just a sharp jerk on his collar. It took a moment for him to realize that he wasn't wet or falling. He was dangling from the roof, a hand latched onto his costume.

If you were to ask Doug Brownie what he was thinking that night, he'd tell you he was only doing his job, preventing a hoodlum from giving him the slip. But if you saw his face, you'd know he'd been sincerely concerned for the boy's safety.

"What are you trying to do?" Brownie yelled as he pulled John up.

"Let go!" John snapped, struggling against the detective's grip.

"The only place you'll be going is the Jersey Home for

Boys," the detective said as he borrowed handcuffs from a nearby officer. He gently clicked the restraints on the boy's wrists.

"You can't put me there," John pleaded, still trying to free himself. "They tried to kill me and—"

"Enough. Do you have any idea what could've happened to you if you jumped into that river? Did you even stop to think about the consequences of your actions? You're just like McGee. Always leaping before you look."

John stared into the man's eyes and realized that Doug Brownie was not the man he'd thought he was. The detective took off his jacket and wrapped it around John's shoulders.

"It's over, son," Brownie said. "Now, come with me."

Brownie walked John down a staircase and through the root beer club. As they passed through the main room, John craned his neck, desperate to get a glimpse of Toadius, but didn't see him anywhere. Officers must have already taken the inspector to jail. John noted that Scotty Moose was also missing, as was Shim-Sham. Most of the patrons had left as well. A half dozen police officers and a couple of workers milled around the space, looking a bit lost.

"You sure made a mess of things," Brownie said as if he were a stepfather at a baseball game. "Though it was only a matter of time, I suppose."

"*A matter of time* for what?"

"For Toadius to overstep his authority. I, for one, have always thought that man was one step from a life sentence."

John struggled to stand a little taller, though it was difficult with his arms restrained. "Toadius McGee is the greatest detective to ever live."

"That he was." Brownie shook his head.

The two didn't exchange another word. Not when Brownie placed the boy in the back of his car. Not when they pulled away from the Blue Moose Jazz Club. Not when they entered the Lincoln Tunnel. And not even when they had traveled well beyond the limits of Manhattan. As the buzz and glow of the City That Never Sleeps faded away, the tense silence kept its hold. John wanted to argue for his release. He wanted to tell Brownie about the night in the alleyway when Wormwood had stolen his locket. He wanted desperately for Brownie to turn the car around. But he knew nothing he had to say would make a difference, and that Brownie wouldn't be swayed.

"It ain't that bad, kid," Brownie said, breaking the silence. "The home, I mean. It's turned out some mighty fine men."

John didn't reply.

"It might just be the perfect spot to help a smart kid like you find his place in the world." Brownie caught John glaring at him in the rearview mirror. "Yeah, I get it. New places always seem scary until you get there."

"You don't understand," John muttered.

"I bet I'd surprise you."

John was trying very hard not to cry. "My life is over. You know that, right?"

"I know it feels that way, but with time, you'll recover. The Jersey Home for Boys will teach you the skills you need to survive in this world."

"Whatever."

"It worked for me." Brownie smiled.

John couldn't believe his ears. "You lived at the Jersey Home for Boys?" Was Brownie part of Wormwood's criminal enterprise? Maybe that's why he refused to listen.

"Yup."

"Then you know Wormwood?" John asked, wondering if Brownie was as dirty as the back seat of his car.

"No, never met the man. He took over years after I left."

That made John feel a little better. "So, you were an orphan?"

"Till I wasn't." Brownie's eyes watered a little. "I got adopted by my folks when I was about your age."

"What about your real parents?"

"My adoptive parents *are* my real parents. If you're asking about my birth parents, I never knew 'em." The detective coughed. "Left me on the steps of the home when I was a baby."

"I'm sorry."

"Don't be. Gladys and Leroy Brownie were the best thing to ever happen to me. They taught me how to be true to myself. Here." The man reached into his pocket, pulled out his wallet, and tossed it in the back with John. "There's a picture in there."

John opened the wallet and, sure enough, between a punch card from Patty's Pancake Parlor and an old baseball card, there was a picture of a family.

The photo was faded, but John could make out the faces of two older people and a robust kid around John's age riding a small horse—obviously Brownie. He was wearing an oversize cowboy hat and had a big smile on his face. A shiny sheriff's badge was pinned to his tight shirt.

"That was my very first birthday. They hired a pony and everything." Brownie's voice was different than John had ever heard it. The detective sounded happy.

"You were a big one-year-old."

"I was ten, or at least that's what we guessed. I remember it like it was yesterday."

John pointed to the star. "Nice badge."

"That was the day I decided I wanted to be a policeman. And look at me now. See, I'm living proof that it doesn't matter where you come from, as long as you have a dream and you don't quit till you get it. Mom was so proud of me that day." Brownie paused for a moment. "Do you have any pictures of your family?"

"I did, of my mom."

"Did you leave them at McGee's? If you want, I could stop over tomorrow and get them for you."

"No, it's not there. Someone stole it." John tried not to think about it.

"Who would steal a picture?" Brownie glanced in his rearview mirror again.

"It was in a locket. They took it."

"I'm sorry to hear that," Brownie said as he exited off the turnpike. "But they won't ever be able to take the picture from your mind. I can still see my mom's big blue eyes when she brought me to my new home. One day, I hope to meet a woman with eyes like hers."

"My mom had red hair—messy like mine—and the brightest green eyes." John didn't know why he was describing his mother. Just that he needed someone else to know.

"She sounds like a real looker. Well, we are here," Brownie said as he parked the car. "Boarhog, if you don't mind, I'm going to need my wallet back."

After John tossed it back up front, Brownie glanced at it and smiled, meeting the boy's eye in the rearview mirror. "You're a good kid, John."

THE JERSEY HOME FOR BOYS is in a town called Newark, New Jersey. Newark is famous for many things, none of them great or impressive.

Brownie exited the car and unlocked John's door. "Come on. I'll show you around my old stomping grounds."

The massive redbrick building towered over John, perched up on top of a hill like a dragon waiting for its prey. Everything in the boy's body made him want to run. The steps leading up to the entrance were also made of red brick, as if the home had unfurled its tongue to entice its victims into its mouth. John swallowed hard as he spotted pale faces peering down from the upper-floor windows.

Brownie knocked on the solid oak door and waited for someone to answer.

They didn't have long to wait. The door creaked open and a shadowy figure beckoned them across the threshold.

"Welcome," an all-too familiar voice said, sending a chill down John's spine. Even though Mr. Wormwood was bathed in shadow, John could tell he was smiling smugly.

"Mr. Wormwood? I'm Detective Doug Brownie. We spoke on the phone." Even Brownie seemed a little hesitant to enter the foyer.

"Please come in, Detective."

Brownie led John into the entryway. At first, the hall was dark, but his eyes quickly adjusted. The room reminded John of his last school, apart from the giant fireplace. Class pictures lined the walls, while a large banner that read THE FIGHTING FISH hung from a rafter.

Brownie beelined to the photos, pointing at a figure in one. "There I am," the large man said, waving John over. "Look at that mug."

John couldn't help but smile. Brownie was twice the size of the other boys in the picture, and he seemed to be stuffed into his suit. High in the middle of one wall hung a giant, ornate, circular frame, inside which was a portrait of Wormwood himself. The painting's smile was just as crooked as its subject. The Wormwood in the painting wore the same plum silk robe as the real version of the man, and it too glowed in the firelight.

"As I explained on the phone, Mr. Boarhog will be staying with you until he can be placed in a proper home," Brownie said, handing John's file to Wormwood.

"Aren't we the lucky ones?" He flashed a predatory grin. "Danny?"

A boy came down the stairs—the crooked-nosed, ginger-haired boy who had stolen John's locket before attacking him. At least John was pleased to note that Danny had a black eye and a fat lip. "Yes, sir?" Danny mumbled, clearly trying not to move his mouth much.

"Please give Mr. Boarhog the grand tour."

"Yes, sir," Danny said gritting his teeth, then winced.

"Oh boy, the tour?" Brownie clapped. "Boarhog, you're going to like it here. You still have that Olympic-sized pool?" he asked, turning back to Wormwood.

"I'm afraid we just put the nightly cleaning chemicals in the water. The fumes are toxic, so unfortunately you can't go into that room."

"That's not how pools work," John said, his eyebrows drawing together.

"Have you spent a lot of time in luxury pools, Mr. Boarhog?" Wormwood asked.

"No, but mom used to take me to the YMCA, and—"

"Well, then you don't know what you're talking about. Shall I show you the living quarters upstairs, Detective Brownie?"

Wormwood led the detective upstairs to a hallway lined with doors. The first on the left revealed a spacious bedroom. It had the largest bed John had ever seen, its own small reading nook, and a TV with big speakers on either side.

At first, John was impressed, too, but then he looked a little bit closer. The TV wasn't plugged in. In fact, there weren't any electrical outlets on the walls. Wormwood was blocking the doorway now, but John was pretty sure that the reading nook was just painted on the far wall. He leaned closer. The bed was wiggling oddly. Was it filled with air?

Brownie let out a low whistle. "Wow. We never had this kind of setup when I was here. What size is that bed, a queen? Looks like you're gonna have a blast, John."

"Can I try out the bed?" John asked as innocently as possible.

"Well, that is the end of the tour." Wormwood put his hands on Brownie's shoulders, and steered him back toward the stairs.

"Not so fast!" Brownie sniffed the air. "Something smells fishy."

"I think what you are referring to is tonight's gourmet dinner." Wormwood motioned to Danny, who closed a large green door behind them before Brownie could see into the room. "Every Monday night, we have our famous fish feast. The boys love it. Isn't that right, Danny?"

"Oh, yeah. We love the fish head stew," Danny barked out.

"Fish head stew?" John tried his hardest not to puke.

"Fishheedstow," Wormwood corrected. "It's French for buttered salmon and kale!"

"Ya hear that, Boarhog? Maybe you can learn some French while you're here."

"I plan on teaching John a lot of lessons." Wormwood grinned hungrily as he tightened his grip on his cane. "Danny? Say your goodbyes now, and see if the other boys are ready for their nightly *bedtime story*."

Danny nodded, but John was sure *bedtime story* had to be code for something ominous.

"What kind of story?" John asked.

Danny puffed up his chest. "It's about how a nosy kid gets his for being too nosy."

Wormwood laughed. "He means 'Pinocchio.' I try to instill in the boys the dangers of lying."

Danny reached out his hand to the detective. "Good night, sir." John watched, horrified, as Danny shook Brownie's hand and very subtly stole the detective's watch.

"Your watch!" John cried out, pointing at the detective.

Brownie looked at his wrist. "Weird."

"What's wrong, Officer?" Wormwood asked smoothly.

"Well, with all the excitement of today, I must have forgotten to put on my watch. But you're right. It is getting late. I should probably go."

"Wait!" John yelped. "We haven't seen what's in this room. The boy opened a random door, but it was just a broom closet. A dirty mop and a shelf full of cleaning supplies was hardly impressive, nor would it help him out of this jam.

"John." Brownie bent over to be eye to eye with the boy. "I know this is scary, but you are in safe hands here. . . ." The detective then shared what might have been one of the most compassionate and wise pieces of advice one orphan could give to another, but John wasn't listening. He watched as

Danny slipped the stolen watch into another boy's hand, and that boy slipped into the room with the big green door.

In the split second before the door shut, John glimpsed what appeared to be some sort of sweatshop. Rows of boys sat at sewing machines, their gaunt faces lit with strange blue light. *That must be where they're keeping all the stolen goods.* This was his last chance. He pushed past Brownie and burst into the room.

"AHA! What's this?"

John was right. The room was filled with boys at sewing machines. Unfortunately, though, there wasn't a giant pile of stolen goods nearby, but a pile of skinny jeans. Enormous screens filled an entire wall, all of them showing the same reality TV show.

"This is our crafts studio," Wormwood explained, strolling into the room. "Every night for an hour, the boys get to watch their favorite show *Keeping Up with the Bachelorette,* while they work on making designer jeans, which we sell on Canal Street. All the proceeds go to our end-of-the-year vacation."

"That sounds great! Where are you taking the boys this year?" Brownie surveyed the room.

"Atlantic City." Wormwood gestured toward the door. "I think we've wasted enough of the good detective's time."

"You're right." Brownie stretched out his arms with a

yawn. "It's time I go. Be a good kid, John. I'm sure you'll end up having a great life here."

And with that, the large man reached out his hand to shake Wormwood's, but he paused midair. Something small, shiny, and heart-shaped had caught the detective's eye. Something hanging around Wormwood's neck. . . .

"That's a pretty locket you got there," Brownie said, his smile stiffening.

"This old piece of tin?"

"Yeah, I've been looking for one just like that . . . for my girlfriend. Say, where did you get it?"

"I really couldn't say. It's been in my family for years." Wormwood flashed his teeth at John sideways, like they shared a secret.

"Oh, may I look at it?" Brownie asked over-politely.

Wormwood yawned deeply. "As you said, it's getting late."

"You're right," Brownie replied, nodding. "Maybe some other time."

John's heart raced. His only hope was that Brownie somehow went against every instinct he had and became a great detective. Alas, Brownie turned away and headed for the door. John wanted to call out, but just as he was about to, Wormwood's hand fell on his shoulder, the man's nails digging into John's skin.

"You know," Brownie said, stopping suddenly, "I just really need to see that locket."

"I don't think you really do," Wormwood said through clenched yellow teeth.

"I insist." Detective Brownie pulled out his badge.

"What are you doing?" John half-expected Brownie to rip off a mask and reveal he had been Toadius the whole time.

"My job." Brownie reached his hand out to Wormwood motioning, for the locket.

At that moment, John learned that sometimes the people you think are *against* you are actually *for* you. Doug Brownie might not have been the best police officer, but he was turning out to be a good man.

"How dare you! I expect better behavior from our alumni," Wormwood snapped, though instinctively he'd raised his hands.

"That locket doesn't belong to you," John said.

"Hand it over," Brownie insisted.

Wormwood considered for a moment, his crocodile smile wavering. With great reluctance he slipped the necklace over his head and handed it to the detective.

Brownie opened the locket to expose a picture of the lovely Sarah Boarhog. Across from her smiling face was the tiny, heart-shaped unmistakable image of John.

"How could you steal from a child?" Brownie demanded, disgusted.

"I didn't steal it."

"Then explain to me why there are pictures of John and his mother inside it?"

Wormwood glanced at the photos, and then in what I can only describe as the worst acting in the world, he began to fake-cry. "Billy?" He reached his hands out to John. "My long-lost nephew, Billy. I thought you looked familiar. I haven't seen you since you were a baby."

"What are you talking about?" John said, taking a step back.

"When Susan died, I thought we'd lost him." Wormwood snatched the locket back out of Brownie's hand. "To all that is holy, a miracle, I tell you. It's a miracle."

Wormwood's performance got more and more ridiculous as he rambled on. At one point, John swore he saw the man splash water on his face from a nearby fishbowl bearing a small plaque that read: MITCH, THE FIGHTING FISH. "Now you have come home to me, your long-lost uncle, Arty."

"You aren't buying this act, right?" John whispered to the detective as Wormwood continued with his rant, insisting that he'd unsuccessfully scoured the world for John.

"Nah. It doesn't take a great detective to tell when someone is lying."

By this point, Wormwood had taken his dramatic act

down the stairs back into the foyer. John and Brownie were forced to follow, mostly because the man still had John's locket. With a great sob, Wormwood threw himself onto one of the large chairs and covered his face.

"You can stop right there, Mr. Wormwood," Brownie said. "If you think I buy any of this tall tale then, buddy, you got another thing coming."

Wormwood's crying morphed into hysterical laughter. The man rose from the chair and began to slowly clap, then cheer, then put his fingers in his mouth and released an ear-splitting whistle. "You got me, Detective. I was lying the whole time."

"Yes, we know," John said. "Now, give me back my locket."

Wormwood's lips twisted into an evil grin. "I'm afraid you're in no position to be making demands."

Brownie raised his badge again. This time he meant business. But before he could make any arrests, a rock flew through the air and struck his hand, sending the badge flying across the lobby. John scanned the room. Up on the balcony, on the stairs, and even blocking the door, stood the wards of the Jersey Home for Boys, all armed with slingshots, baseball bats, and other sports gear.

"You are surrounded." Wormwood sneered, waving his hands as if he were conducting an orchestra. "Danny, take Mr. Boarhog to his new room."

The older boy roughly grabbed ahold of John's arms. "What about the cop?"

"He dropped the boy off, and we haven't seen him since." Wormwood's eyes were gleaming.

John swore for a second that he saw fear flash across Danny's face.

"You mean you're going to kill him?" Danny choked out.

"No, *you* are."

"But—but . . ."

"*But—but*," Wormwood mocked. "Stop being such a baby." Two other boys grabbed onto John as Danny stepped up to his guardian. With one swift motion, Wormwood grabbed at the tip of his cane, and a sharp silver blade slid out of the top. He handed the weapon to Danny. "You know what to do."

Danny's hands were shaking. It was obvious the boy had never held a sword before.

"You don't have to do this, kid," Brownie said in a soft voice.

"Do it," Wormwood ordered through clenched teeth.

Brownie stood taller. "You won't get away with this, Wormwood."

"But, Detective, I already have."

"I wouldn't say that." A familiar voice reverberated through the room.

"Who said that?" Wormwood's gaze darted around, but no one was there.

A puff of smoke shot from the floor. It faded to reveal none other than the world's greatest cat burglar and worst stage magician.

"Who are you?" Wormwood demanded.

"I am THE GREAT GOATINEE-NEE-NEE." He paused. "Nice acoustics."

Murmurs rang out among the orphans. They'd heard of Goatinee. Some of them were awed, while others seemed scared. John even overheard someone say that Goatinee had been the guy who stole his cat.

"The Great Goatinee? What are you doing this far east? You're out of your jurisdiction."

"I've come for John, for I am his—what is the word for when your mother has a brother?" He looked at John, hopefully.

"Uncle."

"Exactly." Goatinee grinned.

Brownie squinted at the new arrival. "You're related to him?"

"I guess that two bodies will be washing up on the Jersey shore, then." Wormwood turned to Goatinee. "I'm a huge fan. I hope you understand."

"As long-a as you understand we will not be going down without a fight."

"Guild rules?" Wormwood asked.

"If that is the way you want to die." Goatinee assumed a fighting stance. "Let us commence, begin, start . . . Do this thing."

DING-DONG!

"What now?" Wormwood whined.

One of the boys raced over to the front door and looked through the peephole. His face went white as a sheet as he turned back to Wormwood. "It's . . . a ghost."

"A ghost? There's no such thing. Open the door."

The boy did as he was told, his hand shaking as he turned the knob, and the ghost shot into the room. Only it wasn't a ghost—it was a museum curator.

"Mr. Van Eyck?" John asked. "What are you doing here?"

Van Eyck thrust out a piece of paper. "I have come for John Boarhog."

"Let me guess. . . . You're his uncle?" Brownie sighed.

"No. I, Viktor Shelby Van Eyck, am the legal guardian of one John Randel Boarhog. The details are all here in these papers."

Sure enough, the old man was holding an official document.

"Guardian?" John didn't know what to say.

"That's not possible. To get full guardianship, a child must be legally placed in a home and live with that adult for over six months," Wormwood protested. "John was placed in the care of Toadius McGee—and that was less than a week ago."

"Yes, but he has been living in *my* museum for exactly six months and four days. It also doesn't hurt that I happen to be married to a revered family court judge. By the way, John, Judi sends her regards."

"What about Toadius?" John demanded.

"There will be plenty of time on the car ride home to talk about the sordid past of Mr. McGee," Van Eyck said, motioning to the door. "Wait, why are you dressed like a pirate?"

"It was a disguise," John tried to explain. "I don't normally dress like this."

"Good. It's bad enough that you're almost a teenager. But if there's one thing I cannot tolerate more than rabble-rousing teenagers, it's people who dress as pirates." The old man harrumphed. "Get your coat. We've taken enough of this man's time. The inspector will be waiting for you."

"The inspector?" Brownie faltered. "McGee's in jail."

"A misunderstanding. But we must get him at once,"

Van Eyck said as he slipped on his driving gloves. "The ruby is in grave danger!"

"The ruby is long gone, pal!" Brownie replied.

"No, it's not. It's safe in my museum," Van Eyck corrected. "The ruby stolen at the Blue Moose was a replica."

Brownie's face had gone red. "What are you talking about?"

"The inspector gave it back to me after he recovered it from the Broadway play. He thought it would be best if we kept that a secret as he continued the charade that he had the real one." Van Eyck motioned for John to hurry up. "Now, if you don't mind, I'll be taking this young man home."

"You aren't going anywhere." Wormwood gave a sharp nod, and the boy shut and locked the door.

"What is this absurdity?" Van Eyck sputtered. "I have no time for tomfoolery. It's much too late for a boy of John's age to be out."

"Hate to disappoint you, old man," Brownie said, motioning to the boys upstairs. "You seem to have walked into the wrong place at the wrong time."

"My word. Are you telling me that you're being held against your will?" John couldn't tell by Van Eyck's lack of emotion if he was afraid, shocked, or just plain annoyed.

"No," Brownie answered.

"Oh, good," said Van Eyck, adjusting his glove. "I was about to fear the worst."

"I'm telling you *we* are being held against our will."

"Oh, my!" Van Eyck exclaimed. "Well, that's not good at all."

"Enough of this chatter." Wormwood waited a second to make sure no one else was going to crash the battle. "Danny, finish the job."

When Danny didn't move, Wormwood raised his arm with such force that John could feel the resulting breeze. Danny cowered back, blocking his face from what he thought would be a backhanded strike. When it didn't come, the teen hesitated, eyeing the sword shaking in his hand.

John knew exactly what the crooked-nosed boy was thinking. He'd felt the same way many times before. Danny was afraid, but not about using a deadly weapon. He was afraid of the man bellowing at the top of his lungs to just get it over with already. All the boys were. John turned to face the three men who were risking their lives for him. They, too, looked terrified. John thought about how afraid Toadius and Pickles must be feeling. He thought about all the times he'd been afraid, from the day his mother died to the fight in the alley to this very moment. His heart was beating so hard, he could hear it. And then time, itself, seemed to slow down.

In life, people will try to put you down. They will tell you that the world is too big or that you are too small. Believe this old professor when I say that the only person who can stop you from becoming the greatest version of yourself . . . is, in fact, *you*. No parent or teacher, no bully or partner, can stop you from finding your path in life. John could have given up. He could've gone back to the world he once knew. But it was at that moment, at the Jersey Home for Boys, John realized it was up to him to choose his own fate.

"Stop! It's over, Mr. Wormwood."

"Excuse me?" Wormwood's mouth curled into what could only be described as the expression of a warthog that had been told a joke. "Who's going to stop me?"

"I am." John took a step forward.

"You?" Wormwood laughed. "You're just a little boy."

"I might be." John cleared his throat. "But so are they." He pointed to the boys on the stairs. "And so are they," he said, waving toward the front door. "And so, Danny, are you. We've all done bad things. We've all been the victims of bad luck, and we've fallen into the wrong paths, but that isn't who we are. A great man once told me, 'There is one moment in every person's life when they must decide to choose their own destiny. Otherwise, they will never be anything more than a puppet.' What are you, Danny? Are you a puppet?" John stared into the young man's eyes. You could've heard a pin drop as Danny pointed the sword at John, holding it steady. For the first time in Danny's life, he knew what he was.

"I'm no puppet," Danny said, letting his hand go limp. The other boys dropped their weapons, too. They weren't killers. They were just doing what they were told. In my experience, if people would just stop doing what they are told and start doing what they know is right, this world would be a better place.

"You fools!" Spittle gathered at the corners of Wormwood's mouth as he shouted. "I said, kill them!"

"No." Danny stood defiantly. "The kid is right. I ain't nobody's puppet."

John handed the badge back to Brownie.

"Mr. Wormwood"—the detective smirked—"you, sir, are under arrest. And Boarhog?"

"Yes, sir?"

"You and your *uncles* need to finish what you started." Brownie gave John a slight nod.

John couldn't believe his ears. "You mean it?"

"Yeah. Just make sure you tell McGee I was the one who saved you. He'll be *so* jealous."

"What about you?"

"We got his back," Danny said, slapping Brownie's shoulder. "Once a Jersey boy, always a Jersey boy."

As Van Eyck hurried John out the door, the boy

looked back over his shoulder to see Brownie handcuffing Wormwood while the other kids cheered. A glint of light caught his attention. His locket was still around Wormwood's neck.

"Come with me, son," Van Eyck urged. "We need to get out of here."

"But my locket."

"We don't have time." The old man pulled John toward the street.

As if on cue, a slick black car pulled up to the curb. It looked like something out of a monster movie, with large bat-like spoilers and tinted windows—a car a super villain would drive.

"Wait! That's my car!" Van Eyck cried. "Someone stole my car?"

John and his new guardian froze as the windows slowly rolled down.

"Do you need-a a lift?" The Great Goatinee's wide grin seemed to glow next to the black leather interior.

"Uncle Kamin? How did you—" John looked back toward the house.

"A magician never tells his secrets." Goatinee revved the engine. "Where to?"

"We have to get Toadius out of jail," John said as he and Van Eyck piled into the back seat.

"That might have to wait till the morning. The courts are closed until then," Van Eyck explained.

"We don't have until the morning. For all we know, the Moth is at the museum stealing the ruby as we speak."

"Amateurs," Goatinee muttered.

"Excuse me?" Van Eyck asked.

"There are many ways to steal a cat," Goatinee said as he put the car in gear.

"You mean to skin a cat?" corrected Van Eyck.

"Why would you want to skin a cat?" Goatinee looked cautiously at Van Eyck. "I'm-a not so sure this is the best guardian for you, John."

John chuckled, then cautiously asked, "Where are we going?"

Goatinee cracked his knuckles. "To steal ourselves an inspector."

CHAPTER TWENTY-TWO

The time John gathered the greatest crime-fighting team of all time.

"G UARD!" TOADIUS YELLED at the top of his lungs.

"What do you want, McGee?" the officer called back.

"What time is it?"

"Five minutes since the last time you asked."

The inspector had now been confined to his jail cell for over two hours, which meant midnight was rapidly approaching.

Toadius had lost the three most important things in his life in just one night. John was surely headed to the Jersey

Home for Boys; the Mauve Moth had stolen his one true love, Polly "Pickles" Cronopolis; and he had been stripped of his badge. He knew that, by now, the Moth had probably figured out that the ruby was a fake and was headed to the museum to collect their prize. If Toadius was right, and the master criminal he'd been chasing was none other than the person who'd killed his mentor, then Polly was in grave danger. "Van Eyck should've been back by now. Something's gone wrong."

"Don't worry, Inspector," said retired boxer Scotty Moose from the cot next to him. "I'm sure your friend will take care of everything, and if you're innocent, then you'll be out just in time for the early bird special." With that, the boxer stretched back, his arms crossed behind his head on the cot.

Toadius punched the wall in his cell. "Owwww!"

"If you's gonna punch something, Mr. Toadius, I suggest you try a face instead of a brick wall."

"Thank you for your advice, Scotty," Toadius grunted, springing up and pacing the small cell as he tried to shake the pain out of his hand. "Next time, I'll consider that."

"You could use my face if you like."

"No good," Toadius replied, grimacing. "I'm afraid punching your face would be *exactly* like punching another wall."

"True, true." Scotty rubbed his cheek. "I got my jawline from my mother."

"She sounds like a beautiful woman." Toadius sat down on his cot. "Can I ask you a question?"

"Shoot."

"Why did you stop boxing? You were undefeated."

The hulking man rose from the cot and walked up to the bars. He rolled up his sleeve so Toadius could see his tattoo. It was a heart with the name *Andy* across it. "I was the greatest boxer of all time, and I loved it. But the day I met Andy, I no longer wanted to fight."

"Because you didn't want to get hurt?"

"Naw, 'cause he made me want more from my life. Before Andy, all I knew was the ring, but he said I could be anything. In that moment, I realized what I wanted most in my life was to be with him." The boxer rolled his sleeve back down. "It was that day I hung up my gloves for good. I promised Andy I'd never punch another man again. You know, a man isn't what he does, but what he's loved for. Andy loves me, not cause I'm a champion boxer, but because I'm a loyal and loving husband."

"So, you're saying that love is the greatest fighter of them all."

"Yeah, unless you count my uncle Walt. That guy is tough as nails. That's probably why they call him the Hammer."

"Well, I'm sorry you broke your promise because of me."

"Even though I don't believe violence is the answer, you

have to always be willing to protect the ones you love. *Defend*, not *attack*."

"Thank you, Scotty."

"You're welcome." The brute of the man gently touched Toadius's shoulder.

The inspector rose and yanked on the bars. "I need to get out of here. Pickles is in who-knows-what kind of danger, and I can't imagine the horrors John will be facing in New Jersey. We need to get him before those boys do something terrible."

"What about the ruby?" a boy's voice asked from behind him.

"I don't care about the ruby. There are more important things—" Toadius froze, then slowly turned around to find his ward sitting on the cot. "*John?* How did you get in here?"

"How many times must-a I say a magician never reveals his secrets?" Toadius spun around again, and found himself face-to-face with the Great Goatinee. "How do you say . . . *TA-DA!*"

Toadius wrapped his arms around the magician and then John. "What are you doing here?"

"Plan B. You stay somewhere safe until I come and find you."

Toadius laughed. "That wasn't what I meant."

"Well, we don't have time to argue about details. We have

to find the Moth and save Pickles." John turned to Goatinee. "Uncle Kamin, how do we get out of here?"

"I thought you'd never ask." Goatinee cracked his knuckles. "Okay, so this is a very easy process. Are any of you left-handed?"

John, Toadius, and Scotty Moose shook their heads.

"*No?* Okay, does anyone have a piece of chewing gum?"

They shook their heads again.

"Well, then, it is not such an easy process." Goatinee reached into his top hat and pulled out a walkie-talkie. "Okay, here's what we do. John, you are skinny, so you'll have to squeeze through the bars on the window. Across the street is a hot-dog vendor. Ask him for today's special. Take it two blocks south to a cop on a horse standing in a parking space. Use the hot dog to lure the horse three spots to the west. Then stand in the original spot until a man riding a hot-pink motor scooter arrives. Give him the spot. He will give you a key to a safety deposit box at the New York Federal Union Bank on Thirty-Eighth and Broadway. Open safety deposit box seven eighty-seven. Inside will be a map of Southern France and a lighter. Meanwhile, Toadius, how good are you at speaking duck—"

"We *could* do that," Toadius said, "or we could do it the old-fashioned way." The inspector put on his hat. "In three . . . two . . . one . . ."

"TOADIUS MCGEE, SCOTTY MOOSE!" a guard called out. "You both are free to go."

"*Finally*. My bail was posted." Toadius tipped his hat at the guard as he walked out the now-open jail cell door. "I'll see you boys out front."

"I hate the old-fashioned way," Goatinee grumbled.

EVEN THOUGH IT TOOK ONLY about fifteen minutes for Toadius to be released, John felt like he'd been waiting on the steps of the jailhouse forever.

Toadius emerged, once again wearing his blue suit and carrying his bowler hat. "There you are, Doctor," he said as he helped the boy to his feet.

"You changed?" John asked, looking down at his own pirate outfit, which was looking worse for wear.

"Rule Number Twelve: *Always pack an extra set of clothing.* Shall we finish what we started?"

"Yes," John replied eagerly. "To the museum?"

"Precisely," Toadius said, slapping the boy on the back. "You're getting very good at this detective business."

"We're going to have to get Mr. Van Eyck's remote control if we're going to stand any chance of getting past the Gotcha 3000."

"Luckily, he's pulling the car around." Toadius placed his bowler back on his head.

"How did you know he was here?" John asked.

"Of course he's here, silly boy. Who do you think posted my bail?" Toadius suddenly got quite serious. "John, we must succeed tonight, or you'll have to go back to the Jersey Home for Boys, I'm afraid."

"No, I won't. Mr. Van Eyck and his wife have become my legal guardians."

"Oh." Toadius swallowed hard, trying to conceal his disappointment. "That's wonderful." He shifted uncomfortably. "How was your short-lived stay in New Jersey?"

"Mr. Wormwood tried to kill us," John said with a little more enthusiasm than he should have had in the moment. "Detective Brownie arrested him for stealing my locket and running an underground crime ring."

"Good show, Doug. I have to say, this has been a very exciting day." The inspector grinned. "Were you able to get your locket back?"

"No." John stared at his pirate boots, suddenly finding them very interesting.

"I'm sorry."

"It's okay," John said quietly. "I don't need it anymore."

The two stood in silence. Toadius opened his mouth to speak, but before he could, John quickly asked, "How long have you been friends with Mr. Van Eyck?"

"I've known Viktor since I was a teenager."

"A teenager? He hates teenagers."

"You draw one mustache on one priceless painting, and the man never forgets it." Toadius shrugged. "I still think she looked better with the mustache."

"Shall we then, gentlemen?" Van Eyck said, pulling on a pair of racing goggles before gesturing to his car waiting at the curb.

Toadius opened the front passenger-side door to find the Great Goatinee already buckled in.

"Shotgun!" The Great Goatinee pressed his thumb to his nose and wiggled his fingers at the other men.

Toadius and John squeezed into the back with Scotty Moose, who took up most of the seat.

Van Eyck may have been slow-moving on foot, but on the road, he was a speed demon. He ran more red lights than an ambulance. At one point, he went the wrong way down a one-way street to "save time." John hated to admit it, but he almost wished Toadius had been the one driving.

The group entered the museum through a secret entrance hidden in the back, which Van Eyck had had built in case the president ever visited the museum. So far, she hadn't, which is not to say that the president didn't like museums—just that, thus far, she had been too busy to visit. John had heard about the entrance when he was living in the ceiling, but he'd never used it. He was surprised to discover that it opened into the Hall of North American Mammals. There were all kinds of neat animals there—bears, mountain lions, and even buffalo—all of which were surprised when they saw the visitors and quickly snapped back into their statue-like state.

"No need to stand still for me," Van Eyck said. "The museum's closed."

The relieved animals all relaxed. It's amazing to me how they're able to stand there completely frozen in time each day. You'd think the museum would want to have the animals moving around, but Viktor had long ago forbidden it. If there is one thing he hated more than rabble-rousing teenagers and people dressed as pirates, it was giant North American mammals moving all willy-nilly about the museum displays.

"So now what?" the Great Goatinee asked, sounding bored.

Toadius straightened his hat. "Viktor, please go to the control room. If need be, you can lock down rooms and trap the Moth inside. I'll go to the Egyptian exhibit and try to lure the Moth out. Goatinee, you climb to the roof and guard the skylights, just in case the Moth tries to escape through the ceiling. Scotty Moose, no doubt the Moth has already taken out the guards. There's a good chance they've brought a crew of their own. You know what to do with any suspicious characters lurking about the museum."

"Punch them in the face?" Scotty asked.

"I was going to say defend the museum."

"That's what I said." Scotty raised his fists. "Punch them in the face!"

"Remind me later to explain to you what a loophole is," Toadius replied, wincing in sympathy for the men about to meet the Moose's fist. "Doctor, *you* will come with me. When we find Polly, your job is to get her to safety. You must promise me that no matter what happens, you'll run, and you won't look back. Once you two are safe, I want you to call Detective Brownie. He is not a good detective, but he *is* consistent, and you can trust that he'll bring every policeman in the city to this museum if it means getting his picture on the front page of the *Confidential Informer*."

"Yes, sir," John said, with a nod.

The inspector took a step back. "We have control of the museum, which means we have an impenetrable fortress at our command. The Moth has no chance against us."

He'd barely gotten the words out before steel containment doors suddenly shut in front of him, locking Toadius in a room away from everyone else.

"TOADIUS!" John yelled.

A muffled voice came from the other side. "Are you all right, John?"

"Yes, Inspector! Are you?"

"I am!"

"Mr. Van Eyck, can you reset this door?" John asked the curator.

"I need to get to the control room to do that," Van Eyck replied.

"Okay, Toadius, hang tight! Mr. Van Eyck is going to reset the doors." The boy turned to the boxer. "Scotty Moose, will you make sure he can get there?"

"Sure thing," the giant of a man said, punching his fist to his palm.

"Thank you. Uncle Kamin, you need to get up to the roof right away."

"Where-a are you going?" Goatinee asked.

"To finish this case." The boy gave the magician a big hug and then started up the staircase toward the fourth floor.

John quickly found out that the wall that had separated him from Toadius wasn't the only one that had been tripped. The museum had turned into a labyrinth. A *labyrinth,* if you have never heard of one, is just another name for a maze. John had read an epic poem about one once. Minotaur—a scary beast, part human and part bull with red eyes and the ability to breathe fire out of its nose—lived in the dead center. John couldn't help but notice the similarities. Only the minotaur at the center of the museum labyrinth was part human and part Moth.

It was a surreal feeling walking down the empty hallways. John had navigated these corridors almost every night for six months. He knew every nook and cranny, every tile on the floor. Blindfolded, he still would've been able to run full speed down the passages without touching a single artifact. But that night, the halls felt like some foreign land. Things seemed different than he remembered—colder, more distant— almost like he was trying to remember a dream.

The old John would have been so lost in thought, he wouldn't have noticed someone creeping up behind him. But the new John was not only aware of his surroundings, he'd been using his time passing through these hallways to devise a plan.

John ducked around a corner and waited for whoever was tailing him to emerge from the shadows. He held his breath, staying as still as he could. Any second now, his foe would step into the light—and then he'd knock them out with the priceless but heavy vase sitting next to him.

Now! He jumped from the gloom, vase held high. The first things John took in were his enemy's dark glass eyes, then its mechanical mouth. For a moment, John thought Van Eyck had purchased robots to patrol the museum. But then John got a good look at the robot's blue bowler hat and realized it wasn't a robot at all, just Toadius McGee wearing a gas mask.

"What's wrong, Doctor?" The mask made Toadius's voice sound muffled and high-pitched, as if he were breathing helium.

John had never been happier to see the inspector. "How did you get out? How did you find me? And why are you wearing a gas mask?"

"John, I am the world's greatest detective. Something as trivial as a four-foot-thick steel containment door could never stop me."

John raised an eyebrow. "Van Eyck got to the control room?"

"That helped a bit," Toadius said with a shrug, then handed the boy a mask of his own. "And as for the mask, after our little adventure with the door, I realized that we may not have total control over our impenetrable fortress after all. We should proceed with caution. You never know what surprises might await you."

The two continued down a hallway, and then took a left turn. As they did, John noticed that the red light on the security camera above wasn't blinking.

"Everything all right?" Toadius's muffled voice asked from behind the boy.

John looked around. "Everything seems different."

"Beyond the museum being transformed into a steel maze?"

"It's not that. The museum has changed somehow."

"Maybe it's not the museum that has changed," the inspector replied softly.

As the pair walked past the break room, John thought about weak coffee and stolen sandwiches, and how they'd taught him how great adventures are found, not bought. As they passed the stegosaurus, John remembered that behind that door was a high-tech security system. From his encounter with the Gotcha 3000, he'd learned that no matter how prepared and careful you are, there is always a chance that something can go wrong. As they approached the Egyptian exhibit, John thought about the hieroglyphs on the wall and realized it takes work to communicate.

And then, he thought about Toadius McGee, the man who'd taught him that having a code of honor, a heart as open as your eyes, and a sense of humor were worth more than any ruby.

John had changed so much since this adventure had started, he hardly recognized himself reflected in the glass of a nearby display case. He didn't mind much. He kind of liked this new young man staring back at him.

Before he knew it, John and the inspector were standing in front of two large limestone blocks. Behind this door was the answer to everything.

"Ready to finally know who the Mauve Moth really is?" Toadius asked, taking a deep breath.

John pulled his gas mask over his face. "As ready as I'll ever be."

"Good. Let's finish this." Toadius cocked his gun and kicked in the exhibit door.

John peeked into the room. The Egypt's Fire wasn't in its display case, but a man had been gagged and tied to the giant, golden throne and was struggling against his bonds.

The room seemed to spin. Tied to the throne was none other than the greatest detective to ever live, Toadius McGee.

CHAPTER TWENTY-THREE

The time John unmasked the Mauve Moth.

ALARMED, JOHN TURNED SHARPLY to find Toadius, or, at least, the man he thought was Toadius, standing behind him, his gun drawn.

"You're the Mauve Moth!" He couldn't believe he'd been tricked . . . again.

"If you would be so kind." Inspector Imposter–McGee waved their hand for the boy to enter the exhibit.

In a matter of seconds, he and both Toadiuses were in the room.

"I didn't want to do this, John," the gun–wielding

pretender said, "but you left me with no choice. Please remove your mask."

John ripped it off, tears forming in his eyes. "Why are you doing this to me? Don't you love me? Weren't we happy? I needed you, Mom. I still need you." John's whole body was shaking. "Why did you leave me? For what, a stupid ruby? What are you going to do, shoot me? I'm your son."

"No, you're not." The soft voice of the real inspector seemed to cast a web of silence over the room. "John, you're not their son, because that isn't Cerise Viceroy." John looked at Toadius, desperate, but the inspector's dark, defeated eyes remained fixed on the figure between them. "Take off the mask. I think it's time we have this conversation face-to-face."

The Moth locked eyes with the inspector for a moment before they dropped their mask to the ground with a *thud*. John watched, horrified, as the Mauve Moth shook out her long, red hair.

"Polly?" A mixture of relief and confusion rushed over John as all he'd discovered over the past few days reshuffled like one of Goatinee's card tricks and began to make sense. The Moth always seemed to be a step ahead of them because she had been with them *the whole time*. And then the betrayal began to sink in.

"I guess this is the part where I tell you how I stole the

Egypt's Fire right out from under the nose of the greatest detective of all time?" Polly laughed coldly.

John felt his heart breaking. He staggered back, bumping into Toadius. John's unexpected outburst had distracted the Moth long enough for Toadius to escape from his restraints.

"Allow me," Toadius said. "You snuck into the exhibit through one of the skylights and hid inside that sarcophagus in the corner, as you'd done your research and knew it was a fake. We found the empty air tank stored inside it the next day. You set an alarm for midnight on your fancy watch—that's why it went off at the diner. You thought you'd been spying on the night janitor, Bart, not knowing it was really John, who'd been sneaking around the museum exhibits after-hours for weeks. You singled him out because he was always alone, whereas the other janitors worked in pairs. You placed the drugged egg salad sandwich in the refrigerator and threw out everything else, ensuring that John would eat the sandwich for dinner. Then you waited for him to get close to the ruby, hiding in the shadows until the Tuta-Tuta-laced sandwich took effect. At first, I thought you used hypnotism to get John to steal the ruby, but something wasn't right. It wasn't until just now that I realized we'd missed a clue. In the sarcophagus, there was an extra janitor's uniform. You didn't hypnotize John—you dressed up like him. When he moved out of view of the camera you knocked him out, then simply took his place, stepping into the light. And from there it was nothing to use the hammer we found to break the display glass. You needed the alarm to go off and the cameras to capture John stealing the ruby. You knew that the police would check the video first thing in the morning, and John, who you thought was Bart, would be blamed. You planted a fake ruby in his pocket to make it appear that the robbery attempt had failed, not that it mattered. If, by chance, the authorities did figure out the stone wasn't the real Egypt's Fire, you'd already be long gone."

"You framed me? So, I was right," John said, turning his attention to Toadius. "It was an imposter."

"Hypnotism would've been more exciting," Toadius muttered grumpily. "But if you want to use clichés like disguises, who am I to judge?"

Polly began to clap slowly. "Very good. I have to say, I didn't know John was living in the museum. I thought the night janitors had been stealing the lunches from the break room. It was kismet that our boy, here, was hiding. No hard feelings, John. I didn't mean to set you up. You just made it so easy for me. I timed it perfectly so that I could step back into the shadows and put on my mask just before the gas was released. But I'll admit there was one thing I hadn't considered. My mask made it hard to see, and when I dragged John's unconscious body back into the light, I dropped the ruby."

"It shattered," John added. "That's why I had glass in my hair."

Polly nodded. "I slipped back into my hiding spot and snuck out when the police arrived, dressed as none other than Jaclyn Star." Polly gestured dramatically as though she were posing for a picture. "The real Jaclyn Star is in Paris following an anonymous tip I thoughtfully provided, so I could borrow her identity, appearing at the crime scene and the pancake parlor without suspicion. That way, I could listen in on—even participate in—your conversations. I went to the Broadway show, hoping to beat you there."

Polly took a bow, just like the mummy had the night of the performance.

"But you know how that turned out. I realized that once the ruby was in Toadius's hands, he'd guard it with his life, so I decided the best thing to do was hang out with the two of you until he made a mistake. You were the ones who suggested a fence, so I found our mutual acquaintance, Shim-Sham, and paid him to set up the meeting at the Blue Moose. It was a smart move hiding that you'd given the real ruby back to Van Eyck, Toadius. I should've known you'd never steal a jewel. It's against that silly code of yours."

John watched Pickles, rage rising in his blood. "I trusted you!"

"Don't look at me like that, John. After I was safely out of the city, I would've sent Toadius a new clue to my next heist. And I'm sure that the night janitor wouldn't have been in jail for long—maybe a week—before his name was cleared. He'd probably even have gotten his job back. The inspector would never let an innocent man take the fall for his mistakes, now would you, Toadius?"

Toadius shifted his weight but remained silent.

"You came back here for the real Egypt's Fire?" John demanded as he took a step toward the inspector.

"Ah, ah, ah." Pickles gestured for him to move back with her gun. "I like you, John Boarhog. We made a good team. Why don't you come work for me?"

"You're a liar and a coward!" John snapped. "I'd rather eat dirt."

"Everyone lies sometimes," she said with a disinterested shrug.

"You spent all this time with me for what? Just so you could use me?" John spat out.

"No, I spent time with you so that I could get my ruby. But I do have to admit that you two helped me a thousand times more than my union-appointed henchmen. I can't believe you fell for everything. I even got you to ask your friend Viktor for the only remote to the Gotcha 3000, so you could unknowingly let us all in." She waved her hand. "You didn't think I came here alone, did you? Oh, boys!" she called out.

Viktor Van Eyck and Scotty Moose entered the room, their hands in the air. On their heels were Rock and Paper, two of the three thugs from the alleyway behind the theater. Each had a gun and was pointing it at John's friends.

"I brought a couple of my friends, too," Toadius announced.

"Put your hands where I can see them!" a loud voice called. Detective Brownie, two uniformed officers, and Danny the redheaded teen from the Jersey Home for Boys poured into the room. John couldn't help noting Danny was wearing a brown suit very similar to Doug Brownie's.

Pickles and her men dropped their guns and put their hands in the air. Brownie nodded toward Toadius. "You all right, McGee?"

"Yes. Right on time, Doug."

"Danny, this is Inspector Toadius McGee. Toadius, this is Danny. I got myself my very own ward!" Brownie said, his chest puffed out with pride.

"I'm sure he'll turn out to be a mediocre detective just like you."

"I sure hope so." Brownie pointed his gun at Pickles. "Put 'em up, dollface. You're under arrest."

"What the blazes is going on?" the chief of police demanded as he and his assistant entered the room.

"I caught the Mauve Moth," Brownie announced.

"Good work, detective. Now drop your gun," the chief ordered, pointing his own weapon directly at Brownie.

"What are you doing, Chief?"

"Taking what's mine. Why couldn't you just sit in jail like you were supposed to, McGee?"

"Because I wanted to make room for real criminals like you. I bet you don't even like jazz," he added, muttering.

"Chief? Is this some sort of joke?" Brownie asked, eyes wide.

"No, you're the joke, Brownie. Why did you think I put you on this case? I wanted the ruby stolen. There's only one fence in town that can handle that kind of merchandise . . . *me*. You don't think you can own a house in the Hamptons fighting crime, do you?" The chief stretched his arm out, motioning with his gun, directing Brownie to join the huddle with Van Eyck, Scotty Moose, and the rest of Toadius's group. John finally got a good look at the man's wrist. There it was—a tattoo of a spider.

Pickles and her men picked up their guns once again.

"Officers, arrest the chief," Brownie called to the cops who'd accompanied him into the exhibit room. The officers didn't hesitate, turning their guns on Detective Brownie.

"Sorry, but they're with me," the chief crowed. "I can see the headline now: 'Hero Cop Chases Ex-Inspector into Museum. Gun Battle Ensues. Many Die.'"

"I like 'Corrupt Chief Gets Taken Down by Mild-Mannered Reporter' better." Everyone turned as the real Jaclyn Star appeared in the room. At first glance, John thought that Pickles's impersonation had been spot on, but when the reporter turned her head, he knew where the actress-now-criminal had gone wrong. Jaclyn Star was the biggest reporter in the city, and she really did have the nose to match.

"I told you it was huge," Toadius murmured.

John was so distracted, he almost missed that in one hand Jaclyn was holding a video camera, recording the scene, while she thrust out a microphone with the other.

"Jaclyn . . . *the* Jaclyn Star?" Pickles stammered. "How did you know we were here?"

"Trick of the trade: I listen in on the police scanner."

Clearly, Pickles had not been prepared for this turn of events. "But—but you were in Paris."

"It's a really great police scanner." Jaclyn turned the camera on the chief. "The jig is up, Quimbly. I have the whole confession on tape. And there's nothing you can do to stop me from exposing you as the crooked cop you are."

The officers turned their guns on Jaclyn.

"We could just take the camera from you and destroy the evidence," the chief said.

"I didn't think of that." The reporter set down her camera and put her hands in the air.

"Does anybody else want to interrupt tonight's jewel heist, or can we get on with it?" the chief demanded, glaring around the room. "Good. Now give me the ruby, Moth."

"Over my dead body," Pickles snapped.

The chief shifted his gun, so it was now directed at her. "That can be arranged."

"You want it?" Pickles reached into her pocket and pulled out the stone. "Come and get it."

Just then, a thunderous roar came from the skylights above. Crashing through the window, diving through the air like an Olympic swimmer, was none other than the Great Goatinee.

"TA-DA!" Goatinee called out as he plummeted toward the museum floor. John noticed an elastic cord wrapped tightly around his waist. The magician bounced down, and with one graceful swipe, snatched the ruby from Pickles's hand. "I am THE GREAT GOATINEE-NEE-NEE-NEE!" he said, bouncing all over the room.

"Get him, boys!" the chief hollered, but it was too late.

The Great Goatinee reached out, and with the power of his mind—or rather the large magnet concealed beneath his sleeve—caused the chief's revolver to fly across the room and into his own palm.

"I, how do you say, absconded with your gun!" The Goatinee winked at John, but a moment later, the magician's arm started vibrating. "Oh, no! This is not good!"

John looked around the room, mesmerized as the arms of every person holding a metal object began to shake. With the power of a thousand moons, one by one, guns, knives, and other weapons flew at the Great Goatinee. With his body now covered in metal, instead of being the world's greatest cat burglar, Goatinee had been transformed into the world's greatest wrecking ball.

Toadius took advantage of the distraction, grabbing John's arm, and the pair ducked behind a sarcophagus. Meanwhile, Scotty Moose knocked out Rock, and Van Eyck hid behind a pillar, crying softly. "Not my beautiful museum," he sobbed.

Brownie lunged at the chief, toppling his boss to the ground. "You're under arrest! You have the right to remand si—"

SMACK! The top-hatted wrecking ball collided with Brownie.

"I AM THE GREAT WRECK-TINEE!" a voice called from the writhing ball of debris. The detective was knocked off his feet and thrown over the chief, and like a professional football player, he tackled Jaclyn Star.

Jaclyn was a very talented reporter but a very poor running back, and she fumbled the camera. It hit the floor with such force, it burst into flames.

She screeched, pushing the now dazed detective off her, and ran for cover, squeezing in beside Van Eyck.

"My museum!" he cried.

"My *camera*!"

Toadius spied the Gotcha 3000's plastic remote lying in the middle of the room. It must've fallen out of Van Eyck's pocket in all the confusion. "John, if we were able to get that remote, we might lock everyone in."

John shrugged. "I'm pretty sure I can get it if I have some cover."

Luckily for them, the two biggest guns in the room had moved on from low-level thugs to focus on high-end corrupt cops. I am, of course, referring to the giant arms of the heavyweight champion of the world, Scotty Moose.

Danny jumped on the back of one of the uniformed officers, while Scotty used the man as a punching bag. Next, Scotty threw a well-aimed uppercut at the other officer.

Then with quick steps, the retired boxer ducked out of the way of the Great Wreck-tinee ball. This fancy footwork gave Toadius an idea.

"John, when I say *Go*, I want you to do your dance from the show, slide and all."

"But I don't remember what I did!"

"Improvise, then." Toadius pushed the boy out from their hiding spot. "Now!"

It was too late. Pickles had already spotted the only control for the Gotcha 3000, and she'd get to it before John could.

He inhaled a calming breath, then followed Toadius's advice. He took three steps forward, then two steps back, avoiding Scotty Moose's fists of fury, before spinning around like a whirling dervish to rid himself of Paper trying to grab him. A quick tumble followed by a cartwheel got him past the chief's assistant. Then a slide step and two claps to get Pickles's attention, and a mighty jazz-hand finale to knock the remote out of the notorious thief's grasp. He raced across the floor as the remote arced through the air, sliding under the chief's legs. John reached out his fingers—inches away—and jerked to a stop.

Pickles had thrown herself on top of the boy, slowing his slide. Using John like a ladder, she climbed up to grab the remote.

"Ha!" she cried. "It's mine!"

"Whatever, lady!" John called as he wrestled with her.

The two were so busy fighting each other for the remote that they didn't notice a third knife-wielding goon also known as Scissors, up on the roof sawing away at a bungee cord.

There was a loud *SNAP*, and the Great Wreck-tinee, top hat and all, plummeted to the ground, though Pickles and John conveniently broke his fall. Not so conveniently, the ruby sprang out of the magician's hand, hitting the remote, sending it once again skidding into a pair of feet. Furry feet. Furry feet belonging to none other than the greatest informant to ever live.

"Eek, eek?" Shim-Sham asked scooping up the remote. Everyone stopped fighting at the command of the monkey. With a quick leap Shim-Sham landed next to the ruby.

"Shim-Sham," Toadius said soothingly. "Give me the jewel."

"Eek, eek!" The monkey pointed the remote at the inspector.

"Yes, a billion dollars would buy a lot of bananas. But if bananas cost a dollar each, then that would mean you want *one billion* bananas?"

"Are there even that many bananas in the city?" Pickles asked.

"All those very high-priced, but very addicting, coffee shops sell bananas—a billion bananas a year," Jaclyn Star piped in helpfully.

"That makes sense. I buy a banana with my venti half-caf soy six-pump peppermint mocha with extra whip every morning." Paper licked his lips. "Mm-mmm. Peppermint."

"Tall Andy loves bananas," Scotty Moose added. "We buy them in bulk."

"What would you do with all those bananas?" John asked Shim-Sham.

"Eek, eek."

"Genius!" Toadius exclaimed. "He who controls the bananas controls the city."

"What about us?" Jaclyn Star asked, annoyance in her voice.

"Eek, eek." Shim-Sham reached out his paw and pressed a large red button on the remote.

Collectively, everyone in the room took in a deep breath and froze.

Nothing happened.

"Well, that was anticlimactic," Jaclyn muttered.

The monkey jabbed the button over and over again.

Still nothing.

The thing about high-tech security systems is that remote batteries drain quickly. With all the orphan-saving and bailing out detectives and prize fighters from jail, Van Eyck had forgotten to charge his remote.

"*HA!*" Brownie snorted. "That thing is useless." Before the detective could react, the remote was flying at his face and hit him square between the eyes. "*OW!* I stand corrected."

"Eek, eek," Shim-Sham said, sticking out his tongue at the detective before he raced from the room.

It took the rest of the group a moment to process what had happened.

"Um, shouldn't we go after him?" John finally said.

CHAPTER TWENTY-FOUR

The time John became a professional rickshaw driver.

Records show that in the history of primates, there have only ever been two evil monkeys. The first climbed the Empire State Building in 1933. The second is the criminal monkey mastermind named Shim-Sham.

Shim-Sham was remarkably agile for a four-pound monkey carrying a two-pound ruby. If you've ever tried to carry half your bodyweight in priceless jewels, you'd know how difficult a task it is. Even so, the monkey was halfway down the steps of the museum before Toadius and the others had passed through the front door.

"Give up, Shim-Sham. There isn't anywhere to run!" Toadius called out.

"Eek, eek!" Shim-Sham squeaked back, dragging the ruby behind him.

Toadius scowled. "Well, that was rude." He waved John over and pointed to a nearby alley. "If we work together, we can cut him off at the pass."

"Sorry, my dear," a melodic voice trilled from behind them, "but I work alone." A moment later, Pickles ran past the inspector, tore off her Toadius costume to reveal a mauve outfit with flowing sleeves, did a perfect front flip over a taxicab finishing in a somersault, and landed right next to the surprised monkey. "Thank you," she said as she snatched the ruby away from Shim-Sham before leaping into the back of a truck full of bananas.

"GET HER!" Brownie bellowed.

"Toadius!" John called out, but the inspector had already hopped into a rickshaw. A New York City *rickshaw*, if you don't know, is a small carriage pulled by a bicycle.

"Follow that banana truck!" Toadius yelled.

John scanned the street for a ride of his own, relieved when he spotted a hansom cab sitting at the curb. A *hansom cab* is a fancy name for a horse-drawn carriage. Many people hire them for romantic tours of Central Park. John didn't have time for a tour, and the two teenagers who'd already hired the carriage were too busy kissing to notice the boy commandeering their buggy.

"Follow that rickshaw!" John ordered.

"Eek, eek!" John looked back to see Shim-Sham perched on the back of a stray dog in hot pursuit.

Jaclyn Star, Detective Brownie, and his new ward weren't about to miss out on the action. Brownie had secured a police motorcycle, complete with a sidecar, while the officer on duty was busy buying coffee at one of those high-priced coffee shops. Danny had climbed into the sidecar, while Jaclyn jumped on the back, simultaneously holding on to the detective and her notepad as tightly as she could.

Scotty Moose and Van Eyck weren't far behind. They'd borrowed a police horse and were bringing up the rear at a gallop. It turned out Scotty Moose was not only a professional boxer but also an accomplished equestrian.

So the banana truck was in the lead, followed by the rickshaw. In the third spot clattered the horse-drawn carriage, leaving the dog, the motorcycle, and the police horse in a nose-to-nose battle for the fourth position (though only two of the three actually had noses).

Pickles, realizing she was surrounded by bananas, had started chucking the fruit at her pursuers.

The horse-and-carriage driver pulled up alongside the rickshaw. "Watch out. She's got good aim," John shouted as the driver's hat was knocked off his head by a banana projectile.

"She should try out for the Olympics!" Toadius cried. He seemed more amused than afraid.

"I'm not sure—*ooph!*" The cart hit a pothole, throwing the two teenagers into John's seat. He was trying to push his way through the tangle of arms and puppy-love talk.

"I love you," one of the teenagers cooed.

"Doctor, this is no time to get emotional. We have a jewel thief to catch," Toadius scolded.

Brownie and Jaclyn Star's motorcycle buzzed past them, and as it did, Jaclyn swung her bag around her head like a lasso, using it to knock the rickshaw driver off his seat. Toadius's vehicle careened out of control, and the rickshaw collided with the horse and carriage, sending all the riders flying into the air. When John landed, he realized everyone had switched places. He was now on the rickshaw's bike while the two teenagers embraced in the back. The pair looked around for a moment, shrugged, and went right back to smooching.

The hansom cab driver was now seated in the back of the carriage; Toadius was nowhere to be seen. John looked over his shoulder, hoping to catch a glimpse of the inspector, but with all the dust kicked up by the speeding vehicles, all he could make out was a bowler hat rolling into the gutter.

"Toadius!" John's heart sank. His mentor was surely injured, if not worse.

"Watch where you're going, Doctor," a voice said firmly. The boy swiveled back. There was the inspector hanging around the neck of the horse.

"Toadius! You're alive!"

"Well, of course I am. How many dead men do you know who can ride a horse?" The inspector shook his head, and with one quick motion, swung himself up so he was astride the galloping steed.

"YEE-HAW!" Scotty Moose's cry rang out from down the street. He and Van Eyck had caught up with John and the inspector.

"Tallyho!" Toadius kicked the release lever, and the carriage unclasped. As the disengaged cart rolled to a stop, John heard the driver say, "That's it. I quit this stupid job."

Not many people know this, but it's very common for horses to be afraid of motorcycles. What is far rarer, however, are motorcycles that are afraid of horses. In this case, neither Toadius's horse nor the motorcycle were afraid of each other; however, they were both quite afraid of a monkey riding a dog.

Shim-Sham, now wearing Toadius's bowler hat, must not have been aware of the motorcycle and horse's fears; he shot right between them trying to catch up to the ticket to his banana empire.

I'm not sure which one saw the monkey-dog team first, but I think it's safe to assume it was the horse, which reared as it let out a terrifying shriek. The inspector, who was more agile than a horse, leaped from the frightened steed and landed on the back of Scotty Moose's horse, grabbing Van Eyck.

The dog, both to avoid the flying hooves and entranced by the horse's amazing two-legged feat, ran into the motorcycle, miraculously landing in the sidecar with Danny. Poor Shim-Sham was not so lucky. He rocketed through the air and smack into the face of the Mauve Moth, hanging on for dear life as she tried to throw another fruit grenade.

The monkey let out a yelp as he reached for the banana, but it was too late. The yellow delicacy hit the road, landing perfectly positioned in the path of Doug Brownie. The motorcycle hit the peel, sliding out of control and sending the detective, the reporter, his new ward, and their little dog, too, into a nearby dumpster.

John pedaled for his life, barely missing the banana trap. Suddenly, a high-pressure stream of water knocked the rearview mirror off the rickshaw. Apparently, the chief, his assistant, cops, and Rock, Paper, and Scissors had found a vehicle of their own—a fire truck. Paper sat on the ladder wielding the pipe nozzle like a water cannon to try knock John and Toadius off their respective rides. Lucky for the good guys, with so many goons crammed into the cab of the truck, steering was a challenge, and the fire truck kept swerving back and forth, making it hard to aim.

Even so, Toadius was having a hard time holding on.

"Toadius!" John yelled, motioning for the inspector to jump into the back of his vehicle.

"Oh, there you are, Doctor. I didn't know you were a rickshaw driver."

"I'm not," John called.

"Well, I hate to tell you this, but you're driving one right now."

"I meant," John said, swerving to dodge another banana bomb, "I'm not a *professional* rickshaw driver."

"My good man"—Toadius flipped off the horse with acrobatic ease, landing in the back of the rickshaw with the teens—"no one is a professional rickshaw driver."

At that moment, the chase hit a fork in the road. A *fork in the road* usually means the road splits in two, but in this case, it meant the group actually ran into a giant fork in the road. A sculpture of a giant fork, that is. It was yet another masterpiece by Master Igon Malik III, from his series *Puns around the World*. This sculpture, unlike his piece at the Blue

Moose, was made of metal, and had been placed in a street that split in two. Pickles's truck took the route to the left, which headed downtown toward the center of Manhattan.

Toadius pointed ahead. "Follow that truck!"

"With pleasure." John found a new burst of energy, switching gears, and pedaled even faster.

Toadius's horse, which no longer had a rider, went right. Caught up in the moment, Scotty Moose followed, taking him and Van Eyck out of the chase.

The Great Goatinee suddenly appeared out of nowhere, pulling up next to John. At first, John thought he was levitating, but a quick glance down revealed that Goatinee was also a skateboard expert. He dodged shots from behind him.

"Toadius," John called out as a water blast almost knocked him off the bike. "We have to shake the cops."

"I'm-a, what do you call it when you take care of things?" Goatinee asked.

"ON IT!" John yelled.

"Eh, close enough." Goatinee waved goodbye, then flipped his board. John couldn't see what was going on behind him anymore, but if he could have, he would've seen his uncle skate straight at the fire truck, jump into the air as his board sailed under the cop's vehicle, do three flips, and shoot fireballs out of his hands, sending the red truck spinning out, before landing with a flourish on the board and rolling away as if it were any other day.

"I AM THE GREAT GOATINEE-NEE-NEE-NEE," John heard from off in the distance, followed by a crash. "Don't worry. I'm-a all right."

There are three things anyone who is new to New York City needs to know. First, Manhattan is an island. Second, every other Sunday, there's some sort of parade. And third, you should never travel downtown while being chased by a horse, a rickshaw, a motorcycle, a dog, a firetruck, and a magician on a skateboard, without checking the traffic report ahead of time.

As the banana truck turned the corner, it screeched to a halt. A combination of New York's Annual Big Apple Parade, an accident shutting down the Lincoln Tunnel, and the general lack of planning on the Møth's part had led the group into the biggest traffic jam in New York's history. On top of all that, in an attempt to avoid the parade, twenty-seven garbage trucks had rerouted to the center of the island, converging in a few tiny blocks. The downside of this, of course, was that the trucks were stuck, and no one was going to move until the parade was over. On the plus side, sanitation workers get bored easily, so they were all walking around picking up trash. I do believe it was the cleanest street New York City had ever seen.

The Moth didn't waste any time leaping from the banana truck, throwing Shim-Sham from her face, and racing into a nearby building.

A man who'd just put his coins into a newspaper vending machine forgot all about retrieving the paper as he stared agape at the odd sight. Incidentally, Shim-Sham landed inside that same newspaper vending machine on a stack of not-yet-purchased papers, and the man was so startled, he released the door. It closed with a snap, trapping the outraged, bowler hat-wearing monkey inside.

The skyscraper Polly happened to run into was the world-famous Chrysler Building. The Chrysler Building is one of the tallest buildings in New York City at 1,046 feet high and seventy-seven stories tall. It boasts thirty-two elevators and two hundred flights of stairs.

The inspector and John pulled up to the building seconds after the Moth, and Toadius jumped out of the rickshaw and raced inside. The two teenagers still had their faces stuck together. John shot them an exasperated look, then left them there, following the inspector into the lobby just in time to see the Moth slipping up one of the staircases.

"She's headed for the roof!" Toadius bellowed before he, too, disappeared from view. John was racing across the travertine floor when he heard a *ding* on his right, and a set of elevator doors slid open.

He stepped inside. "Seventy-seventh floor, please."

"I can only take you up as high as the sixty-first floor," the elevator operator said. "That's where the four giant eagles keep vigil over Manhattan. There's also a wraparound observation deck, where you can take photos, get engaged, or have an epic battle with your archnemesis while overlooking the entire city."

"Then take me to the sixty-first floor," John said, a note of impatience in his voice.

"NEXT STOP, THE SIXTY-FIRST FLOOR!" the operator shouted, and pressed the button. There was a long pause as the pair stared at each other awkwardly, waiting for the doors to close. They did so, very slowly, and after a delayed ding, the car began to rise.

CHAPTER TWENTY-FIVE

The time John went to the top of the Chrysler building.

DARK CLOUDS FILLED THE AIR as John waited near the door of the stairwell on the sixty-first floor for what seemed like a century. It had begun to rain. Apparently, no one was interested in taking pictures or getting engaged that day, so he was alone. He scanned the observation deck, searching for anything he might use as a makeshift weapon, but everything was bolted to the ground. He had found a set of umbrellas hanging on the far wall meant for visitors on a rainy day. He took one.

Unfortunately, there was really no place to hide on the

observation deck, either, so he decided to crouch down behind one of the observatory telescope machines and hope for the best.

As a flash of lighting illuminated the sky, John spotted the silhouette of Polly rounding the corner. Little did he know that Polly was not only a master thief but also skilled at limbo. *Limbo* is a game where you bend backward as you try to walk under a horizontal bar. Right as John swung his umbrella, Pickles bent back and slid underneath it. Regrettably, Toadius's limbo skills were quite average, and the swinging wet umbrella connected with his head.

The inspector fell flat on his back, though he recovered quickly. But as he rose, it was to find Pickles holding a sharp hairpin to John's neck.

"Up, up," Pickles demanded.

"Polly . . . release the boy."

"Don't come any closer," she warned as the cold metal pressed into John's skin. "It would only take a little bit of pressure."

"Polly," Toadius said very calmly, "let him go, and we can work all of this out."

"There isn't anything to work out." Her hand began to shake.

"I promise you, Polly, I can still fix this." He reached out, but Polly jerked away.

"Just like you fixed things at the circus?"

"I tried to save him. I never meant for any of it to happen. I loved him with all my heart."

"And what about me?"

"Do you even have to ask? I love you more than there are earthworms."

"You left me there all alone." She adjusted her grip on the boy.

"He's here for you now," John cried. "We both are!" For a moment, the adults had forgotten he was still being held hostage. "We're together now. *We* can be your family!"

"It's too late." Tears hung on Polly's lashes, mixing with the rain.

"Why? We've all made mistakes and lost people we love. But like you said, you can't lose your way if you listen to your heart. It'll always bring you home," John pleaded. "We can be your home."

"Pickles," Toadius said as he reached his hand out again.

"I swear, if you take one more step, I will kill him, Toadius," Polly insisted, her voice shaking.

Toadius shook his head sadly. "Please. It's me you're angry with. John is just an innocent bystander."

"Fine." Pickles pushed John away into Toadius. "We'll do this the old-fashioned way."

She grabbed an umbrella off the wall and swung it around as if it were a sword.

John took the cue and tossed his umbrella to Toadius. The inspector gave it a couple of good swipes, just to test the weight and resistance, then took his stance. "Very well. En garde."

The clashing of their plastic umbrellas echoed off the buildings and through the alleyways below. The pair seemed almost to be dancing, locked in a lethally choreographed routine. John worried one of them was about to take their final bow.

After trading blow after blow, Toadius had succeeded in backing the Moth out onto one of the giant decorative eagle heads. The rain was pouring down.

John ran to the railing, eyes wild. "Toadius! Polly! Please! Enough!"

With a grunt, the inspector deflected a strike from Pickles's umbrella. There was a great clamor—John couldn't tell if it was a thunderclap or the sound of the umbrellas bouncing off the building. Pickles pushed Toadius back. His shoes slipped on the slick stone, and he danced to keep his balance. She spun to knock him off the platform, but Toadius fell onto his rear, barely dodging the attack.

The momentum of Polly's swing was too much. Her feet

slipped out from under her, and she landed hard on the eagle's head. Both the umbrella and the ruby flew into the air.

The umbrella dropped down sixty-one floors, stabbing straight into the pavement below. Luckily, it just missed the man still gaping at the monkey in a newspaper vending machine.

Toadius and Pickles both grabbed for the ruby, but it was too late.

Without a thought for his own safety, John jumped into action, leaping over the railing. With one hand, he grabbed the Egypt's Fire, and with the other, he grasped onto the end of a flag hanging off the building. Using the cloth as a makeshift rope, he swung himself back and forth, waiting for the exact moment to release his grip and fling himself back to safety. *One-one thousand. Two-one thousand. And . . . three.* He let go, reaching for the railing, but his hand found only air.

"JOHN!" Toadius scrambled forward, moaning as he looked down at the drop.

"I'm here," a faint voice called. The inspector looked over the edge and, sure enough, there was John dangling from a ledge a couple feet below the observation deck. Toadius fell to the ground, stretching as far as he could, just reaching where John was clinging to the wall.

"Doctor, I need you to give me your other hand."

"I can't." The boy whimpered. His fingers were still tightly wrapped around the Egypt's Fire.

"John, let go of the ruby." The rain was still pouring down, and Toadius could feel his grip on the boy slipping.

"But our case?" John tried to shake the water from his eyes. "We have to get the ruby back to the museum."

"It's just a case. Please! You have to give me your hand."

"But Rule Thirty-Five! You have to follow the case until it is finished!"

"Forget the rules, John! Give me your hand!" Toadius's voice was shaking. Their hands were too wet—the boy's fingers slipped. *If only he had pockets.*

"But the ruby!"

"It doesn't matter. You are far more important than any case. Let it go!"

John stared up at the inspector. He hadn't seen that expression for many years. The last person to look at him that way had been his mom. He uncurled his fingers from the stone, and it fell from sight as the boy pushed his arm up and grabbed the inspector's hand.

"*NO!*" Pickles screamed as she watched the ruby plummet to the ground.

With one great swing, Toadius tossed the boy back up over the railing. John landed on his feet face-to-face with Master Criminal Polly "Pickles" Cronopolis.

Although she would never admit it, he knew she was glad to see him alive.

"It's over, Polly," John said softly.

"So it is." She raised her hands into the air. "Look. You finally caught the Mauve Moth."

Toadius came up behind the boy and pointed his umbrella at her. "I have only one question. Why the Moth? You couldn't be the original Moth. You were oceans away when your father was killed."

"My mom," John said quietly. All the pieces made sense now. "Cerise Viceroy was the original Moth, but when she found out she was pregnant with me, she decided to leave behind her life of crime. She faked her own death."

Polly gave a dainty shrug, then shifted her attention to Toadius. "That's entirely possible. When you came home, you were obsessed with finding Dad's killer. You locked yourself in the study. I saw the drawings in your book, Toadius. All your notes about the Mauve Moth. I tracked down all the members in the circus, save one."

"Cerise Viceroy." John gulped. "My mother."

"I thought she was dead, and I didn't think a dead woman would mind if I assumed her identity, at least for a little while. It was the perfect plan. You wanted your Mauve Moth, and I gave her to you."

"You knew I would try to stop you."

She gave a small, sad smile. "I knew you wouldn't be able to help yourself. At least, this way, I wouldn't lose you. Not entirely, anyway."

"But that wasn't your only reason," John said. "You were hunting your father's killer, too. Being the Mauve Moth gave you the perfect opportunity to trick Cicada into coming out of hiding."

Toadius was fuming. "You *wanted* Cicada to come after you?"

"I welcomed it," Polly said without emotion. "I plan to make Cicada pay for what he's done. I lost my father because of his stupid set of rules, and I knew I was going to lose you, too. The Rules of Crime Fighting just get in the way, Froggy. The reason Cicada beat you both was because he didn't have to follow any. He could do whatever he wanted. I won't make the same mistake. I will do whatever it takes to avenge my father."

"By endangering yourself? By becoming a criminal, just like the man who took your father from you?"

Polly gave another shrug. "Cicada stole my life. I just decided to steal it back."

"Why the Egypt's Fire, though?" John asked. "How does a billion-dollar ruby bring Cicada out of hiding?"

"It doesn't matter now." Polly looked down. "You destroyed my only way of finding him."

"No, if he's out there, we'll find him," Toadius said, stepping in front of John. "But, Polly, I'm afraid you're going to have to come with me."

She shook her head defiantly.

"Come with *me*, Polly. I can help you."

"It's too late for me, Froggy," she whispered.

"I still love you."

"I hope you find what you're searching for," she said softly.

With one quick motion, she stepped up to the inspector, threw her arms around his neck, and kissed him.

John had read dozens of books—had seen hundreds of movies—where people kissed, but this kiss was not storybook love or some cliché Hollywood interpretation. This was *true love*, and John would never forget the difference.

Finally, Polly pulled away, and whispered in Toadius's ear, "Rule Thirty-Six."

She took a step backward, then another, until she was at the very edge of the eagle's head. "I'm sorry, John," she said, her eyes meeting his one last time. Then she lifted her arms straight out from her sides in a *T* and leaned back.

Toadius lunged to catch her, but he wasn't fast enough. John watched as the Mauve Moth plummeted toward the ground. She seemed to be smiling, and a break in the clouds allowed the sun to illuminate her like an angel. The long cloth of her mauve sleeves fluttered in the wind, and John couldn't help but think she looked like a giant butterfly.

John and Toadius watched helplessly as her body fell sixty-one floors, until it disappeared into the back of one of the garbage trucks stuck parked on the street below.

How could she do this? How could she have done any of this? John sank to the ground and covered his face with his hands.

Toadius remained perfectly silent and still. He'd spent his entire career on the trail of the Mauve Moth, all to win back the woman he loved. Yet, he'd lost the Moth and his beloved forever.

Numerous words in the English language can be used to describe the pain and beauty of love lost, but the one I am most fond of is *sillage*. *Sillage* is the scent that lingers in the air, the trail left in water, the trace of someone's perfume—the impression made in space after something or someone has been and gone.

The sweet fragrance of lilacs lingered in Toadius's nose as the biting winds of New York City blew away his tears.

CHAPTER TWENTY-SIX

The time when John learned Rule Thirty-Six.

S EVERAL DAYS HAD PASSED since Polly's dramatic demise, but it felt like a year. John hadn't seen Toadius since the Chrysler Building umbrella battle. Viktor and Judi were nice guardians. Their house wasn't very kid friendly, but they had a huge library, and John even had his own room with a real bed. They'd even gotten him glasses. Judi wanted John to attend private school in the fall, but he couldn't think that far ahead. All he wanted to do was see Toadius and talk about everything they'd been through together. Finally, he was going to get his chance.

John looked into the mirror. His wounds from the alleyway had almost completely healed, but he worried the pain in his heart might never go away. Judi had laid a nice blue suit and red tie on his bed. John couldn't help but notice how the clothes looked like Toadius's.

He picked up the tie and wrapped it around his neck.

"Here, let me help," Viktor said from the hall. "I feel like tonight is a Double Windsor kind of night, don't you?"

"I have no idea what that means," John said as Van Eyck adjusted the knot.

"There you go." The old man took a step back so John could see the full effect. He really did look like a smaller version of the inspector. He placed his cabbie cap on his head and smiled for the first time in a week. He stared into his own warm brown eyes with surprise. In the past when he looked into a mirror, he always wished his eyes were green like his mother's, but he finally liked what he saw. His eyes were deep and intelligent, and they sparkled with life, courage, and curiosity.

"I'm not sure that hat goes with that suit." Van Eyck turned his head as if he were facing down a painting with a mustache on it.

"I like this hat," John said. "Toadius gave me it to me."

"Yes, that fellow is an odd duck." Van Eyck shrugged, then scanned the room. "How are you enjoying your stay here?"

"It's a lot better than living over a bathroom," John said. Although the snug space he'd built for himself had been very comfortable, he really didn't want to live there. And he liked Judi and Viktor. They were very good to him—more than he could ask. But he missed Toadius.

"Well, we should be going," Van Eyck said awkwardly. "If there's one thing I hate more than rabble-rousing teenagers, people who dress as pirates, and North American mammals running willy-nilly around my museum, it's arriving late to a museum opening."

John laughed.

"What's so funny?" Judi stood in the doorway in a red dress that matched John's tie. She handed Viktor a hat with a red feather. "Oh, John, I love that hat. It really suits you."

John glanced up at Van Eyck, who just shook his head.

"I was explaining to the boy that we can't be late." Viktor extended his arm to his wife. "Shall we?"

Thankfully, the trio arrived at the museum on time. Big spotlights bounced off the pink brownstone exterior of the massive building. People dressed in extravagant gowns and tailored suits were escorted up the red-carpeted steps by actresses in peacock costumes.

"I hired the cast from *Asp Me Why I Love Her*," Van Eyck boasted as the car pulled up in front of the entrance. "Brings a bit of flare to the evening, don't you think?"

John was awed at how beautiful everything looked. And then he remembered Pickles, and felt the sharp pain of how much he missed her.

Banners draped down the outside of the museum, golden with bright crimson words that read EGYPT'S FIRE AND THE SECRETS OF AN EGYPTIAN TOMB! But John wasn't looking at the banners. He was focused on the figure standing beneath them—the greatest detective who ever lived, Inspector Toadius McGee.

John leapt from the car, but before he could reach the inspector he was surrounded by peacock dancers and members of the press.

"John, how did you catch the Mauve Moth?"

"Is it true that you lived in the ceiling of the museum?"

"What will you do now that you're no longer a suspect in the case?"

John tried to push past, but when he cleared the flashes and feathers, Toadius was gone.

"Leave the kid alone!" a voice boomed, silencing the crowd. Doug Brownie pushed the gawkers back as Van Eyck and Judi shepherded John up the steps and into the museum.

"Sorry about that, son," Brownie said as he dusted off John's suit. "How are you feeling?"

"A little overwhelmed," John replied honestly.

"I would, too. The press will eat you alive."

"All the press?" a woman's voice called before Jaclyn Star sauntered over to the group. Danny, the redheaded orphan and new ward of Brownie, was hot on her heels.

"Well, not *all* press," Brownie stammered, turning a bright shade of pink.

"Daniel, say hello," Jaclyn gently prodded.

"What's up . . . I mean, good evening," Danny said, bending into an awkward bow.

"I got you a soda." Jaclyn smiled, handing Brownie a root beer. "You are simply not allowed to talk to the press with low blood sugar."

"Yes, my dear." Brownie took a sip from the glass as Jaclyn fussed with his hair.

"Monday, we'll get you in with my stylist. The chief of police must always look his best."

John was amazed at how different Brownie seemed compared with the first time they'd met in this very spot.

"I see you two are getting along." Viktor grinned knowingly.

"Well, it turns out Ms. Star and I have a lot in common." Brownie offered her his arm.

Jaclyn looked up at Brownie, admiration shining in her eyes. "Who wouldn't love a man who takes in an orphan, uncovers the biggest underground crime ring in New York City, and becomes chief of police all in one day? I don't believe there's an attribute more appealing to a woman than a man with ambition, unless it's heart."

"And I love a woman who knows what she wants—and gets it," Brownie replied.

"And I love a man in a brown suit."

"Well, I love a woman who has brains and fashion sen—"

"We get it. . . . You two were meant for each other," Danny interrupted, rolling his eyes.

"Are they like this all the time?" John whispered.

"What can I say, dude? We Jersey boys love hard." Danny thumped his chest and grinned.

John searched the reception for Toadius but didn't see him. In the center of the display was the Egypt's Fire. Even from across the room, the ruby seemed to glow.

As if he were under a spell, John walked toward the ruby. Peering into the priceless gem, he realized he was back where he'd started.

He missed his mother. He missed her smile. He missed the sound of her voice and the smell of her perfume. But deep down inside, he knew it was time to move forward. That didn't mean he loved her or missed her any less. It was just that the hole in his heart had begun to heal.

At that moment, John realized there are different types

of family—the ones you are born into, and the ones you choose. As he gazed into the facets of the ruby, it was as if he were staring into a thousand vermilion mirrors. This time, instead of seeing only himself, he saw the reflections of all the people he now considered family. His three "uncles" stood in the corner. Brownie was showing Van Eyck his shiny new chief's badge, while the Great Goatinee dazzled Jaclyn Star and Judge Judi with a very bad card trick. Scotty Moose was over to one side talking with reporters and showing off his left hook. Danny stuffed his face with hors d'oeuvres while Mindy scowled, pretending not to notice him from behind the table her grandmother had put her in charge of. Patty zoomed around the exhibit hall on her roller skates, serving guests bite-size pancakes and root beer floats. They had all become his family, and even though they were a curious league of detectives and thieves, John was sure that his mother wouldn't have wanted it any other way.

"I hope you aren't planning to try steal that ruby," a familiar voice said as someone in a bowler hat filled all the reflections.

"*Toadius!*" John called out.

"Hello, Doctor," the inspector said, as if no time had passed since they'd last seen each other. "It is rather breathtaking, isn't it? And to think a billion-dollar ruby was so thoughtlessly thrown into the back of a garbage truck."

"If the person who had hold of it had pockets, he wouldn't have had to drop it in the first place."

"Quite so. Fate is a cruel mistress. You know, if you ever decide you don't want to be a doctor, you might try for a golfer. *Hole in one*, as they say."

John wanted to tell the inspector he wished they'd found Pickles safe and sound in the back of a garbage truck instead of the ruby. He wanted to say he'd give anything to go back in time and change the outcome of last week to get her back. Instead, what he said was, "It *is* very shiny."

"Yes, very." The party roared cheerily around them, but the pair stood silent, each lost in his own thoughts. "What about you? How are you doing? I see Viktor and Judi got you a pair of glasses."

"Yeah, I didn't realize how much I needed them until I finally got them."

"I believe I understand." Toadius eyed John for a moment. "Judi informed me you have your own room now. That will be useful for storing all of these presents."

John hadn't noticed the large table full of wrapped gifts. "Are—are those all for me?"

"Well, I'd assume so . . . unless there's another John Boarhog who recently stopped the world's greatest criminal mastermind."

"Why?"

"Why would there be another John Boarhog?" Toadius shrugged. "Yet another mystery to solve, I suppose."

"Toadius?" John cleared his throat. "How are *you* feeling?"

"Sad," Toadius said. "I assume I'll feel this way for quite a while."

John had similar mixed feelings about Pickles. She had been his friend, and even though she turned out to be a criminal, she had saved his life. "It's a paradox."

"I suppose it is." Toadius was still staring into the ruby. "If only we had the power to start time over."

"We don't have that power, do we?" John asked. At this point, after all John had experienced with Toadius, he felt like anything was possible.

"Alas, no. I'm afraid we are mere mortals," replied Toadius, placing his hand on John's shoulder.

"What will you do now?"

Toadius shrugged. "I was thinking about going on holiday. Maybe it'll help keep my mind distracted for the time being."

"Where are you going to go?" John felt a wave of panic wash over him. The truth was, he didn't want Toadius to go anywhere.

"Well, my friend Amelia just sent me this note." Toadius reached into his pocket and drew out a postcard, then handed it to John. On the front was an enormous ship, only the sails had been replaced with giant wind turbines. It looked like a mix between a cruise ship and a helicopter.

"'Her Majesty's Royal Air Armada,'" John read out loud. "'A luxury air cruise line. Why sail the friendly seas when you can float the peaceful skies?'"

"Sounds exciting, doesn't it?"

"It sounds dangerous."

"Exactly!" Toadius's eyes gleamed. "I knew you'd understand. They just landed in New York on their way to Rio de Janeiro."

"Rio de Janeiro?" That sounded so far away. John had lost his mother, and now it seemed he was going to lose the closest thing he'd ever had to a father.

"And how are things with Judi and Viktor?"

"Okay. It's nice there. They have a library, and I get my own bed."

"So, then . . . you hate it."

"I don't hate it." John sighed. "I . . . just don't feel—"

"—like it's home?" Judge Judi had quietly come up behind them. A crease of concern had formed between her eyebrows.

John turned pink as Van Eyck made his way over to join their group.

"We've been talking all week," Toadius said quietly as he

took off his hat. "We've decided that the choice should be yours."

"What choice?" John asked.

"Why, where you want to live," Judi said, straightening John's hat.

"I don't think I can compete with Judi's library"—the inspector glanced over at the judge—"but you would have your own room."

John's eyes had grown to the size of golf balls. "Are you saying I can live with Toadius?"

"If that's what you want," Van Eyck confirmed with a nod.

"But you're always welcome to stay right where you are," Judi added. "We care about you, and you'll always have a home with us."

"I want to live with Toadius!" John couldn't contain his enthusiasm.

"I thought you would, which is why we brought the paperwork for the inspector to sign."

"You did?" When John turned to Toadius, tears stung his eyes. It was the first time since his mother's death that he felt like he had a real home.

Judi leaned in to give John a hug.

"Consider this our present," Van Eyck said with a wink.

"Thank you!" John wrapped his arms around the old man, who patted him on the head, as if he were a small dog.

"Speaking of presents . . ." Toadius waved Brownie over. "Doug, it's time. I do believe this is yours." Brownie stretched out his hand, and when he opened it, he was holding John's locket.

The silver heart had been repaired and polished. Even the hinge was fixed. John opened it gently. Inside was the picture of his mother on one side, and on the other, a picture of Pickles.

"I thought Polly would've wanted you to remember her," Toadius said quietly as he patted John on the shoulder.

"How did you get—Where did you get—?" John wiped his eyes.

"Let's just say, you aren't the only detective written up for breaking a major case." Brownie pulled out a magazine from his breast pocket and flipped the pages before pointing to a brief article in the back. A small black-and-white picture of Brownie arresting Wormwood was stuck in between an ad for Lucky's Laundromat and a coupon entitling the bearer to ten percent off their all-you-can-eat meal at the Shrimp Shack. The caption below the photo read, "New York Detective Doug Brownie uncovers New Jersey child crime ring."

"That's incredible," John said, shaking the newly appointed chief's hand.

"That's not even the best part." Brownie pointed to his lapel. Neatly pinned there was a brand-new shiny S.O.S. pin.

"You got in?" John asked.

"Yep. Solved a crime, got written up in the trades, and was sponsored by the greatest detective to ever live," Doug said, nodding to Toadius. "And because a bet's a bet . . ." Brownie pointed down at his shiny black wingtips.

The inspector patted Brownie on the back. "I did say if you kept swinging, eventually you'd hit a home run. I only hope you will prove to be as good a chief of police as you are a man."

"I'm so happy for you, Chief Brownie. I hope one day I can follow in your footsteps and become a member of the S.O.S., too," John added.

"Speaking of that"—Toadius reached into his pocket—"Doctor Boarhog, I was wondering if you would accept my invitation into the Society of Sleuths." The inspector uncurled his fingers to reveal a white S.O.S. pin.

"Really?" John asked, eyes wide.

"Yes, but I must warn you, this is just a probation pin. You have to complete the trials before you become a full member."

"Trials?" John eyed the pin. "How many are there?"

"Three."

"Are they dangerous?" John asked.

"Almost certainly."

John laughed. "Then I'm in!"

"I thought you'd say that," Toadius said as he fixed the S.O.S. pin to John's jacket.

"Thank you, Toadius. Thank you." John threw his arms around the inspector.

"You are very welcome, John," Toadius murmured, holding the boy tight. "Now, I still have a couple of things to sign to make this arrangement permanent. Why don't you go look at the other presents? I've always found that opening a present makes me feel a lot better."

On the table sat gifts of all sizes. Large boxes. Small bags. One package was even wrapped with old newspaper. John admired a thesaurus, no doubt from the Great Goatinee, a pancake-shaped hat, and what appeared to be a slingshot with the words *Made in Jersey* carved into the handle.

John was grateful for all the many presents, but a small purple box resting in the middle of the table was the one that most caught his eye. It was the box's tag that made John lean in closer. At first glance, it appeared to have an illustration of a purple butterfly, but it wasn't a butterfly. It was a moth. A *mauve moth*. John turned over the tag. On it was a single sentence:

My obituary was greatly exaggerated.
—P. C.

John scanned the room. No one was wearing purple. He looked at the door but saw nothing amiss. Next, he turned his gaze up to the skylights and then to the ruby, but the stone sat where it was meant to be. The Moth had let them win this round.

Still, he knew he had to tell Toadius. The inspector was leaning over a table, signing his name on a small stack of documents.

"Toadius!" John held out the package. "Look, look!"

"One second, Doctor." Toadius signed the last sheet of paper. "We are officially partners in—" But at the sight of the box, the inspector's eyes glazed over, as though he'd seen a ghost. "Where did you get that?" he asked gruffly. John might as well have been handing him a rattlesnake dressed in a tutu.

"From the table. It's from Pickles."

Toadius carefully opened the package. Inside was a small white card with purple writing and a smaller box labeled for John. Toadius took out the card and handed the rest to the boy.

A QUEEN'S CROWN AND THE BOUNDLESS SKIES,

HIDES WHAT YOU SEEK, MY ROYAL PRIZE:

WHAT SEASONS, SQUARES, AND SUITS ALL SHARE,

STORM'S A-BREWING. SAILORS, BEWARE!

"What do you think it means?" John asked, trying not to let his excitement overtake his voice.

"Rule Thirty-Six!" Toadius chuckled. "I'll call my friend Amelia. Doctor, we have a ship to catch!"

"You mean . . . ?" John looked down at the postcard.

"A *queen's crown!*" Toadius pointed to the airship in the photo. "The Moth is going to stow away and steal something in midair." He clapped his hands together. "Rule Thirty-Six! I can't believe it!"

"What's Rule Thirty-Six?" John asked.

"*There will always be another mystery to solve, as long as there is someone willing to solve it.*"

John turned his attention to the small box with his name written on the top. When he opened it, he felt overwhelmed. Inside, wrapped in a handkerchief, was an old brass compass. He gently picked it up, examining it carefully. Engraved on the back was a message:

C. V.,
I hope you find what you are searching for.
Yours,
T. M.

His mind raced as he tried to understand what the message could mean. He had no idea what was in his future, what dangers were lurking ahead, or what intriguing riddles were waiting for him to decipher, but there was no denying Rule Thirty-Six. There was a new mystery brewing, the Mauve Moth was still on the loose, and John was willing to solve it.

"Shall we, Doctor?" Toadius pointed to the door.

"I'm not a doctor." John tipped his hat. "I'm a detective."

ACKNOWLEDGMENTS

THE NUMBER ONE RULE of being a writer is knowing that you can't write alone. I mean, the typing part and the endless hours of existential dread may make you feel like you are alone, but it is a giant lie. The secret to writing a book is a lot like trying to get to Mordor. You can't simply walk there alone. You need a fellowship, or giant eagles, but since eagles are a protected species in the USA, I suggest you get a ragtag group of people who love with reckless abandon, live with their heads in the clouds, or belong to some sort of fruit-of-the-month club. I didn't do this alone. Usually, it is frowned upon to name names, but I was never good at following rules . . . so here we go.

First, Tom and Lori Phillips, I don't know what you fed me as a child, but this book is your fault. How dare you be such perfect parents who set an example of what love, family, and mini-golf courses should look like. My sister Sherry for dropping me on my head and sending me bootleg *X-Men* cartoons while I was doing three years of hard time (middle school). My best friend and sister, Annie. I must keep this short, kind of like you, but seriously there isn't an aspect of my life I don't owe to you. You are my Jedi master, fairy godmother, and luck dragon wrapped up in a small but very brilliant package. To Alan, thank you for being an example of how to be a father and a man. To Aunt Suz, thank you for fostering my creativity and keeping Dad alive with every cow joke. And last, my nephews Ethan and Eli, thank you for the many hours of listening to my book and teaching me the values of love, friendship, and Minecraft.

To my wife, Autumn. YOU FOOL. I tricked you into believing I could write a book, and then forced you to be the best creative partner ever. We did it, baby, mostly because you challenge me to be a better man, writer, and speller. You are my heart. Thank you for beating so hard, I couldn't hear the voices in my head telling me to quit and go find a normal job like party clown or fire juggler. To my in-laws, Kay and Eric, I can't express how much your support, love, and advice mean to me. When I married your daughter, I didn't realize I'd be joining a family that was so obsessed with chicken wings, wine slushies, and Catan, but I sure am lucky to have you even when you won't take my sheep.

To my tribe: Scott Redder, Tanny Nanda, Randel Davis, Jarrett Sullivan, Jess Ayers, Steven Parker, Jaclyn Freidlander, Justin Liebergen, Aadip Desai, and Tamela D'Amico. I couldn't have a group of people I love more than you idiots. Thanks for keeping me alive and being the inspiration for the characters in this book. (No, you don't get any of the royalties.)

Thank you, Jan Powell, John Redder, Donna Lyons, Ellen Caps, Peter Ivanov, Dr. Jack Delmore, Dr. Richard Buys, Anthony Abeson, Heather Waggoner, and the teachers of Grand Lake Elementary for giving this dyslexic monster the love of learning and the skills necessary to make it in this crazy world. There isn't a day that goes by when I don't feel bad for all of the pain I must have brought you. You all deserve a statue built in your honor, or a stiff drink. Whichever you prefer.

LeVar Burton, Sangita Patel, and Isabelle Redman Dolce at LeVar Burton Entertainment: When you said, "I can go twice as high. Take a look, it's in a book," I took it to heart. Thank you for supporting me through this crazy roller coaster of emotions. Mark Wolfe and Mike Matola, I can't even begin to thank you for all the guidance and support you have given me.

To my agent, Ann Rose, I cannot thank you enough. You are single-handedly the best agent on this planet. You loved my book more than anyone (even me). Thank you for not giving up on us. I will never be able to repay you, but hopefully this book will sell enough copies to make a dent.

I want to thank my editor, Alison Weiss. You picked my book out of a sea of books, and instead of throwing it back into the water, you put it in a bowl and fed it book food until it became a whale. You get me on a level that only few have been able to achieve, and not go mad. You made my dreams come true, and I will always be grateful.

To Bethany Buck, for not only captaining the Pixel+Ink ship, but also giving my book a home, a name, and a chance. You are like the Santa, if Santa was a brilliant book editor with a Diet Cherry Pepsi addiction. IT'S SO GOOD! Jay Colvin and Stephen Gilpin for bringing my characters to life. The illustrations are nothing short of sorcery, and if you keep this up, I will report you to the Ministry of Magic; you aren't supposed to use magic outside of Hogwarts. Basil Wright, thank you for helping me continue to grow and be the ally my readers deserve. Melissa Kavonic and Pam Glauber, thank you for making sure I didn't have 663 exclamation marks, and that my book reads like a person who didn't fail every spelling test in his life. Miriam Miller and Erin Mathis, thank you for introducing the world to my characters and Zooming at 1 a.m. in Germany. I hope I never have your work ethic, but I am grateful I have you in my life.

They say it takes a village to raise a child, and my village is filled with the most talented people collected since the A-Team. (Look it up, kids!) Thank you to Derek Stordahl for leading this village. None of us would be here if it weren't for you.

The greatest team of marketing/publicity ever assembled, Aleah Gornbein, Sara DiSalvo, Michelle Montague, Alison Tarnofsky, Terry Borzumato-Greenberg, Mary Joyce Perry, Alex Howard, Annie Rosenbladt, Elyse Vincenty, Darby Guinn, and Carmena Jarrett. Seriously, you are the Avengers of the book world and I want to put your symbol on a T-shirt and wear it to every book signing like the true fan I am. The production team who deserves an Oscar, or whatever they give to book folks—an Ernie? A Bert? I have no idea, but Raina Putter, Jamie Evans, Rebecca Godan, Courtney Hood, and Melanie McMahon Ives, you deserve a gold statue and speech so long they play you off the stage with music. A special thanks to Julia Gallagher and Erin Valerio, for the endless hours it took to get all of my demands into the contracts. I know most writers don't demand that the contract folks get an extra week of paid vacation, and I am sorry it didn't make it into the final contract, but you did get me an extra five ARCs, so it evens out in the wash.

In the wise words of Charles Dickens, "Family not only need to consist of merely those whom we share blood, but also for those whom we'd give blood." You all are my family, and the heart of this book is because you found me, and I found you, and together we made a curious league of detectives and thieves.